HIS CURVY HAPPINESS

A SMALL TOWN CURVY GIRL ROMANCE

BOOK BOYFRIENDS WANTED
BOOK TWENTY

MARY E THOMPSON

Copyright © 2025 Mary E Thompson

Published by BluEyed Press, All Rights Reserved

No part of this book may be reproduced in any form or by any electronic or mechanical means, including information storage and retrieval systems, without written permission from the author, except for the use of brief quotations in a book review.

This is a work of fiction. All characters, businesses, locations, and events are either products of the author's creative imagination or are used in a fictitious sense. Any resemblance to real persons, living or dead, is purely coincidental.

NO AI TRAINING: Without in any way limiting the author's exclusive rights under copyright, any use of this publication to "train" generative artificial intelligence (AI) technologies to generate text is expressly prohibited. The author reserves all rights to license uses of this work for generative AI training and development of machine learning language models.

Book Cover Copyright © 2024 Mary E Thompson

Photos sourced from depositphotos

Ebook ISBN: 978-1-953879-77-6

Print ISBN: 978-1-953879-78-3

Discreet Special Edition Print ISBN: 978-1-967463-36-7

Audiobook ISBN: 978-1-953879-79-0

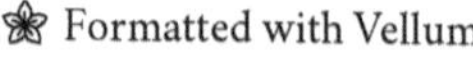 Formatted with Vellum

BOOK BOYFRIENDS WANTED

We're finally here, my beautiful cupcake. The last book in the Book Boyfriends Wanted series. It's a sad day and a beautiful day. This series followed twenty couples as they found love, found themselves, and found family. I love every one of these books, and I am so honored you came on this journey with me. From the bottom of my heart, thank you.

Never miss a thing when you sign up for Mary's newsletter. *Romancing the Curves* comes with subscriber exclusive freebies, sneak peeks, and a first look at everything Mary has to offer. Be the first to know about new releases and sales and all the curves ahead!

SUBSCRIBE NOW AT MARYETHOMPSON.COM

Happy reading!

To you... Thank you for joining me on this journey. We're not done yet.

CASEY

I slammed my car into park and yanked the handle. I tumbled out, nearly dropping my phone on the asphalt. Being late was a sin in the newspaper industry, and I was a perpetual sinner.

I grabbed the latest edition of the MacKellar Cove Gazette on my way into the building, wanting to know what my coworkers were writing and wanting to see my name in print. I was still getting used to it. Since my divorce, I'd gotten a few good assignments, but not enough for me to quit my two other jobs and work full time as a reporter.

Newspapers were quickly dying out everywhere, but our small-town paper was solid. I had no doubt that was thanks to the influx of money from the locals over the last few years, not to mention the low-key notoriety of some of those locals.

As I raced into the office, I realized I had a stain on my light pink blouse. Crap. I held the paper in front of it, but it was only a matter of time before someone noticed it.

"Thanks for joining us, Casey," my editor, Gretchen, said with a sneer.

I nodded, choosing not to speak and cause even more of a disruption.

Gretchen continued, giving me a chance to set my over-sized handbag on the floor next to my chair and grab my notepad out of it. She was old-school and refused to allow anyone to take notes on their phones. It was paper or nothing.

Gretchen assigned stories to the full-time reporters and opened the floor for other ideas. A few were rattled off, and approval was given for them to be chased. When the conversation slowed, I cleared my throat, anxious to pitch my story.

"Mayor Knight is getting married next month," I said.

Gretchen stared at me. "We are all aware of this. Why are you mentioning it?"

"I was thinking I could do a series about the wedding. A behind-the-scenes thing. Talk about the local vendors they're using, how he's handling the wedding with running the town. Stuff like that."

Gretchen held my gaze for a long moment, her eyes narrowing as she considered my proposal. "What's your angle?"

"Angle?"

Gretchen sighed as if I were the world's biggest moron.

Maybe I was because I was fairly sure I'd just told her what my angle was. Highlighting the town. The mayor. Making MacKellar Cove more appealing to visitors as a destination for major events.

"Yes, angle. Why does anyone care?" Gretchen was new to MacKellar Cove, but not new to the newspaper industry. She came to MacKellar Cove when the previous editor, Erik, resigned.

Erik ran articles about Mayor Omar Knight that were both misleading and damaging to him. He allowed me to publish stories that showed Omar positively, but Erik was a fan of the mayor Omar replaced. When I came forward with an article outlining all the things that happened before Omar stepped into the position, Erik resigned. He was willing to publish articles intending to get Omar removed from office, but when he saw all the evidence against his buddy, he walked away. Gretchen was brought in afterward, with no loyalty to either side.

I looked around the room at the others. MacKellar Cove was a small town. Life in a small town differed from that in a city. It was all about the community, the town being a place where everyone was respected and worked together. Omar had been a champion of that since he'd taken over as mayor, and his getting married was big news.

"I've read your other articles about him. It's obvious you have a personal attachment to him. Maybe a crush? I will not approve anything that's more of the same. More about how great the man is. You need to give me something new. Something different. Unless you just want to write about the mayor. We don't really need someone who only covers one thing." Gretchen's gaze slid around the room, waiting for anyone to argue or agree.

Unfortunately for me, there were more nods than anything else. "I'm not... That's... I thought it would be a good personal interest story. We always talk about work-life balance and how to handle family and having jobs, and I thought it could be a good take on it."

"That's been done. A million times. What else do you have?" Gretchen asked, sounding bored.

"Um, I mean, they're using a lot of local vendors. It could be a highlight of what MacKellar Cove has to offer couples looking for a small-town destination wedding."

"No one is looking for that."

"Oh, okay. I... I don't know."

"We need excitement. We need scandal." Gretchen looked

around and again got heads to nod with her. "Is he secretly sleeping with his secretary? Is he still not over his ex-wife? Can we call her? Maybe have her show up? Does the bride have secrets? Who is she? What can we find out about them?"

"Um, I don't think either of them has any secrets like that."

"Then your story is a boring fluff piece. Do we really need more of those?"

"It wouldn't be boring," I mumbled.

"Then give me an angle that would make it interesting. We don't need more sunshine and rainbows about the mayor. We need something to get people to buy the newspaper. You might think this job is easy, but every day more newspapers are closing. If we're going to stay open, we need more than the small-town mayor is getting married. We need something to grab attention."

I nodded and chewed the inside of my lip. Tears stung my eyes, but I refused to let them fall. I thought it was a good idea. Something that would be an easy series. But Gretchen had no interest in it.

The meeting wrapped up a minute later, and again, I had no assignments. I shoved my notepad into my bag and slung it over my shoulder as Gretchen stopped in front of me.

"Come see me," she said, walking out before I could reply.

Shit.

A few snickers followed me out of the room, but I ignored them. What choice did I have? Most of them were regular columnists. I was still a freelance reporter. The other freelancers worked throughout the Thousand Islands region, writing stories and publishing in a bunch of local papers. With a sixth grader at home and an ex-husband who wasn't reliable when we lived under the same roof, I couldn't travel to chase a story.

I knocked on Gretchen's door, even though she'd just left the conference room and told me to follow her.

She looked up, surprised that I was there, then waved me in. "Close the door."

I gulped and squeezed my eyes shut to stop the tears. I already worked three jobs to afford my apartment and keep Mikayla in the activities she enjoyed. Losing this one would mean saying no to something.

"Have a seat, Casey," Gretchen said, gesturing to the chairs on the opposite side of her desk.

I sat, letting my bag slide to the floor. I folded my hands in my lap, belatedly remembering the stain on my shirt.

Gretchen didn't miss it. Her lips pursed, but she didn't comment. "Your article about back-to-school was good."

Not what I expected her to say. "Thank you." When Gretchen assigned the article to me, I was flattered. With a sixth grader, I was well versed in the *intricacies of back to school*. Gretchen's words, though not untrue. She was a single woman with no kids, happily so, and shuddered at the idea of having to ever go back to middle school.

I'd worked my ass off to write a good article. One that covered the expense of school supplies, the added load on parents to handle all the things expected of students, and the lack of time for working and single parents, and that exposed the pressure on the teachers who didn't receive enough funding to provide for their classrooms and were frequently using personal funds to create spaces that were comfortable for the students.

I was proud of the article. I interviewed teachers and parents, getting both sides of the story and presenting a position I felt was fair. My own daughter struggled the first few weeks in middle school with the increased responsibility. My opinion, and that of the parents I spoke to, was that the elementary school teachers hadn't prepared the kids for the change, and I suggested changes to help students succeed at all levels of education.

"That's what I want to see," Gretchen said, again surprising me. "You have to have a perspective. You can't just write articles that do nothing. There has to be a reason for the article."

"I understand."

Gretchen was quiet for a minute, her hands steepled in front of her, elbows on her oversized glass desk. Her desk was the neatest I'd ever seen in a newsroom. A single box sat in one corner, empty. A laptop was closed in front of her, no cords visible. A single pen rested next to the laptop, lined up perfectly with the edge.

Gretchen leaned back, crossing her ankles and her arms.

"What do you know about the mayor's first marriage?"

I shook my head. "I don't really know anything about it. I'm not obsessed with him like you said. I don't have a crush."

She shrugged, uninterested. "You know what divorce is like. You've been through it, recently from what I hear."

I wasn't sure if she expected me to respond until she met my gaze and her brows went up. "Yes. Last year."

"The mayor is boring. Writing another article about how great he is isn't going to get people to pick up the paper. You know what life is like after a divorce. I've never bothered with the confines of something like marriage, but I've read enough about the damage a divorce can do to a person. What can we find out about the mayor?"

"His divorce was a long time ago from what I know."

"So? The ex never lived here, right? Has anyone spoken to her? Maybe she's not over him. Maybe he's getting remarried because of the scandal between him and the bride. From what I've seen, no one ever came forward and said it was her in that picture, but it obviously was. Did she trap him? Or did he trade a marriage with her for funding that summer camp of hers?"

"Nothing like that happened," I argued.

Gretchen's brows arched expertly. Her lips curled up at the edges. "Since you seem to know so much, you can surely find out more. Use your connection to them. We need a reason to write this story. I think you can make it good, but we need more brainstorming. More ideas. Or the story is dead before you start."

"I understand."

"Find out more about the mayor, and the bride, and..." She trailed off as she opened her laptop. She tapped a few keys, then continued. "Be back Friday at eleven. I'll put you on my calendar. If you have a good enough pitch, I'll let you roll with a four-article series. If not, I'll hand it over to Mike."

I swallowed my groan and nodded. Mike was a shark. He never let anything go until he found dirt, whether the dirt was relevant or not. I could not let Omar and Natalie be exposed to him.

"Not fluff, Casey. A story," Gretchen said, her gaze sliding to the door, then back to her computer, dismissing me.

I took the hint and let myself out of her office, closing the door behind me as Gretchen picked up the phone.

I had four days to come up with a story. One about Omar and Natalie that wouldn't be fluff and wouldn't make them look bad. And I had zero ideas of what to write.

Two days later, I was still trying to come up with ideas about Natalie and Omar that weren't bad for them, or the town. Out of options, and with two more days before my meeting with Gretchen, I showed up at the Community

Center, hoping to catch Natalie before the kids got out of school and flooded the afterschool program.

"Can I help you?" a voice asked when I buzzed the door for the Community Center.

"I'm Casey White. I—"

"Oh, Casey. How are you? How's Mikayla?"

The door buzzed to let me into the building. I heard footsteps approaching and saw Amelia Rucker. "Hi, Amelia. We're good. Mikayla misses coming here." My daughter joined the afterschool program as a fifth grader, something she hated, but after I had to get a job, and then two more, to support us, I insisted. Amelia and the rest of the staff made it fun, and Mikayla stopped fighting me after the first few days.

Amelia chuckled. "That's what we like to hear. But I'm guessing you're not here to convince us to take her in. What can I do for you?"

"I'm actually looking for Natalie. Is she here?"

"Natalie!" Amelia shouted, turning her head away from me as she bellowed. "Visitor!" Amelia smiled at me. "She has a tendency to hide, and if she thinks she can get away with it, she pretends not to hear me."

"I don't do that," Natalie said, appearing from a door on the far side of the gym with a look that said it was exactly what she planned to do.

"Yes, you do. Be nice and talk to Casey. She always writes nice things about us. You should thank her for that," Amelia said, giving Natalie a scolding look tempered by a slight grin.

"I do thank her. Every time. How are you, Casey?" Natalie smiled at me.

"Good, mostly. I need your help, though."

"We don't really have space for Mikayla to join the program, and a lot of older kids fight when they come. We don't have anyone her age this year." Natalie scrunched her face.

"I already asked about that," Amelia said.

"Oh." Natalie shook her head, her dark ponytail flicking over her shoulder. "Then what can I do for you?"

"I wanted to write a series of articles about your wedding. A behind-the-scenes kind of thing. Maybe highlight some of the local businesses. Something about the two of you balancing work and the wedding. Something like that."

"That sounds fun. Sure. Do you want to come to appointments and stuff with us?"

"Um, well, yes, but I also need something more."

"More?" Natalie looked at Amelia, who shrugged, then back at me.

"My editor thinks a basic story about your wedding isn't interesting enough. She wants something…"

"She wants dirt," Amelia provided.

"She… yeah," I agreed. "I'm sorry."

"Dirt? On me and Omar? Like what? We're not dirty people."

Amelia snorted.

Natalie flashed her a mock glare. "You know what I mean. That came out wrong. Please don't print that."

I shook my head. "I'm not here to trash you guys. But if I don't come up with a good angle on the article, she's going to give it to someone who will twist things and not care what it looks like."

"Ugh!" Natalie cried. "We've been through hell already. Why can't they just leave us alone?"

"I'm sorry. It's my fault for proposing something. I just thought it would be a good article. Something residents would enjoy."

"I don't blame you. I would love to read a story about the mayor getting married. If I weren't the one he was marrying." Natalie smiled sheepishly. "There's nothing special about us except his job. We're just two people who ended up falling in love."

"What about his first wife? Or your summer camp? I know the funding was all above board, but did working together change things? Maybe I can talk about how that factored in?"

Natalie exchanged a look with Amelia that I didn't understand. Amelia shrugged.

"What?" I asked.

"I was the woman in the picture with him," Natalie confessed.

I nodded. "Um, yeah. I know."

"You do?"

"Yeah. I think Melody told me. I never told anyone else, though. But my editor knows. I don't know how, but she mentioned it. She wanted to know if you traded favors after that picture or what the deal was with it."

"Favors? No. It was taken out of context, but that scandal brought us together. He was protecting me. The night that picture was taken, we weren't together. He chased down the photographer to try to get it back, but the guy refused. I thought it was going to tank the summer camp project, but they were only after Omar."

"I can pitch it. See what she thinks," I said. "Will it hurt you, though?"

Natalie shrugged. "I don't think so. The summer camp is growing every year. We're taking as many kids as we can. And the wedding is coming up. The picture wasn't what it looked like, but I still get people asking me if I know who the woman was and if I'm worried she'll try to stop the wedding."

"If they only knew," I said.

Natalie chuckled. "Right? If you run with this as an article, they will."

"I don't know if it'll be enough for Gretchen. She seems pretty set on there being more to a story."

"She has a job to do," Amelia said. "Her job is to sell newspapers. It makes sense she's going to look for something juicy that would help with that."

"But why does it have to be about me?" Natalie asked. Her whine was well-earned.

"Again, I'm sorry about that. I'll talk to her about doing something leading up to you being the woman in the picture, and I'll let you know what she says." I hoped it would be enough. If not, I was afraid Mike would take over and make things really uncomfortable for Natalie and Omar.

"If she approves it, you can have full access to everything for the wedding. All the ugly behind-the-scenes stuff. Whatever you want to see," Natalie said, shuddering. "I think Omar is more excited that I am."

"You're going to have a great day," Amelia said.

"I hope so. The best part for me will be when it's all over and I can sneak away with my husband." Natalie's cheeks flamed red. "I mean… That sounded bad. I didn't mean it like that."

I snickered. "I know what you meant. It's one day. What really matters is the marriage, not the wedding."

"Yes, that's what I meant. Jeez. I feel like I need an editor to sit in my brain and change the words before they come out of my mouth."

"That would be handy," Amelia teased her.

Natalie laughed again. "Let me know what your editor says, and we'll figure it all out. Thanks, Casey."

"Thank you. I'll be in touch."

I let myself out of the Community Center feeling a little better. Hopefully, Gretchen went for it, and Natalie and Omar didn't have any dark secrets dug up before the wedding.

And if I were really lucky, maybe this article would seal a future for me at the paper. And give me the opportunity to have only one job and more time with my daughter.

LANDON

I plunged my hands into the soft dirt, inhaling a deep breath as the pungent scent of earth surrounded me. It grounded me in a way nothing else ever had. Reminded me I was fine. Everything was fine. I had no reason to worry about the fact that I was thirty-five years old and still single. With zero prospects.

I used that frustration to dig out weeds from my garden. The sun was warm on my neck, the late-September air cool as my sleepy little town woke up.

Mornings were my favorite time of day. The minimal amount of traffic that trickled past my home hadn't picked up, and the only sounds to reach me were those of nature. Where I was happiest. Where no one judged me or made me feel like I wasn't good enough.

I moved from one section of my garden to another, watching the delicate plants that were starting to show off. In a week or two, I could harvest the first of my fall flowers and vegetables. I dreaded the first frost, and the impending winter, and seeing all my beautiful blooms get buried in snow and go dormant for a few months. But spring was always around the corner.

Maybe by then I'd have my shit together and would feel like I had something to offer a woman.

I snorted. Not likely. I accepted that the only thing I had to offer was my garden. I was definitely better with plants than people, and desperate was not a good look on anyone.

I finished my weeding and checking on the plants, then went back inside to get ready to open the store. Blossom & Grow was my life. I'd planned to share it with Reegan, but that dream…

That dream would never come true. It had been a year since things ended between us, and I was finally at a place where I could admit that and accept it. She was braver than I was. Stronger. She knew we weren't right together, but after three years, I couldn't see a way out. Everything about our lives had intertwined. I'd accepted it. I loved her, but I wasn't in love with her anymore, but I didn't know how to move on without her.

I held on to a lot of anger toward her for the first nine months after things ended, blaming her for our breakup. I was finally getting better, accepting my part in it and understanding that her refusal to move in with me was really for the best.

It still fucking hurt, though. To know I spent so many years planning a future that wasn't ever going to happen. Even if a part of me was relieved that it didn't happen.

I'd been stuck since then, trying to find a new dream. A dream that didn't leave me feeling empty inside.

I shook off the thoughts that plagued me most mornings as I went through my routine alone, always alone, and opened the door to Blossom & Grow.

It wasn't long before the first visitor of the day walked in. I smiled and helped the older couple find something for their fall garden. When the husband picked out a bouquet for his wife when she wasn't paying attention, then presented them to her as a surprise gift before they paid, I held back the bitter jealousy that surged through me at their sweet connection.

I wanted that. Too much.

"Thanks for coming in," I told them before they left, smiling and wondering if someone would ever look at me the way she looked at her husband.

When the store was quiet, I placed orders for the winter, needing to keep flowers in stock as much as possible. My greenhouse couldn't keep up, no matter how much I wished I had the space. I chose seeds for the spring plants I wanted, marked up my calendar for when I would plant everything, and helped customers shopping for gifts through the day.

I was finishing up with my last customer of the day when I heard the back door open and close, followed by the steady footsteps of my closest friend, Andre Davidson.

Andre was two years older than me, and I reminded him as often as possible. He'd also spent the summer falling hard and fast for a woman who ran from her wedding to a man she didn't love and ended up in MacKellar Cove and never wanted to leave. It took me a little while to get past my unfair resentment that Andre had found someone when he wasn't even looking, but Joelle was amazing and absolutely perfect for Andre. I was happy for them.

And a little jealous.

But mostly happy.

"Yo," Andre said as I locked the door and turned. "You going tonight?"

Every Thursday night, a bunch of local men got together at O'Kelley's, a bar in town. A lot of them grew up together and had known each other for years, but some, like us, were newer to the group. Andre had made more than a few business connections. I couldn't say I hadn't benefited from the group, too, but I was the only single one and sometimes felt like I was the last single man in town.

"I haven't decided yet," I told Andre.

"Why not? I thought you were going." Andre picked up a stepping stone that read *Life's Better Dirty* and smirked. "Nice."

I chuckled. I liked that one, too. It helped inspire my online screen name, not that Andre knew that. "I don't really have anything to add to the conversation these days. It's all babies and weddings and happy couples."

"We talk about other things. Plus, you love weddings."

I resisted the urge to roll my eyes. Yes, I loved weddings. Any florist would tell you weddings were both a giant pain in the ass and something that helped keep them afloat. Back when I thought I might have my own wedding, I used all the weddings I provided flowers for as a bit of research.

Now…

"You'll find someone," Andre said, far too astute for my liking.

"Maybe. But that's irrelevant."

Andre's brow went up, giving me a look that said he knew my words were shit.

"I don't know if I want to sit around and listen to everyone talk about how great life is when I'm looking at another long and lonely winter alone."

"Even more of a reason to come. Maybe you'll meet someone."

I snorted. "At O'Kelley's. Where everyone who goes there is already a local and either not single, or already dated someone else I know."

Andre's hands went to his hips. He studied me carefully, his gaze assessing me in a way that made me want to squirm.

"I thought you were in a good place with Reegan. Are you wishing—?"

"No," I blurted before he could finish his thought. "No. It's not Reegan. Jesus. Fuck. I'll go."

Andre looked at me again, trying to find something that wasn't there to find. "I'll drive."

I rolled my eyes and followed him out the door. The fucker. All he had to do lately was ask if I was mooning over Reegan, and I caved like a fucking wimp. I wasn't. Not at all. It was better we were done, and after a year, I could admit, to myself and no one else, that I was happy we were done. I was happy when it happened. Okay, maybe not happy, but relieved. Which was a total dick thing, but true.

My phone buzzed in my pocket, and I dug it out before I opened the door to his truck. I smiled when I saw a notification from Book Boyfriends Wanted.

TOOBUSY

Again, I leave you hanging. It's a good thing I know you don't mind. A compliment I've never forgotten? I had to think about this one for a while, but I'd have to say the first time my kid said I was the best mom ever. I think it was because I baked her a cake, but still, it was pretty damn nice. What about you?

I started to text back, but Andre blew the horn and snapped my attention back to where I was.

He rolled down the window and leaned down to look at me. "Who are you texting?"

"No one." I locked my phone, shoved it into my pocket, and climbed in the truck.

"That didn't look like no one. Are you seeing someone?"

"No. It's nothing."

"You do know you saying that makes me think it's something. Who is it?"

"I matched with someone. We talk sometimes."

"Whoa, what? When?"

I shrugged. "A month ago? Maybe a little longer."

"Seriously? Have you met? Who is she?"

"We haven't met. She has a busy life, and I do, too."

"Are you going to meet?"

"What the hell is with you?" I barked.

Andre leaned back in his seat and shifted the truck into drive. He eased around the edge of the building and pulled out onto the road before he answered. "Is it Reegan?"

"Are you kidding me? I already told you I'm not still hung up on her. We're done. It was a good thing. It is a good thing."

"Okay, but—"

"No. Don't do this. Okay, when things ended with Reegan, I was pissed. I was… I'm good. I know it was for the best. We're not seeing each other. I'm not talking to her on Book Boyfriends Wanted. It's all fine."

"How do you know it's not her?"

"I just do, okay. Can we drop it?"

Andre opened his mouth to say something else, but I glared hard at him, and he snapped his trap shut.

Thank fuck.

He parked along the street, three blocks from O'Kelley's. We said hello to a few people as we walked toward the bar, but otherwise, Andre was quiet.

O'Kelley's was crowded. We pushed our way inside, fighting for space as we worked toward the bar, where everyone met on Thursday nights. Hudson Grant, the owner, jerked his head toward the end of the bar where the other guys were sitting and standing, huddled together and glaring at anyone who tried to take one of the open stools they'd commandeered.

"Thank you," Ian Jameson said, taking his hand off the

back of an empty stool. "I thought I was going to have to fight someone. Good to see you guys."

"Thanks for saving seats," Andre said. "What's going on tonight?"

"New local band asked if they could play. I agreed, but I had no idea they would bring in this big of a crowd," Hudson explained.

"Good for business, though," Andre told him.

"Yeah, but I wish I had a few more servers and another bartender to help out," Hudson said.

"I did some bartending in college. Need a hand?" I offered.

Hudson raised a brow. "Yeah? You wouldn't mind?"

I shook my head and slid off the stool I'd just taken, nodding to Ramsey Holland as he walked up. Ramsey took the stool before anyone else could steal it, and I walked around the end of the bar to join Hudson.

Hudson gave me a quick rundown of where everything was, then left me to handle our group while he checked on some of the other patrons. I took orders and handed over drinks before easing my way down the bar to help the rest of the waiting customers.

The band started to play, a heavy rock sound with a beat that had their fans on their feet and dancing, singing along with most of the music. Hudson and I worked well together, filling orders and keeping the customers happy as the band entertained the crowd.

When the band took a quick break, Hudson thanked me for helping out. "I don't know what I would have done without you. I never would have kept up."

"Not a problem. It's been a while since I've been behind the bar. It was fun."

"Like riding a bike?"

I chuckled. "Something like that."

"You drink for free forever," Hudson said.

I shook my head as James Rucker shouted, "Hey! Why don't I ever get that offer?"

Hudson flipped James off. "When have you ever gotten off your ass to help?"

James scowled. "I'm a cop. I think there's a law against me being allowed to serve drinks."

"Then sit your ass down and shut up about it," Hudson said, a teasing light in his eyes. They were two of the originals, men who'd been friends for years.

I smirked at their easy banter and thought about TooBusy. Talking to her was like that. Easy. There wasn't any pressure between us, which was nice and new for me. I had no idea who she was, but she said she lived in MacKellar Cove, so I wondered if maybe I did know her.

I shook off the thought. There was no way. She was a single mom, and she said she worked a lot to be able to take care of her daughter. I didn't know any single moms. Even if she wasn't a single mom, I didn't know anyone I felt such an easy connection to. Someone I could say things to that I didn't admit to anyone else.

The band started to play again, and the crowd pressed in to listen and dance and sing along. When they announced they were done for the night, they told everyone to get one more drink and to come back to O'Kelley's soon as a thank you for letting them play that night. The bar was slammed, three people deep, with happy and excited customers waiting for another drink.

An hour later, the crowd had thinned, and most of the men in the group had left to go home to their families. Andre stuck around, which was nice since he was my ride home, but his nose was in his phone and the smile on his face was his *Joelle smile.*

"You ready to go?" I asked him.

He shoved his phone away before I could see what they'd been texting, but I didn't need to see it to know I didn't want to see it.

Hudson thanked me again for helping out and reiterated that I would drink free whenever I wanted. I thanked him, knowing I owed Hudson way more than one night behind the bar. If it weren't for him, I'd still be nursing my resentment toward Andre and Joelle and would probably have ruined the only relationship I had left that wasn't blood.

"I didn't know you were a bartender," Andre said when we were in the truck.

I nodded. "Two years in college. It was a good job. Decent money, lots of phone numbers, and the hours never interfered with classes."

"You didn't have morning classes?"

"Sure, but I had enough time after I got off work to get a few hours of sleep and be up. You know I like the morning."

Andre chuckled. "Yes, you do." He pulled in behind my shop and slid the truck into park. "Are you doing okay?"

"Yes, Dad, I'm fine."

Andre flipped me off. "We worry about you."

"Tell Joelle I'm fine. I promise. I want what you two have, but I know Reegan wasn't the one for me to have that with. It's all good. It would be even better if you stopped asking me if I'm hung up on her or talking to her or want to get back together with her or whatever the hell else you're going to come up with."

Andre smirked. "Yeah, but how would I get you out if I didn't do that?"

"Asshole," I mumbled as I opened the door. "Thanks for the ride."

"See you in the morning."

I waved as he backed out, turning around and disappearing around the side of the building.

I let myself in the back, then went up the stairs to my apartment. I loved living in the same building as work. At first, it was cheap, and I was sinking all my money into making the store a success. After years of living and working under the same roof, it was home. It certainly wasn't special, and it wasn't fancy, but I loved being there. It was just big enough for me, and that was all I needed.

I turned on the TV and grabbed a beer from the fridge. I sat down on the couch and pulled my phone out, reading TooBusy's message again before I typed out a response.

DIRTYLIFE

I think that's a pretty nice compliment, too. Sounds like you have a great kid.

I didn't expect a reply from her since it usually took a few days before she wrote back, but three dots appeared next to her name, then a message popped up.

TOOBUSY

I meant, what's a compliment you've never forgotten? But yeah, she is pretty great.

DIRTYLIFE

I honestly can't think of one.

TOOBUSY

None? No one has ever given you a compliment that you never forgot?

DIRTYLIFE

Nope. I've had people tell me they like my work or they appreciate me, but something like what you said? Nope.

TOOBUSY

I'm guessing that means you don't have kids.

DIRTYLIFE

No kids. No wife. No husband. Not even a pet.

TOOBUSY

What makes you feel appreciated?

DIRTYLIFE

In a relationship or what?

TOOBUSY

In general. In whatever way you want or need to feel appreciated.

DIRTYLIFE

My work is important to me, so I guess hearing I did well is good.

TOOBUSY

What about in a relationship?

DIRTYLIFE

I thought you said in general.

TOOBUSY

I changed my mind. What would you need in a relationship to feel like you were appreciated? To feel like it was good.

DIRTYLIFE

That's easy. Someone who wants the same things I do. A family, a future together, a commitment. What about you? What would you need?

TOOBUSY

Um, sorry. I need to go. I'll talk to you soon.

She signed off the app before I had a chance to say anything else. Was it me? Or did she really have to go?

3

———

CASEY

I hadn't been so nervous for a meeting since I was fresh out of school and trying to get a job as a full-time reporter. I changed three times before I groaned and went with what I had on. Gretchen already knew me. Impressing her wasn't possible, and it wasn't going to change anything. Either she liked the pitch or she didn't.

I was early for our meeting, choosing to forgo coffee before the meeting since it usually left me jittery and half the time I spilled it. I was going to nail my proposal, and it would all be fine. Totally fine.

"Casey!" Gretchen shouted as she opened the door.

I was sitting next to it and jumped. "Here."

"Oh. I didn't see you." Gretchen left the door open for me to follow her inside. "Close the door."

I was already doing so, but nodded. The first rule was don't piss off your boss.

"What do you have for me?"

"Okay, well, I was thinking we can run with what you said about Natalie being the woman in the picture with Mayor Knight. It was never public knowledge that it was her.

The man who took the picture was working for the former mayor and trying to get rid of Mayor Knight so he could run for office again."

"And you already exposed him, and he ran away and hid. Why is it worth bringing all this up again?"

"I spoke to Natalie, and—"

"You what? You told her we are doing a story?"

I shifted in my seat. "Well, yes. If I was going to get access to her for the article and follow her around as it got closer to the wedding, I figured it only made sense she was aware of it."

Gretchen leaned back in her chair and sighed heavily. She twisted her neck until it cracked, then twisted it the other way.

Not intimidating at all.

"I guess if you are going to publish something, yes, you will need her approval. What did she say?"

"She admitted it was her in the photo."

"And?" Gretchen's perfectly sculpted brows rose.

"And… um, she said it wasn't public, but she would be willing to share the story."

Gretchen was quiet for a long minute. She steepled her fingers in front of her face, then rested her chin on them. "We still need more. Is this just one article? Once we expose the truth, no one will care anymore. What else are you going to talk about?"

"Um, well, she said people keep asking if she's worried about the woman in the photo. We could go with the angle of Mayor Knight being married before and a man in power settling down with someone after a scandal that pushed them together."

Gretchen's brows popped high again. "Pushed them together?"

"Natalie said he was protecting her. He went after the

photographer to try to get the picture, but the man wouldn't delete it. Omar… Mayor Knight was trying to keep Natalie safe and make sure the summer camp didn't suffer because of that picture."

"Well. That is interesting." Gretchen's smirk was not friendly. "I think you might have a story after all. I'll approve it. Start working with her ASAP. Find out what you need. Go to all her appointments with her, and get on his calendar. I want you to get both of their sides. And see if you can find out anything about the ex-wife, the family who donated the land, and anyone else in their lives. Sort of a public interest angle. You can layer all of this into what they're doing to get ready for the wedding."

I nodded, unsure I liked the way she was presenting it all. "But positive, right? Because they're good people."

"Yes, positive. I'm not going to be accused of throwing the mayor everyone loves under the bus."

"Okay."

"When is the wedding?"

"Four weeks."

"Perfect. I want your first article on my desk Monday to run in Tuesday's edition. If you can make it compelling enough, we can make this a regular column leading up to the wedding."

"That would be great. Thank you, Gretchen." A regular column? That would be more than just a good piece. It would mean getting into the paper every week. It would mean knowing I had income coming in.

Gretchen turned to her computer, ignoring me.

I stood to leave, grabbing my bag and closing the door behind me as I let myself out of her office. I fought my smile, not wanting the others to see that I had gotten a good assignment. Not everyone who worked in newspapers was ruthless, but there were more than a few who were happy to swoop in and steal your story.

Especially if they had a stronger connection to the editor and a regular seat at the table.

I headed for the door, needing to get to my second job so I could get home on time when Mikayla was off the bus. I knew better than to change in the paper parking lot, but I couldn't sit in the driveway of the house I was scheduled to clean either. I drove a few minutes away, then changed quickly. I tugged jeans under my skirt and unbuttoned my blouse. In my fitted tank and jeans, I dug for my tee. My hand grabbed the cotton and pulled it over my head.

Cleaning houses gave me a peacefulness that my other jobs didn't. The work was routine and easy. I didn't get grossed out by things that other people did, and the money was decent. The company was local, owned by two cousins who loved being able to help people make their homes clean and beautiful. They hired me without a lot of fuss, and I could take on whatever jobs worked within my schedule.

Even better, I never worked nights or weekends and was paid by the job, not the hour.

I rang the doorbell of the house and smiled when Mrs. Gentry opened the door. "How are you today?"

"Hello, Casey. We are doing our best. How are you?"

"I'm good, thank you. Regular cleaning today, right?"

"Yes. I've been trying to keep up with everything, but you know I'm not very good at it."

I patted her hand and shook my head. "You are a treasure, Mrs. Gentry. Please don't worry yourself. That's why I'm here."

She tutted and fluffed her bob. Mr. Gentry insisted on hiring someone to clean the house when Mrs. Gentry fell off a stepladder. In the year since, I'd been the one to clean their house every other week. They were in their eighties, and Mrs. Gentry always had a spotless home, but it was good for them to have someone who handled the high and low things. I cleaned the entire house, but she always insisted she could handle the basics. I still did it.

I carried my mop and vacuum inside with the bucket of cleaning cloths I used. My bosses were adamant about using non-toxic products and as few chemicals as possible.

Mrs. Gentry went to the living room, where Mr. Gentry was in his chair, reclining and watching TV. "Casey is here."

"Hello, Casey!" Mr. Gentry called, waving to me from his seat.

"Hi, Mr. Gentry. How are you today?"

His face pinched. "Feeling a little slower this week. We had a lot going on last week, didn't we, Love?"

I was enamored with the way he called his wife Love. More than sixty years of marriage and he still talked to her as if she was the most precious thing in his world. "What did you have going on?"

"The kids are all doing something these days," Mrs. Gentry said. "Between sports and events and even just the activities, it gets busy."

"And you're not the kind of grandparents, or great-grandparents, to not be around and involved," I said with a smile. They'd shared with me that their three kids had all stayed in MacKellar Cove and gotten married and had kids who also stayed in town. Of the five grandkids, four of them were married with kids, and the fifth was finishing medical school and looking to come back to the area within the next year.

Mrs. Gentry laughed. "We want to soak it all in as long as we can. My fall was a reminder that I'm not invincible."

"None of us are. And being healthy means you can do all the things you enjoy. Even if it exhausts you."

"Oh, I can do that," Mrs. Gentry said, moving toward me as I grabbed plates in the sink to load into the dishwasher.

I waved her off. "I know you can. And you do when I'm not here. But when I am, it's part of what I do."

She smiled, her dark-brown cheeks lifting with her grin. "You are too good to us."

"I am happy to do whatever I can. And you know you can call me if you need anything else. I know you have a lot of family around, too, but I'm not far from here."

Mrs. Gentry nodded. "Thank you, dear."

"You are very welcome." I loved cleaning their house. They told me stories about their lives and what the town was like over the years. Mrs. Gentry always tried to tell me she could do something I was paid to do, and I gently reminded her it was part of my job.

If I were ever going to miss being married, it would be when I was spending time with them. Most of the time, I didn't think twice about not having a partner. Kyle was mostly only good for one thing, and in the end, even that wasn't always that good. An accidental pregnancy after a few months of dating tied us together for far longer than either of us wanted.

He stayed with me, though. He was never a great husband, but I wasn't a great wife either. I resented him for getting me pregnant, for taking away my dreams. He felt the same. We tried, for years we tried, but divorce was inevitable.

Kyle was the one who finally said it. He wasn't happy and hadn't been for a long time. He needed a change and decided that change was in another woman's bed. Not while we were married, but he didn't waste any time finding someone else's sheets to fall into.

It left me more than a little jaded. I wasn't looking for another husband. But there were times I missed the physical connection of sex. It was the only time Kyle and I were happy. The only time I felt like we were okay.

And that was why I still hadn't reached out to DirtyLife again. He wanted a family. A relationship. A connection.

I should have expected it. Why else would someone be on a dating app? It wasn't why I was on it, but I had to assume that, with all the options for dating apps, the one that didn't allow pictures wouldn't be the one people would go looking for a hookup.

I let my mind wander as I cleaned the house, talking to Mr. and Mrs. Gentry as I worked. At their age, I didn't think there was a lot of sex happening. Not that I wanted to picture it, but when she broke her hip, sex was not an option. Other things held them together. Things I'd never experienced.

Things I wasn't sure I ever would experience.

When I was done cleaning, Mrs. Gentry asked about my dating life, and I knew it was time to go. I made my excuses for getting out of there, even though I was going to be really early to meet the bus, and told them I'd see them in two weeks.

I didn't waste any time backing out of their driveway, ready to escape the inquisition.

I decided to take the long way home. I didn't live far from the Gentrys, but since I had time, I drove to the edge of town for a few minutes of peace.

Leaving their neighborhood, I noticed Blossom & Grow just down the street. The flower shop was beautiful. Stopping was unnecessary, but I couldn't resist when I saw the bright, friendly sign outside.

I couldn't remember the last time I'd gotten flowers from anyone. Kyle certainly never bothered. Was it as far back as my wedding?

I made my way inside, weaving through the displays that held more than a few bouquets exploding with color and fun and vibrancy. I heard voices, but I mostly tuned them out until I heard the woman say something about a wedding.

Blossom & Grow was the only florist in town, and I assumed Natalie would use it for her wedding.

I moved closer to where the people were speaking to listen in on their conversation. I couldn't see them from where I stood, but that wasn't as important.

"Flowers say all kinds of things," a man said from behind a display. "Roses are always a favorite, but if you want something unique or different, there are so many options."

"Like what?" the female customer asked.

"Well, peonies are a symbol of a happy relationship. Carnations mean affection." He laughed.

"I'm not a fan of those," the woman said.

"That's okay. There are so many more. Orchids are elegant and strong. Gardenias symbolize beauty and hope."

"What's this one?" the woman asked.

I moved closer so I could see what she was looking at. I caught sight of the man who was speaking. He wore an apron around his waist, stuffed with tools and sprinkled with dirt. The look in his eyes was one of pure adoration and love.

I found myself jealous of the woman he was speaking to.

"Sweet peas are one of my favorites." He picked one up from the container they were in. "They mean blissful pleasure, which is fitting for your wedding day. They're a great addition to any bouquet, and they work very well as centerpieces. You can even add a few to your honeymoon suite for a reminder when you get back after a long day of happiness."

The woman laughed softly. "I think we definitely need some of those."

"I had a feeling you might."

I moved closer, needing to know more. Just listening to him talk had me wanting to hear more.

"What about daisies?" she asked.

He laughed. "I would say they're fitting for you. Did you know they symbolize true love and new beginnings?"

She sniffed. "I love that."

"It's perfect."

"Thank you so much for helping with this, Landon. It's amazing."

Landon? Reegan's Landon? Oh, no. I had to go. Being there was a bad idea.

I turned to go, and my oversized handbag slapped the side of a display. The tower of black containers, all full of flowers, teetered.

I stood there, watching the tower as it swayed. It seemed to be happening in slow motion. Too bad I was moving even slower.

I reached, hoping to steady the tower, just as it took its last dip and fell to the floor with a crash that drew the attention of Landon and the bride he'd been speaking to.

"Shit," I hissed, watching as water poured from each of the black funnels. I grabbed the tower as I felt someone crouch next to me.

"Don't worry about this. Are you okay?"

I looked next to me and found myself captivated by the light dancing in his chocolate eyes.

I guess I didn't answer quickly enough because he touched me. His hand on my arm startled me, and I jumped, nearly knocking another tower down on top of us.

"I'm so sorry. Were you hurt? Did I scratch you?"

I shook my head, my voice finally catching up with my brain. "I'm good. Sorry. I... I am so sorry. I wasn't paying attention to where I was going."

"It's not a big deal. I'm always covered in dirt, so clearly I'm not going to worry about a little water." That light sparkled in his eyes as he smiled. Little lines appeared next to his eyes, like he was someone who enjoyed laughing and did it freely.

I breathed a laugh, appreciating the fact that he was not

yelling at me for making a mess. "Thank you. I'll just—" I reached for the tower again.

"Don't worry about it. I can take care of it in a few minutes."

"I didn't mean to interrupt your meeting."

"Things happen. As long as you're okay?"

"Yeah. Yes. I'm good. I'm fine." I stood, nearly hitting another tower. "I'm going to go before I ruin your entire store. I'm so sorry."

"No big deal. I promise."

"Yep. Okay. Thanks. Bye!" I clutched my bag to my side and hurried toward the door, getting as far from Landon and his too-tempting eyes as possible.

Too bad his eyes weren't the only tempting part of him.

4

_I_ made it home before the bus, my cheeks still flaming at the way I'd behaved. Landon. Shit. Listening to him talk was hypnotic. I could have stood there all day. The way he described flowers as if they were erotic.

I fanned my face. I could not think about him like that. I couldn't think about him at all.

Reegan wasn't a good friend, but we had friends in common. They were a couple everyone expected to get back together, eventually. After three years together, they were enmeshed in each other's lives. It was inevitable that they would work it out.

It didn't matter that it had been a year since they broke up. I was not wading into the middle of that.

Plus, I didn't want a relationship.

A fling would be—

No! No. I could not think about a fling with Landon. He wasn't really available. And I was too old for him.

The bus rumbled down the road toward the building, giving me the distraction I needed to pay attention to what really mattered. My daughter.

When we moved into the apartment, Mikayla was embarrassed. She hated we had to give up the house we'd lived in since she was a baby. I felt the same, but I couldn't afford it on my own, and Kyle didn't want to stay there. Before we were even officially separated, he'd found someone to live with, so selling the house meant he had money in the bank and I had money to pay for Mikayla and me for a while.

After a year in the apartment, she was getting used to living here and liked it. I had a suspicion her favorite part was that she got off the bus without me being outside and had her own key to get into the building.

She didn't have to know I watched from the window and rushed to the kitchen and pretended to be casual by the time she made it to our apartment.

"I'm home!" Mikayla called as she walked into the apartment.

I emerged from the kitchen, wiping my dry hands on a dishtowel. "Hi, honey. How was your day?"

"It was so good. I got to sing the solo in chorus today, and Mr. Johnson said I should try out for the lead in the school musical next week!" Her smile lit up her entire face, her blue eyes sparkling with joy.

"Wow! That's amazing. If anyone knows, it's your chorus teacher. When are the auditions?"

"Thursday. You have to sign my paper so I can do it. And you have to pick me up from school because there's no bus."

"I have to pick you up?" I did mental gymnastics as I processed what that would mean.

"Yeah, but you're always home anyway, so what difference does it make?"

The preteen in her was coming out. She wasn't wrong, but damn, did she have to say it like that? "It will probably be fine, but you could ask instead of demanding."

"Sorry," she murmured.

I counted to ten, knowing I wouldn't get the request. "Are you going to ask?"

She sighed like I was the most ridiculous person ever. "Can you pick me up after auditions on Thursday? Please?"

"Yes."

She grinned before I opened my mouth to continue, then scowled.

"I need a schedule for rehearsals and all the things that you're going to need to be there for. And you need to make sure you're still getting your schoolwork done. Finish homework, stay on top of anything you miss, and don't fall behind."

"I won't. I promise." The excitement was there, waiting for me to officially agree.

"Okay. We will figure it out."

"Yay! Thank you, Mom!" She threw herself at me, hugging me tight around my middle.

I hugged her back and kissed her head. She wiggled immediately, pulling back.

I let her go, missing the little kid years.

Before I'd gotten pregnant with her, I'd hoped to have a big family. Three or more kids, preferably more. But things didn't go as planned. Kyle and I talked about more kids, but it never felt right. After a decade of marriage and a few short months for the divorce, I was left half relieved we didn't have more and half disappointed I was almost out of time.

Thirty-eight hit me hard a few weeks ago. The likelihood that I'd have another kid was pretty close to zero. Even lower when I had no interest in a new relationship. But I knew that was the right choice for me. I couldn't handle the ups and downs of another person's emotions anymore. Not when I was going to be dealing with a teenager's emotions soon enough and had my own to handle.

Mikayla got a snack, then settled on the couch for an

hour to watch TV, like she always did when she got home. We argued about her starting homework right away, but she said she wanted time to relax before she did her work. She negotiated for that hour with the promise that she would do things my way if she didn't get her work done. After almost a month of trying it her way, she proved she would do it, and I backed off.

I took advantage of that hour to write and finish up anything for my upcoming articles, when I had one. Since I was meeting with Natalie and Omar the next day for wedding preparations, I wanted to review the plan for the day.

Shit. They were looking at flowers. At Blossom & Grow. Where I'd embarrassed myself just an hour ago. Of course they were. I couldn't start when they were tasting cake or making a seating chart or… anything except returning to the place where I made a fool of myself.

I had to get the hell over it. I was a big girl. And I was going to be there for a story. Not for Landon.

My phone vibrated with a message, and I took advantage of the distraction. I smiled when I saw a notification from Book Boyfriends Wanted.

DIRTYLIFE

You never answered my question. What do you need from a relationship to feel appreciated? What are you looking for?

I sighed heavily. How did I admit to him that I didn't really want a relationship? That I wanted to feel desirable but without the weight of dedication to one person who would inevitably let me down?

TOOBUSY

I guess I don't really know. I told you I'm divorced, and my marriage was okay for a while, but mostly it was like we were roommates. I'm not looking for that again.

DIRTYLIFE

So you want passion. You want someone who makes you feel like you are the only thing they think about when you're not together. Someone who lives and breathes for you.

TOOBUSY

That's exhausting. I don't think I could handle someone who didn't have their own sense of independence. Someone who didn't have interests and a life outside of me. I have my kid to think about, and work, and I don't have time to be everything to someone else.

DIRTYLIFE

It's funny because I never thought about passion that way. As something that could drain someone. With my ex, when we were together, it was good. Great even. We fit. But there was always a part of me that knew it wasn't right. Not that I had the guts to say that to her, or anyone else.

TOOBUSY

I get that. I was the same with my husband. Nothing was specifically wrong, but it wasn't right either.

DIRTYLIFE

Yes! That's it exactly. It's hard to walk away from something that's not wrong.

TOOBUSY

Because sometimes it's better to not be alone.

DIRTYLIFE

Yeah.

TOOBUSY

Yeah.

DIRTYLIFE

But what I've realized since that relationship ended is that it's also exhausting to try to hold something together that isn't meant to be. We didn't want the same things. And trying to make it happen would have meant us hating each other.

TOOBUSY

That's not fair to anyone. I feel the same mostly. Although I'm angry that I'm the one acting like the responsible adult and my ex gets to live without responsibility.

DIRTYLIFE

That sucks.

TOOBUSY

It does. But I have custody, and I love having time with my kid, so I really can't complain. He doesn't make time for her, and even though I hate it for her, I also know if she did see him much, it wouldn't be better. He was never a great father.

DIRTYLIFE

Sounds like she's lucky to have you.

TOOBUSY

I think I'm the lucky one.

"Mom, can you help me with my math homework?" Mikayla asked, dragging her backpack to the table and sitting next to me.

As she pulled her folder out and searched for a pencil, I read DirtyLife's last message.

DIRTYLIFE

How anyone could walk away from that amazes me. It's all I've ever wanted. But my ex wasn't looking for a family. She didn't want kids.

TOOBUSY

Not everyone is meant to be a parent. My daughter wasn't planned, but she's the best thing that's ever happened to me. And she needs my help with homework, so I need to go.

DIRTYLIFE

Talk soon. Enjoy your evening.

TOOBUSY

Thanks. You too.

I flipped my phone over and focused on Mikayla. She was the most important thing to me. She had to be. Always.

I LOADED Mikayla up on Saturday morning and drove to her bestie's house. Melody Holland had become a close friend over the years since the girls became friends. Melody and her husband, Ramsey, went through a separation years ago, but they were able to find their way back together. Still, she understood how tough marriage and parenting and life could be and was always there for Mikayla and me.

Mikayla tore out of the car, racing to the open door as Amber appeared. I followed more slowly, the girls disappearing into the house before Melody walked out.

"Good morning," Melody said, reaching to hug me. "How are you?"

"Good. Tired."

Melody nodded. "It's not easy doing it all yourself.

Ramsey said he'll be happy to have Mikayla here if you ever want to join me for book club again."

"Thanks," I said, knowing I wouldn't take him up on it. I'd leaned on them too much over the last year. Asking them to watch Mikayla when I needed to do assignments and meet with my lawyer and work. I was not going to ask them to help out so I could socialize.

"I know that really means you're never going to ask, but Ramsey said it's good for Amber to have time with her friend. It's not a bother for us. Ever. Mikayla is an amazing kid, and we love that they have stayed so close for so long."

"I love it, too."

"So, you'll agree? How about tomorrow?"

I exhaled a laugh with my sigh. "You know I don't like asking you guys."

"Which is why we're offering," Ramsey said, appearing behind Melody in the doorway. "I adore Mikayla, and we all adore you, Casey. Plus, it makes my job easier and gives me bonus points." Ramsey winked at Melody.

Melody's cheeks turned pink, and she swatted him away.

Ramsey leaned down and kissed her in a way that made my cheeks warm. Kyle never kissed me like that. Not in front of people, and not in private. It was the kind of kiss that said he couldn't wait to get her alone and have his hands, and other parts, all over her.

I wanted that.

I couldn't bring myself to want another relationship, but sex? I missed sex. Even if it wasn't as passionate as the kiss Melody and Ramsey shared, sex was still fun. It was a release, a moment to pause and not think about all the other things in life. It was exciting and made me feel good, and I missed it.

Melody was still blushing when Ramsey disappeared back into the house. "Sorry about him."

I shook my head. "Nothing to apologize for. You guys deserve that kind of happiness."

"So do you," Melody said, looking affronted that I dared suggest otherwise.

I laughed mirthlessly. "I think I missed the boat on happiness. I'd settle for some good sex, though."

"Then have some. Didn't you tell me you have a match you've been talking to?"

"Yeah. We talk about our failed relationships. Hardly sex-talk."

"Then flirt with him."

"I don't think I know how to flirt."

"Everyone knows how to flirt."

"Then maybe I forgot."

"You're an intelligent woman with endless resources. Figure out how to flirt and find a man who'll have some good sex with you."

"You make me sound so undesirable."

"You're not undesirable. You just have to have a little confidence. There are always single dads at school. I still get hit on sometimes. Ramsey gets angry about it, but I kind of love that it makes him a little jealous."

I laughed with her. "You're bad."

She shrugged. "Maybe, but it's not like I encourage them. You should volunteer at school sometime."

"I wish I could, but I'm barely earning enough with the three jobs I'm already working. I don't think I could add volunteering into my day."

"Maybe one of the events on a weekend then. I don't know. Or just flirt with the next guy you see. Who cares how it goes? Practice."

I snorted, then realized where I was going and who I would see. The master of flirtation. Who was both not really single and had the ability to make me weak at the knees with his words alone.

He could teach me a thing or two about flirting.

"Mom! We're going outside!" Amber called from inside the house.

"Okay!" Melody called back. She turned back to me. "Don't worry about Mikayla. We'll feed her and let them play outside and tire her out. Take as long as you need today."

"Thanks, Mel. I really appreciate it. Thank you to Ramsey, too."

"I'll let him know. See you in a few hours."

I nodded and waved, turning to go and knowing my daughter was in good hands.

I just wish I had the same confidence in my own situation.

I parked outside the flower shop and took a deep breath to steady my nerves. Walking in there again, knowing the day before I'd made a fool of myself, was not my favorite plan for the day. But I had no choice. I pitched this column. I had to follow through.

Voices led me into the shop and toward the back, where I found Natalie and Omar staring at a book with Landon talking about the flowers he offered.

"Fall flowers have rich, deep colors that are stunning against a white dress. The burgundy and orange and yellow colors of hydrangeas, plus a few lighter and brighter colors to balance the whole thing. Or you could do one single stem of a large, bold flower that brings simplicity and elegance instead of a full bouquet."

"Simple is definitely my style," Natalie said.

Landon looked up and saw me standing a few feet away. "You return. Give me a minute, and I'll be right with you. If you think you can avoid destroying things today."

His smile and the light in his eyes told me he was joking,

but the subtle mention that he remembered me sent heat to my cheeks. The man could flirt with a post. Which was pretty close to how I felt as I stood there without speaking.

Natalie and Omar turned to see who Landon was speaking to, and Natalie smiled brightly. "Casey! You made it. We started without you." She stood and came over to me, hugging me warmly before tugging me to the table where the three of them sat.

"Hi," I said, letting Natalie shove me into the open seat. Between her and Landon. My knees bumped against Landon's, and a jolt went through me.

He cleared his throat, almost sounding as startled as I was when we touched. He offered his hand to me. "I'm Landon Boyd. It's nice to meet you, Casey. Natalie and Omar have filled me in on your articles planned. I'm happy you could join us."

"Thank you," I said, my voice coming out breathy, like I was trying to talk him into the bedroom. I cleared my throat and forced a smile to my flaming face. "Nice to meet you. And I promise to keep my destruction to a minimum."

Natalie and Omar looked at us, confusion written all over their faces.

"I stopped in here yesterday on my way home. I... The brightness of it drew me in, but then I knocked over a display tower and ran off before I could buy anything. I was planning to never come back again."

Omar chuckled. The man was polished and perfect and had probably never had an embarrassing moment in his entire life.

Natalie laughed heartily and put her hand on my arm. "That's totally something I would have done. You know how I am. As they say, a picture is worth a thousand words. It's good because I had none when I fell to my knees and groped him."

Landon choked, his blinking gaze struggling to figure out what he'd missed.

Natalie chuckled. "I was the woman in the picture with Omar."

Landon looked astounded. "You were?"

Natalie nodded. "I was. And it wasn't like it looked. I came out of the bathroom and someone slammed into me, and I fell. Omar was just there, and unfortunately for him, slowed my fall. With his crotch."

A laugh burst from Landon. One he covered up before he winced. "That… um… I have no words. Ouch?"

Omar cracked for the first time, a laugh falling from his lips. "Yeah, ouch was the first word I thought of, too. Followed by a few others I shouldn't say to anyone besides my future wife."

I swear to God, I swooned. These damn men. Ramsey, Omar, hell, even Landon. How in the hell did I end up with Kyle when there were men like these others out there? Why couldn't I find one of them now?

Nope. Nope. I didn't want one. I wanted sex. I wanted flirtation and desire and a few really good orgasms. Not a relationship. I wasn't looking to pick out flowers and a white dress and promise to love someone for the rest of my life. Been there, done that, was not going back.

Ever.

5

LANDON

*W*ell, well, well. The pretty woman who knocked over my display was the reporter following Natalie and Omar around for the month leading up to their wedding. That wasn't what I expected.

When Natalie and Omar showed up early for our appointment, Natalie was apologetic about the whole situation and springing it on me. I assured her it was fine, but seeing who the reporter was definitely made it more than fine.

Casey was beautiful. A little older than me, if I had to guess, but close enough to my age that I didn't feel like a child next to her. She had an easy laugh and was adorable when her cheeks flamed red every time she was embarrassed.

And man did I like seeing that when I flirted with her. She made me feel like I wasn't destined to be single forever since everyone in town had decided Reegan and I were still a couple and would eventually figure it out and get back together.

Even Natalie made a comment about us reconnecting at the wedding since we were both invited.

Kill me now.

The last thing I needed was to have my dating potential eliminated because the town decided Reegan and I were meant to be when we'd decided we weren't. That was only part of why I was enjoying online dating.

Or online conversing. It hadn't progressed to actual dating yet, but I had hope.

"This is gorgeous," Natalie whispered as she flipped the pages of the display book I kept on hand.

"Sunflowers are pretty classic for fall weddings. They're simple and fun and make everyone smile," I told her. Flowers were my love language. The meaning behind each flower was something I found fascinating, even if sometimes I felt like flowers should say whatever the hell you wanted them to say. If a bride loved chrysanthemums, I wasn't going to tell her they symbolized grief in some cultures. The meaning of a flower was what a person made it, not always what someone said it should mean.

Then again, I was never able to decipher classic literature in high school either. If the author wrote one thing, I couldn't make the jump that they really meant something else, which was a metaphor for another thing, and what they really intended was nothing close to what was written. I was too literal. Or so I'd been told.

I was more of the say what you mean mentality. And that translated to flowers.

"I like simple," Natalie said for the second time.

I glanced at Omar and noticed the hint of a smile on his face. I smothered my own grin, but not fast enough.

"What?" Natalie demanded, her eyes flipping between Omar and me. "You seriously think I'm complicated?"

"I think you're beautiful and smart and kind. But simple is not a word I'd use to describe you," Omar said, ending his statement with a kiss.

"How am I not simple? I can't do complicated. I get over-whelmed, and my anxiety takes over, and I lose it. I like simple." Natalie huffed, arms crossed as she scowled at her fiancé.

"All of that is true. But nothing about this wedding has been simple. You wanted a band and a DJ, so people could enjoy both. You asked for hors d'oeuvres that could be served when we're taking pictures, more for when we arrive at the reception, and then dinner. And don't forget the three flavors of wedding cake because you couldn't decide what you liked best." Omar smirked throughout his entire diatribe.

Natalie's scowl morphed into a grin as she lost her fight to hold on to her mad. "Fine. I'm not simple. But I really want to be."

"All those things sound like you're trying to create a wedding that will make your guests very happy," Casey said. "Maybe the flowers should be more about what would make you happy?"

My chest expanded with joy. Damn. She got it. I was about to say the same damn thing. "What she said."

Omar and Natalie chuckled.

"I like simple," Natalie reiterated. "I want simple. During the wedding, I'm going to have to hand off my bouquet or flower or whatever to Daisy anyway, so simple makes sense. And it'll look really nice with my dress."

She looked up at Omar as she said that last part, and he groaned. "Stop teasing me." He kissed her, then met my gaze. "She keeps telling me all these bonkers things about her dress, and I'm pretty sure they're all lies, but I promised not to look, so I'm left wondering if her dress is really as elabo-rate as she makes it sound."

"You think I would lie to you?" Natalie asked in fake offense. "Why would I do that?"

We all laughed, enjoying the sweet bickering of the couple. I lifted my gaze to Casey's and found her watching me back. The moment stuck, and our gazes held, the two of us lost in a tiny world of our own. My blood pulsed hot in my veins. My cock swelled without conscious thought. My entire body wanted this woman.

This woman whose name I didn't know yesterday. Who created an avalanche of chaos in my store. And who was currently creating the same inside me.

Casey tore her gaze from mine, a sharp end to the moment that left me fighting for my next breath and wondering what in the hell just happened.

And how soon I could experience it again.

"So, simple?" Natalie said. "Our colors are navy and white because I couldn't really think of something I liked with navy. Do you think sunflowers would work with that?"

I held up one finger, then walked toward the refrigerated cases up front. I searched through for what I was looking for, grabbing one bright yellow sunflower and a handful of navy roses. I arranged them with the roses a bit below the sunflower, letting the sunflower shine and take all the attention.

I carried the small bouquet back to Natalie and Omar, offering it to Natalie to see.

"Oh, wow," she breathed.

I couldn't stop my smile. I loved what I did, but that right there, that exhale of perfection, that's what did it for me. I wasn't always around to see it. Usually someone bought flowers and took them home, but when I was able to see the joy on the face of a customer and know they got it, they really understood what flowers could say, that made my day.

"So simple but not a single flower?" Omar asked with a grin.

Natalie chuckled. "Fine. I'm not a simple person. But you love me anyway."

"More than anything else in the world." The sincerity in his tone and gaze hit me hard.

Had I ever felt that way about Reegan? I didn't even have to ask the question. I knew I hadn't. I was drawn to her originally because she was vibrant and fun and the chemistry between us was electric, but over time, we were just comfortable. The spark that brought us together faded, and instead of parting ways, we held on. We made plans for our future because we were so wrapped up in each other's lives we couldn't see a future that didn't involve us.

But I never loved her the way Omar loved Natalie. I never looked at Reegan and knew I'd do anything to make her happy. Toward the end, I was spending more time trying not to make her angry than trying to make her happy.

That wasn't how I wanted my next relationship to be. Or any relationship ever again.

I cleared my throat and forced a smile. "What does work? If one single flower isn't it, we can do something like you're holding where it's a sunflower in the middle of the navy roses, or another dark flower. We can add some white if you'd like to balance all the colors. We can do three sunflowers instead of one and see if you like that instead. This was just to show you the colors together. Do you like them?"

"I love it," Natalie said. "Thank you. And... I have no idea what I want. Can I see some options? Is that possible?"

"Of course," I told her, getting up from my seat and returning to the cases. Natalie followed me, with Omar and Casey trailing behind us.

I flung open the case and grabbed flowers, picking white and navy plus a few others that could work if she wanted more variety.

Natalie shook off ideas to add more colors, and we worked out the perfect bouquet for her and her maid of honor. Daisy was going to get the simple bouquet I put together first, with a single sunflower and a bunch of navy roses. Natalie was getting the same thing, but with three sunflowers and some small white roses added in for depth. Both bouquets were stunning.

She decided on single sunflowers for the men's boutonnieres before we moved on to the flowers for the tables.

"You can also get silk flowers to save yourselves some money," I suggested. "As many tables as you're going to have, it could get pricey."

"Let's see what it costs before we think about other options."

I nodded. "Sounds good. I would suggest either something very short or something very tall to foster conversation. If you go for short, you could do potted plants, which people can take home afterward. If you go tall, you're going to need to think about how elaborate you want to go, but simple could be single sunflowers in a narrow vase, so it doesn't block lines of sight or conversation, but they look nice."

Casey's quick inhale had me looking at her. She was writing something in her notebook and not looking at me.

"What if we did some of each?" Natalie suggested.

Omar and I laughed.

He kissed the side of her head and said, "Definitely not simple with you."

"Oh, Landon is used to me. Although I have a feeling Andre makes decisions before he comes here so you don't have to be exposed to all my crazy," Natalie said.

I shook my head. "I know nothing."

Casey snorted. Omar laughed. Natalie's cheeks turned red.

"You are not a problem, I promise you. And I love what I do. I can't imagine a job that didn't allow me to get dirty all the time."

Casey choked. Her cheeks went beet red. I winked at her, and they darkened even more.

"It's important to enjoy what you do," Natalie said. "I never imagined I'd be running a summer camp and working at an afterschool program, but I can't imagine anything else now."

"Life gives us what we need, although sometimes we don't like it."

"Very true." Natalie looked up at Omar, their gazes shining with something that made me jealous.

I looked away and focused on the options for centerpieces.

"What are we looking at for everything if we do half and half with the centerpieces?" Omar asked.

I went back to the table where we started the meeting and put in everything we talked about. I gave him a number that made Casey's eyes bug out.

Omar nodded. "That works. And you can have everything done for the wedding?"

"Absolutely," I told him. "It won't be a problem at all. I can deliver everything to the Retreat that morning, get it all set up so you don't have to worry about it, and I'll bring the boutonnieres and bouquets to you if you want."

"That would be perfect. Thank you so much," Natalie gushed.

"Of course. I'm happy to do it. If you think of anything else, let me know, okay?"

They nodded, stars in their eyes as they focused on each other. Four weeks until the wedding and they were ready. I could see it. I'd seen more than a few couples come in before their wedding, and some had that look of love in their eyes, and others looked like they were stressed out and annoyed. I preferred the happy ones.

"What else do you need from us?" Natalie asked Casey.

Casey smiled and shook her head. "Nothing. I'm just following along and figuring everything out. Before I publish anything, you're both going to see it, okay?"

"We trust you," Natalie said, hugging Casey.

"Still. After everything you two have been through, I want to make sure you see it all. I will send it to you tomorrow at the latest."

"Thank you, Casey. That means a lot." Omar hugged her, too.

I felt like I was missing out. I didn't get to hug Casey. But it wasn't like I could ask her for a hug. That would be weird.

"Are you walking out?" Natalie asked when she turned toward the door, and Casey didn't follow.

Casey looked at me for half a second, then shook her head. "I was going to pick out some flowers to take home. Something to brighten my place up."

"Oh, fun. We have to run, if that's okay."

"Yes, of course. Don't let me hold you up. I'll be in touch soon."

Natalie hugged Casey again, then followed Omar outside.

Casey stared after them, her teeth sunk into her bottom lip.

Was she worried about me? About being alone with me? She didn't seem to be, but why was she—

"I want you to teach me how to flirt," Casey blurted without looking at me.

"You... What?"

She drew a breath and let it out slowly, then faced me. Her brown eyes were wide with fear or excitement, maybe both. Her cheeks were stained with a blush. Her chest rose with the rapid breath she sucked in. "Flirting. You're really good at it. And I feel like I wouldn't know what to say to a man if my life depended on it. I need lessons or something. I don't want to cross any lines with you or anything, but I was hoping you could help me... Oh, my God, what was I thinking."

She started toward the front of the store, half-running away from me.

All I could think was *stop her!*

"Wait!" I called out.

"Please forget I said anything. I don't know—"

"I'll do it!"

That stopped her. Her handbag swung, narrowly missing a large display near the front of the shop. She spun around slowly, as if she would spook me if she turned too quickly. "What?"

"I'll do it. I'll teach you about flirting."

"You will? Why?"

I shrugged. "Because you asked."

"Just like that. You'll teach me about flirting."

"Sure. I like flirting. And there's certainly nothing objectionable about spending time with a beautiful woman."

"Well, I'm not sure your girlfriend would agree."

My brows shot high. "Uh, I don't have a girlfriend."

"Reegan. I mean Reegan. I know you two broke up, but everyone knows—"

"Nothing," I interrupted her. "Everyone knows nothing. Reegan and I are over. We're not getting back together. I hope she finds happiness, but it's not going to be with me. We're not right for each other, and we both know that. That's why it's over."

Casey took a tentative step toward me. "You sound pretty sure about that."

I exhaled a laugh. "That's because I am. Not that you asked, but when things ended, I was angry, but she and I have talked. We know we're done. It's everyone else in town who has trouble with that idea. Which is why…"

"Which is why what?" she asked when I didn't continue.

Could I do this? Could I really say what was on the tip of my tongue?

Fuck it.

"I'll teach you about flirting. About whatever you want to know. But I need a favor from you."

She gulped. "What sort of favor?"

"I'm assuming you're going to the wedding."

Her brows furrowed before her eyes widened. "Natalie and Omar's wedding?"

"Yes. And I'm assuming you're going alone since you're asking about flirting lessons."

"I am."

"Then for payment, I want you to go as my date."

"What? Why? No. Reegan—"

"Is not in the picture. But she will be there. And if I show up alone, everyone will be trying to push us together all night. I can't deal with it. Dating in this town is hard enough, but dating when everyone thinks I should still be with my ex is borderline painful. I need to make it clear to everyone in town that I'm not with Reegan."

"And you think showing up with me is going to make people stop talking?"

I grinned. "I guarantee it won't. It'll make them talk more. But they won't be talking about me getting back together with Reegan."

Casey considered my offer. Her eyes narrowed, then she nodded, almost to herself. She took a step closer and extended her hand. "Deal."

I smiled and stepped closer. I grasped her hand in mine,

clasping it between both of my hands. I watched as her eyes widened. She tried to tug her hand back, but I held firm. "We have a deal, Casey."

She sucked in a breath, her pulse fluttering under my fingertips.

This was going to be so much fun.

6

CASEY

I had to have lost my mind. Had to. Propositioning him? To teach me how to flirt? What was wrong with me?

Too late now, though. He agreed. And in exchange, I was going to what? Make Reegan jealous? That wasn't what he said, but was it the plan? Everyone knew they were going to get back together. It was as inevitable as me never getting married again.

Which was why I agreed. I knew a man who was in love with someone else was safe. He wouldn't be a threat to my heart. And if he was using me to get back together with the woman he loved… Well, I didn't want to end up with Landon, so it was fine. It was all fine.

I was halfway home when I realized I forgot to buy flowers. Again. It was a good thing I was not going to fall for Landon Boyd because he had the ability to make my head fuzzy without even trying.

I spent the rest of my day with Mikayla, helping her with homework. We cooked dinner together and watched a movie on the couch before she got a call from Amber and raced to her room to talk about preteen stuff.

After I cleaned up the kitchen, I checked my phone to see if I'd missed anything. I had a message from Book Boyfriends Wanted and clicked over to see a new match.

His profile was only a few days old. He mentioned skiing and fishing as his two favorite hobbies. No kids, no ex-wife. And no sense of grammar.

He sounded funny, but the complete disregard for typing out full words and using proper grammar made me snarl. Rational? Maybe not. But I was a writer. I had a really hard time accepting that people weren't willing to even try. Not everyone was as particular as I was, but I couldn't even read past his first few answers before I was annoyed.

I closed the app and decided I'd deal with that later. I poured myself a glass of wine and grabbed my notes from the meeting with Natalie and Omar to collect my thoughts.

Four hours later, Mikayla's room was quiet, and I was falling asleep on the couch. My article was almost done, so I packed my things up and went to bed.

Only to remember I was going to book club tomorrow night. Crap.

I had to think of an excuse to get out of it. Not that I didn't like Melody and her group of friends, but I felt out of place there. The single mom who had to rely on others to live my life. The woman with no dates and no hope for any in the near future.

Unless I counted my fake date with Landon, but I didn't. I couldn't.

Sleep evaded me for far too long, but when it finally came, I had dreams of a sexy florist with a devilish smile and a talent for making me hot.

SUNDAY WAS A RUSH. I was up early and finished my article, sending it to Natalie in case she wanted to change anything. Then, I had to get to the grocery store so I could get things ready for the week. Mikayla helped to make lunches and dinners so we didn't cave and go out to eat on the nights we had a lot going on.

So I didn't cave. She wouldn't fight me if I said I wanted to grab a pizza or something.

When I finished, Mikayla had her shoes on and stood by the door.

"What are you doing?"

"Amber said I was going to her house for a little while tonight because you are going out with Ms. Melody," Mikayla said. Her brows pinched, and confusion lit her features. "Was she wrong?"

Before I could answer, my phone buzzed with a text.

MELODY

I hope you're not backing out of tonight. Ramsey has dinner almost done, and Amber is so excited to have Mikayla over on a school night. I promise we won't stay too late. Everyone has things to do in the morning.

I swallowed my groan and thumbed a quick reply.

We were just getting ready. Be to you soon.

I looked up at my daughter and nodded. "Let me change my shirt and we will go."

"Yay! Thanks, Mom. You're the best."

I smiled and kissed the top of her head as she threw her arms around me. Little victories.

Everyone was fairly casual for book club, but I didn't want to show up in a stained tee and sweatpants, so I searched for something that made me feel less like a frumpy mom and more like me. Oh, and I needed a bra.

Ten minutes later, with me in yoga pants and an oversized shirt, I pulled into Melody and Ramsey's driveway. Amber raced out to meet Mikayla before the two of them rushed back into the house and disappeared. Melody came out before I could get to the door.

"Let's go."

She said the words like she was running away, and all my instincts lit up. "What's wrong?"

She chuckled. "Nothing. I promise. Amber's just been up my butt all day. She's getting into a needy phase, I guess, and I want to get away before she clings to me again."

"Oh," I said, feeling more than a little jealous. Mikayla definitely was not in the same phase.

When we got into the car, Melody sighed. "Amber got her first ever period yesterday."

"Really? Wow. How did she handle it?"

Melody chuckled. "She was fine. She said she knew all about it between what I'd talked to her about, school, and what she saw online. But it was still a shock and a little bit of a moment for her. Did Mikayla start yet?"

I nodded. "Last year."

"Amber said a lot of girls had already started. She was anxious about it for a while. Truth be told, I was starting to worry, too. I was going into fifth grade when I got mine. For her to start sixth grade and not have it yet, I was wondering if something else was going on."

"I think there are more girls who haven't started than have admitted it. You know how kids are. They all want to fit in. It's not like they are in the stalls together. Something like this is easy to hide."

"True. I'm just happy she's okay. You hear stories about girls who never got their period, and it was some major medical issue that no one knew about until they were much older. One tiny bit of relief for this stressed-out mama."

I chuckled with her as I parked a few spots from the front of Book Boyfriends Unlimited. "I can only imagine. We have enough to stress about. We don't need to add something like that on you."

"Exactly." Melody climbed out of my SUV and waited for me on the sidewalk. "How are things going with work?"

I groaned.

She laughed. "That good?"

I sighed. "Gretchen wants me to dig up dirt on Natalie and Omar. Natalie gave me permission to share that she was the woman in the picture last year, but I don't want to trash them. They're good people, and this is a good town. I don't love that Gretchen is out for blood."

"Isn't she always? You said that was her reputation."

"Whose reputation?" Finley MacKellar asked as she unlocked the door to let us in. Finley owned Book Boyfriends Unlimited and married Trent MacKellar, the man whose family founded the town we all called home.

"My editor's," I told her. "She wants dirt on Natalie and Omar."

"Natalie's already here," Finley whispered, locking the door behind us again.

"She knows. I told her about it. I am not looking to destroy anyone who doesn't deserve it," I said.

Finley's brows shot up. "Who gets to decide if it's deserved?"

"I get what you're asking. As a reporter, freedom of speech is important to me, but so is telling the truth. When former mayor Levine was trying to undermine Omar, I wanted the truth exposed. The fact that it tanked his chances of getting reelected was his own doing. He was trying to ruin Omar's reputation with half-truths and blatant lies. I'm going to report on that. I didn't go after him for a vendetta. I went after whoever was twisting things to take down someone who'd done nothing wrong. It led to someone who hid behind the reporter he fed information to. That's not what I signed up for when I decided to be a reporter. Just like we don't have to reveal our sources, we also shouldn't print things without verifying their truth. My former colleague didn't do that."

"No, he didn't. And he ended up losing his job for it," Natalie said from the center of the group that had already gathered. "Thanks to you wanting to print the actual truth."

"There have been a lot of times people have printed things about Trent and his family that just weren't true. There's a fine line from his experience, and now mine. I struggle with a lot of it," Finley said, reclaiming her seat.

"Would you feel more comfortable if I weren't here?" I asked her. If she was worried about me reporting anything I overheard, she wouldn't be comfortable in her own shop. That wasn't fair.

"No," Finley was quick to say. "I know you're not going to deceive any of us. That's never been something I've worried about."

"Okay. Thank you." It meant more than she knew to hear that. It gave me the security to take a seat in the circle arranged toward the back of the romance-only bookstore. Finley said she always wanted to read romance novels and couldn't find many in town, so she opened her own store to cater to the others who felt the same way.

"Casey is on the right side of things," Natalie said. "If Omar was dirty, she would expose it. She's not going to pull punches, but she's also not going to dig up stuff that doesn't need to be unearthed. Unlike her boss."

"That's what Casey was saying when they walked in. She's always out for blood," Finley told the group.

"It's a newspaper thing," I said with a sigh. "It's the part of the job that gets you ahead when you work in a city. First to get a scoop. First to find out someone is cheating. First to expose a scandal. I think it's important to report on what's actually happening and to expose people who aren't doing the things they should be doing, but is it anyone's business if Omar's ex-wife ended the marriage or if he did?"

"She wants to know that?" Natalie breathed.

I nodded. "She asked me about it when we talked the first time. Before I came to you. I don't see what that has to do with anything, and I told her so."

"She really does want to stir shit up," Finley said. "I don't like that. It makes me feel like people don't have a right to privacy and a personal life. If Trent had an affair, I would be crushed. I wouldn't want to read about it in the newspaper. Just because he is a business owner, it doesn't mean everyone should have access to every minute of our lives."

"I agree," I told her. "I wanted to write about Natalie and Omar's wedding because I think it's a great story. A feel-good kind of thing. The town's mayor is getting married. In a place like MacKellar Cove, we don't have a lot of scandals or major news stories, which I like, and a personal interest kind of thing is what people want to read about. Gretchen doesn't really get it."

"Gretchen? Oh, I think I know her," Blake said, her eyes going wide. "Mid-fifties, white. Brunette bob with zero gray. Clear-frame glasses, perfectly arched eyebrows, red lipstick, and always dressed like she's ready for a business meeting?"

I nodded. "Sounds like her."

"She comes into Cracked every week. Sits in my section most of the time. I tried to introduce myself and get to know her, but never got past her first name. I don't think she likes me," Blake said with a wince.

"She doesn't like anyone," I told her. "She is good at her

job, but I think she sees coming here as a punishment. At first, with everything going on around Omar and Levine and Erik publishing stories without fact-checking, I think she thought it would be a good assignment, but she's bored."

"She needs to get laid," Elise said. Known as the one who wasn't afraid to speak her mind, Elise always said people needed to get laid.

I couldn't really argue with her on that one, though. Gretchen didn't talk to people, so my guess was she hadn't had sex in even longer than me. Which was saying something.

"Ooh, Casey, you should tell her Omar and I were matched on Book Boyfriends Wanted. That we didn't like each other, but we were matched. I ran away from him," Natalie confessed.

"No, you didn't," I gasped.

Natalie nodded and looked at Daisy, her best friend.

"She did. We came here for book club the next night. That was when she realized he'd messaged her... how many times?" Daisy asked with a smirk that said she knew the answer.

"Thirteen times," Natalie said with a wince. "I freaked out, okay. He was sort of my boss, and I knew he didn't like me, and when he was the one I was matched with, I just ran."

"What did he say?" I asked, knowing I was the only one who didn't know the story.

"Well, before we met, I made him promise he wouldn't walk out as soon as I got there. Then I did that, and he called me out on it."

"Wow. Listen, none of this is on the record, but that would make a great story about how you two met. It would be good to put with the article about you being the woman in the picture."

The collective gasp around the room said no one else knew Natalie told me to run that in a story.

"I told her about it," Natalie defended. "Omar is sick of people asking if I'm jealous of the woman in the photo and if that woman is going to come back and cause problems for us. I told Casey to do a story about it."

"Are you sure about that?" Finley asked.

"I trust Casey. And if we tell the whole story, with matching and all that, maybe it'll help other people who are on the fence about signing up for Book Boyfriends Wanted. Like Gretchen. Not that I would really want to meet someone from there just for sex, but maybe it'll lead to more for her like it did for all…most all of us." Natalie flashed me a sympathetic smile.

"I think it's a great app to meet people for sex," Elise said. "I did that all the time before Colin and I got together. Hell, it's how Colin and I got together."

"What?" Daisy asked. "Are you kidding?"

Elise snorted. "No. Not even a little. I pissed off Karissa and Hudson all the time."

"Why?" Daisy asked, glancing at Karissa, who'd been quiet so far.

"Because I wanted my app to be used to create connections. To find the person you're meant to be with. Not for hookups. There are enough apps out there for that," Karissa said.

"And Hudson was pissed because I would always meet people at O'Kelley's. I knew he would make sure I was safe when I was there. And he would know who I left with if I wasn't there," Elise explained.

"That's smart," I told her.

"Thank you!" Elise cried. "Finally, someone who gets it. You're single. Are you living it up with the app? Wait, are you on Book Boyfriends Wanted?"

"I am on it, but living it up… not so much," I confessed.

"Why not? If I were still single, I'd be hooking up with as many men as possible," Elise said.

"Same," Willow agreed.

"I don't think I would," Natalie countered. "I never felt like I could relax and enjoy casual sex."

"If you're looking for something serious, then yeah, it's not easy to enjoy it. I was never looking for that. I had no intention of ever getting into another committed relationship," Elise said with a shiver.

"But then Colin swept you off your feet," Blake said with a grin.

Elise snorted. "More like he waited me out until I got my head out of my ass and realized how amazing he is."

"Which is what you needed to be swept off your feet," Blake said.

Elise wrinkled her nose. "True. I was stubborn."

"You were wounded. Emotionally," Chelsea, Elise's cousin, said. "You didn't know how to trust a man after what happened."

"No, I didn't. I could screw them senseless, but if they even thought about something serious, I would run screaming. Until Colin." Elise trailed off with a dreamy smile that made my heart squeeze.

Did I want that? A part of me said I did, but I wasn't sure. Kyle was less than great as a husband, and the sex was the only part of being married I ever missed.

"As the one who's only ever been with one man in my entire life," Melody began, "I don't have a point of reference, but sex has definitely gotten better over time."

"I agree with that," Blake said. "Sex with Ian was better than with William from day one, but over the years, it's only improved. We have more of a connection. It's not just sex for the sake of sex. There are days when I'm exhausted and feel like I can barely keep my head up, but he's there for me to rub my feet and take care of things at home to ease my burden, and when we finally get into bed, that partnership continues. Everything about it is better."

The others around the room nodded, adding their own stories to the conversation.

I sat back and listened, feeling like I had nothing to contribute. Not just because I was single, but because sex with Kyle was good, but it was for the sake of sex. It was the only link we shared over time. We got married because of sex. We stayed together as long as we did because of sex.

And when it came down to it, we both knew we couldn't survive in a marriage that was only about sex.

I enjoyed sex, but sex was an act. It was a momentary connection. It wasn't something that made me want to spend the rest of my life with someone. No matter how many of the women in the group said it brought them closer to their significant others.

I just wanted an orgasm or two. I could get that from anyone. I didn't need more than one night.

7

andon texted me first thing Monday morning. I was packing Mikayla's lunch, wearing my mom hat, and blushing like a child.

LANDON

Good morning, beautiful. I can't wait to see you. Are we still on for lunch? I had a dream about you and your bottomless brown eyes.

Heat rushed through me. I tingled all over. Then I remembered why we were meeting.

He was giving me flirting lessons. The man who was flirting with me. Had the lessons already started? Was he flirting because he couldn't help himself or because it was part of teaching me how to do it?

It didn't matter. We weren't going to be anything beyond what we were. Student and teacher. Friends, sort of. Fake dates to the biggest story of my career.

It was all part of the plan. I asked him to give me lessons because the man could flirt without breaking a sweat.

Whereas I was hot and bothered over the tiniest bit of attention from an attractive man.

No way was I getting laid that way.

I brushed the breadcrumbs off my hands and channeled my inner seductress. She was passed out in the corner, maybe dead from boredom. I'd never called on her before, so it took a minute to come up with something to write back.

> Still on for lunch. I'm looking forward to soaking up all your knowledge.

Was that flirting? This was why I needed lessons. I had no idea what I was doing.

> You'll be beating them away with a stick…
> even more than you already are, beautiful.

"Mom," Mikayla said, interrupting the conversation I was doing very little to advance.

"What? Yeah? Huh? Did you need something?" I jammed my phone into my pocket and tried to push down the heat rising in my cheeks.

"I asked if my breakfast was ready."

"Oh, um, yeah." I turned and grabbed the milk from the fridge, pouring her a glass and setting it on the table with the bagel she wanted. Not the best breakfast ever, but mornings were not my strong suit. Nor hers. We were lucky if we got out the door without a fight every day, and I was not going to pick new ones about healthy breakfast.

Mikayla sat down and took a bite of her bagel, chewing with her eyes half closed. I went back to packing her lunch, ignoring the pull to text Landon back. He could wait a few minutes. I could wait a few minutes.

Mikayla finished her bagel without another word, then grabbed her lunch and stuffed it into her backpack. She shoved her feet into her sneakers and slung her backpack over her shoulder. "Bye, Mom."

"Hold on," I told her, reaching for a hug.

She indulged me for a few seconds, then extracted herself and walked out the door.

"Have a good day!" I called before it slammed shut behind her. I waited a few seconds, then went to the window to watch her get on the bus. When she stepped on and smiled at the bus driver, I finally breathed a sigh of relief.

It was a good morning. For us.

I cleaned up the kitchen and made a quick pass through the bathroom. I had a house to clean before lunch. I'd already submitted my first article about Natalie and Omar to Gretchen, and I was confident it was a good story. No bombs, no big reveals, just a good story about a sweet couple who wanted to share their love with everyone.

In other words, none of the drama Gretchen wanted. But I had hope it wouldn't end up cut.

The house I was cleaning belonged to a couple with two kids. They both worked full time, so I was usually in their house alone. I didn't mind the quiet, and it meant I got a lot more done than if I had someone to talk to. Most clients were happy to let me work, but some of them liked the company. Any other day, I wouldn't mind chatting, but I had a lunch date to get to.

The house was picked up as usual, and I was able to work through one room at a time. The work was soothing and rhythmic for me, allowing me to daydream about Landon and his flirtatious nature.

By the time I finished cleaning the house, I was more than happy to get something to eat and enjoy an hour or so with an attractive man.

Landon was already at Cracked when I arrived. He suggested the popular spot for lunch since it would put us in front of as many people as possible. I didn't love the idea, but I was reaping the benefits of it without having to do something truly embarrassing like pay someone to teach me to flirt. Or worse, pay someone for sex.

Landon stood when he saw me open the door. His smile lit up his face, his eyes crinkling at the edges. He looked like he was honestly happy I was there, and it made it impossible for me not to return the smile.

"Hey," he said, pulling out my chair. He hovered next to it, and I wasn't sure if he was waiting for me to sit or hug him or what.

"Hi," I said, smiling and taking the seat.

He pushed it in as I scooted forward, then let his hand linger on my shoulder before he gave it a soft squeeze.

I felt it all the way down my body. What was wrong with me?

"How was your morning?"

I shrugged. "It was fine. My daughter is in sixth grade, so after she got on the bus, I had to work."

"Middle school is tough. Is the newspaper busy every day or is there a day that's quiet?"

"Um, I don't really know, actually. I only freelance at the paper, so I write articles when the pitch I give is something the editor is willing to print."

"Oh. I didn't realize that was how it worked. Were you working on an article today?"

I picked up my water and shook my head. I always felt a little ashamed that I didn't have just one job. Or two. "No, actually, I was cleaning a house. It's my second job."

He shook his head. "I didn't know you had a second job."

"I actually have three. I do some data entry at night, too."

"Wow. You're making me feel like a slacker." His grin was kind and encouraging, but I felt my cheeks heat with embarrassment.

"I don't get any financial help from my ex, and it's expensive here. None of my jobs pay for insurance, so I basically have one job to cover the cost of insurance for us, one to pay for our living expenses, and one to try to have a little bit of fun sometimes."

He reached across the table for my hand, holding it until I looked up at him. He smiled kindly. "You have nothing to be ashamed of. I'm amazed by you. Not everyone would be willing to work their asses off to make ends meet. I admire it. I have an apartment above my shop that basically came with the building, and I live there because I had the space available. Before I bought the place, with a gigantic loan from the bank, I had roommates. And I was only worried about myself. Not a kid."

"You're being nice."

He shook his head. "I'm being honest. Andre lives in your building, but before that, he was living at home with his parents. A lot of people I know had some kind of support in one way or another. Don't discount how hard you work to make your situation work."

"Thank you," I whispered.

He squeezed my hand. "You moved into the apartment a year ago?"

I nodded. "Yeah. When my divorce went through. We had a house, but without my husband's income, I couldn't afford to stay there. We sold the house and split the money."

"I sense a but in there."

I chuckled at his insight and nodded.

"Are you guys ready to order?" Blake asked, not missing that Landon was holding my hand. Her brows went up, and her lips pressed together in a smile she swung my direction.

I shook my head and pulled my hand back.

"I need some coffee to start. And I'll have a BELT sandwich to eat."

"A what?" I blurted. I hadn't looked at the menu and had no idea what he was ordering.

"It's a BLT, but we add eggs," Blake explained. "So it's a B.E.L.T. sandwich."

"Oh, that sounds good. I'll do the same." I smiled at Blake.

"Coffee for you, too?"

I nodded. "Yes. And a water, please."

"Coming right up." Blake winked at me before she walked away, and I knew I was going to get grilled next time I went to book club.

"You two are friends?" Landon asked.

I nodded and shrugged at the same time. "Sort of, I guess. Melody… Holland, do you know Melody and Ramsey?"

Landon nodded.

"Their daughter and my daughter are best friends, so Melody tries to get me to go to book club."

"Book club?"

"Melody and Blake and a bunch of local women meet at Book Boyfriends Unlimited on Sunday nights."

"Ah, nice. A bunch of the guys meet on Thursday night. Sounds like it might be the other halves. Ramsey and Ian are usually there, and a bunch of guys they're friends with."

"Do you go?"

"Sometimes. Not every week. Andre has been going more lately, and he's dragged me a few times. It's not always easy being the only single one, though."

"Tell me about it," I murmured.

Blake delivered coffee and water to us, pausing to see if she could catch more of our conversation before she sighed and walked away.

Landon snorted a laugh. "I guess she's curious."

I nodded. "It seems so."

"And you don't want people to get the wrong idea about us."

"Yeah. I mean, I know we're going to the wedding together, and you need people to know you and Reegan are done, but..."

"But you're looking for..."

He trailed off, giving me space to answer the unasked question. "Sex."

He barked a laugh, then snickered when I didn't laugh with him. "Really? A gorgeous woman like you needs my help in that department? I don't believe it."

I snorted. "The last time I had sex was with my husband before we decided to separate."

He had just picked up his coffee and stopped with it halfway to his lips. "You said you've been divorced for a year."

I nodded.

"And separation takes time."

"A year."

"Are you telling me it's been two years since you've had sex?" he hissed.

"Longer, but close enough."

"What the hell is wrong with the men of this town?" He shook his head in wonder.

"They are just like all men. Not interested in a divorced single mom with more than a little extra weight."

"They don't know what they're missing if they judge you on any one of those qualities."

"You don't really know me, though. How can you say that?"

He leaned closer and smiled. He was magnetic, and I found myself leaning toward him. "I know enough about you to know any man who gets to know more is a lucky guy."

I snorted a shook my head, leaning back. I knew he was just saying what he thought I wanted to hear. What would be good for me to hear. It wasn't about romance or getting me into bed. It was about teaching me how to flirt.

"You are really good."

"At what?" he asked, finally taking a sip of his coffee.

"Flirting." I breathed a laugh. "You have me believing you mean all the things you're saying. It's impressive."

He stilled, frozen for a second, then he set his coffee down. "I'll share the most important rule of flirting. Are you ready for it?"

I leaned closer, eager for his knowledge.

"Never lie."

I blanched. "What?"

"Never lie. For one thing, it's shitty. For another, people can see through it. You believe what I'm telling you because it's the truth. I'm not making it up. You are beautiful, and I consider myself lucky to be spending time with you, for however long you want me around."

I sucked in a breath as he leaned back, stunned by his admission. It had to be a part of it, though. Reegan wasn't a small woman, but she was stunning. She had long dark hair that fell in gorgeous waves to her waist. She was funky and sexy and, yes, curvy, but she carried her curves in a way that I always envied. She was confident in her body and could go from casual teacher clothes to sexy night out clothes and look just as good in both.

As for me, I was lucky if I could squeeze myself into fancy clothes, let alone feel confident.

"Your BELTs," Blake said, depositing plates in front of each of us. Both had fries covering the rest of the plate and toothpicks sticking out from the end of each of the four sandwich triangles. "Can I get you two anything else? More coffee? Or ice water?"

Landon chuckled. "I could probably use some more ice water. Cool me down some."

Blake smirked at him and nodded. "I'll be right back."

"When your brain adjusts to what I just told you, I'll share the next secret with you."

My head snapped up. "What is it?"

"Flirting is really about talking to someone. Some people are natural flirts and seem like they are flirting with everyone they speak to. Others only flirt with someone they find attractive. But flirting, in any form, is about having a conversation and making sure the person you are talking to knows you think positively about them, whether that's sexual or not."

"Your ice water," Blake said, with a hint of humor in her tone. "I'll leave the two of you to…enjoy."

My cheeks flamed as she walked away. I was never going back to book club.

Landon chuckled again. "Is it really so hard to believe I could be attracted to you?"

I shoved my sandwich in my mouth so I wouldn't have to answer.

"Okay, then how about this? Your first lesson is convincing someone you want something from them. Flirting can be fun, but it can also help you to get something. You want sex, but you're probably not looking to flirt your way into someone's bed. Am I right?"

I nodded, still chewing the overly large bite I had taken.

"Step one becomes something smaller. Something more reasonable. Maybe a kiss. Or a date."

I nodded. That sounded like what I needed to do. Maybe I could practice these lessons on my match. I enjoyed talking to him, and if we met up, maybe it could lead to more than just a date, but first, we needed to meet.

"It's old-fashioned, but a lot of men like to be the ones to ask a woman out. Not all men, but a lot do. It's part of the protector instinct. That's not to say a man shouldn't be able to step aside and let his partner be strong and independent, but he wants to feel like he can be there for her. He can provide for her, in some way, not always financial, but in some way."

I nodded, feeling less and less sure about this whole thing.

"The other side of this is that when a woman asks a man out, she will stand out. She will be showing that she's assertive and interested. And men are basically scared teenagers forever."

I laughed.

He grinned and nodded. "I mean it. We are terrified of rejection, but we also like to be the ones who ask a woman out. It's the worst conundrum ever."

"Then maybe men should be okay with women doing the asking."

"I hope it's getting there."

"What about you? I asked you to teach me about flirting. Did that bother you?"

He shook his head. A wolfish smile curled his lips. "I think it's hot as fuck when a woman asks for what she wants. Dating, sex, everything. It tells me where I stand, and it makes me feel good."

"Is that why you flirt? Because it's the same thing? It tells a woman where she stands with you?"

"Absolutely," he said without hesitation.

"So, how do I do it? How do I ask out a stranger without coming across as creepy or weird?"

"What would you say to me?"

I opened my mouth, snapping it shut before I said anything. My mind went blank.

Landon grinned. "I'm already here, so clearly you said something to get me here."

"Yeah, but I can't ask every man I meet to teach me how to flirt. That kind of defeats the purpose."

He laughed again, the crinkles around his eyes telling me he laughed a lot.

It was appealing. A man who enjoyed laughing. Kyle rarely laughed at anything. Not with me. If I were ever going to consider another relationship, it would have to be with a man who made me laugh.

"What are you thinking right now?" Landon asked, his voice dropping low and hitting me in all the good spots.

"I was thinking I like that you laugh. That you make me laugh. And that I'd want that in someone I dated or whatever."

"Have you ever laughed during sex? Been so comfortable with the other person that laughter isn't mockery, it's just a part of the experience sometimes?"

I shook my head.

He smiled, this one not as bright. It was a sad smile, of missed chances and love gone wrong.

It was the reminder I needed that, no matter what he said, he had a past that hadn't completely let go of him. He might claim he wanted to start dating again, but whatever the reason was, it wasn't because he was ready to move on.

"Laughter is important in a relationship to me, too," he said after a minute. "So, what would be a good date that lets you express your sense of humor?"

"Please don't tell me to go to a movie."

He shook his head. "No, that's not a place where you can get to know someone."

"I agree. But an even bigger problem than that is my time. Because I have my daughter all the time, and I'm not ready to leave her home alone while I go out on a date."

"So, we're talking lunch dates only. And something that makes you laugh. That has the potential to end up in bed. No pressure, though. It just has to be perfect."

I snorted. "Easy, right?"

8

LANDON

*C*asey was the most fascinating person I'd ever had lunch with. Not because she was beautiful or funny, but because she was honest in a way that was refreshing and made me believe in people again. Reegan wasn't a bad person, but she spent most of our relationship lying to me about what she wanted. That was the hardest thing about it all ending. I felt like I misjudged her, and if I didn't know what was going on with a woman I spent three years with, how was I ever going to figure out a new person?

But sitting with Casey was like coming up for air after a deep dive into a pool. My entire body was filling with her oxygen, reborn and refreshed after nearly suffocating.

And then she laughed and stole all that breath away again.

My chest tightened, my heart squeezing at the expressive twists of her face. Damn, she was stunning.

I reached across the table for her hand, forgetting my place. It wasn't a date. It wasn't the beginning of something. I was teaching her how to flirt so she could have sex with someone else.

Fuck.

79

I changed the path my hand was taking and grabbed my water, downing half of it in an attempt to cool my body. This woman was more capable of flirting than she realized. She thought she was turning men away, but anyone who didn't see how amazing she was didn't know where to look.

But it was my victory that she was sitting there with me. I was the lucky one.

"You're the expert. What's a good date that will let me get to know someone, see if he has a sense of humor, and not take me away from my jobs or my daughter?" Casey asked.

Expert. It was funny she thought I had any sense of what the hell I was doing. Self-serving prick was more like it. But if it meant I got to spend more time with her, I was going to fake it all the way home. "This time of year, things are much quieter around here. You're not going to have the events of summer to try new things. So you're left with the normal everyday stuff. Unfortunately, there aren't a ton of options."

"I know! That's the problem," she blurted.

I chuckled. "I get it. But the good thing is it gives you a chance to do something you're comfortable doing. You're not going to be presenting a side of yourself that isn't real. I know you're interested in something temporary, but it's better if you see each other for who you really are instead of pretending to be someone you're not." Do as I say and not as I do, said the pot to the kettle. I was an asshole pretending to have good advice for her when my sex life was just as dormant as hers.

"That makes sense," she said, looking contemplative instead of skeptical. "Just because I haven't had a lot of luck with men doesn't mean I need to hide everything about myself." She stared off for a minute, her mind working through something.

I wanted to ask her what was going through her mind, but I kept my mouth shut. I took a bite of my sandwich and chewed slowly. Casey did the same, the far-off look still in her eyes. We ate in silence for a few minutes, half of my sandwich disappearing before Casey looked at me again.

"Having lunch with someone is good. It gives me the chance to talk to someone. As a reporter, I like to talk to people. Lunch is less intimidating than dinner. But it also feels boring."

"It's economical. Everyone needs to eat lunch. You can start with a lunch break, then move on to something more significant. If you have a chance for that. Or an interest in it. I think that's what people do. Meet for coffee to see if there's a connection, then move to something more serious."

"I hate all of this," she mumbled.

"Everyone does."

She looked up at me with a doubtful smirk. "Not you. You seem right at home flirting."

I leaned back and inhaled. "Part of it is my job. I work in sales. People come to me when they know they're ready to buy something, so I'm not talking anyone into something they don't want, but I'm still selling. In order to do that effectively, I have to talk to them. Find out who they are, what they're really looking for, what makes sense."

"That's true. The first time I was in your shop, I heard you talking to that woman about flowers and what they mean. It was..."

She trailed off with a grin that had me leaning in.

"It was seductive."

She looked up as she whispered the word, her gaze hitting mine and knocking me off balance. I leaned back in my seat, my breath and heart working harder to keep me upright. My dick thickened, all of me wanting to take advantage of the desire lighting her eyes. The spark between us.

We were two lonely people, hurt and broken by the people we were supposed to love forever. But in that moment, with her dark brown eyes locked on mine, her mouth parted slightly as her gaze dipped to my lips, the world fading around us, we were just two people. Two people with a connection neither of us expected.

A crash in the kitchen snapped us apart. The sound was loud after the entire restaurant had faded away while I was lost in Casey's eyes.

She leaned back, as if she had leaned closer to me, drawn in the same way I'd been. She chuckled, pulling her bottom lip between her teeth. She looked away, then picked up a fry and popped it into her mouth.

What the hell just happened? And how can I make it happen again?

CASEY HURRIED off not long after our moment, claiming she had to get to work. I didn't argue with her, and I didn't do any of the other things I wanted to do. Like ask her to come back to my place. Or ask her out on a real date. Or tell her I'd break her dry spell and mine if she wanted.

I kept my mouth shut tight and waved when she took off down the sidewalk the opposite direction from my truck.

I was not going to get pulled back into a relationship with a woman who wasn't interested in the same things I was. My ego couldn't take it. And neither could my heart.

Blossom & Grow was quiet when I made my way back. Gail and Carson were a two-for-one package who wanted to work at the shop. They started working for Andre over the summer, expanding his business with their knowledge and skills. Best friends and roommates, the two of them worked well together. Their jobs with Andre were part time, and they were looking for more work. They approached me with an offer I couldn't pass up and took them on as part-time employees in Blossom & Grow. Their knowledge about landscaping and planting had proved to be invaluable in the few weeks they'd been working for me.

"How was everything while I was gone?" I asked, directing my question to both of them. They were equal partners in everything they did.

"Good," Gail said. "We had a few customers come in. Carson sold an older couple a great bouquet for their anniversary, and I took down information about an office building that wants to get a quote from you for weekly maintenance on indoor plants."

"Indoor plants?" I took the note from Gail. "I've never offered that service before."

"That's what I told him, but Mr. Holland said he was hoping you would consider it."

I chuckled. "Ramsey?"

Gail nodded.

I rolled my eyes. "He's asked a few times." I was quiet for a minute and eyed the two new employees. "What would you two think about something like that?"

They exchanged a look. Gail spoke first.

"Potted plants would be best, since they won't die and require replacement frequently. Since the season is almost over, you can take up some of the plants that haven't sold yet and make money on them. Depending on the location, you would be able to mix colors and scents, or limit everything to one scheme if a customer wanted to do that."

"And," Carson continued, "you could offer bigger plantings for places that have an outdoor space or a foyer or lobby where people will be to brighten up a place."

"You sound like you have something in mind," I said.

Carson nodded. "We went to MacKellar Theater this weekend. The lobby is great, but there's a lot of chaos at times. They have those black retractable things to create lines, but they get knocked over and people duck under them. If you anchored the ends of the line with tall planters, you could make things more streamlined."

I thought back to the last time I was there, with Reegan so it had been a while, and remembered the same chaos. "That's a good idea, but Xavier didn't come in and ask for that. We can't really go to a business and demand they pay us money to solve problems they don't see as problems."

"But if they want the help…" Gail trailed off like she knew something I didn't.

"Sure, but we don't know if they do."

"Actually, my mom is friends with Genevieve. She works there. She's the business manager or something. She said she wished we offered something like that. She's tried to come up with options, but nothing has worked because it isn't her expertise."

"What has she tried?" I asked, curious to hear about this new opportunity.

"I don't really know, but we could talk to her and find out," Gail suggested.

I sighed, letting out a laugh. "Okay, then this becomes part of your duties." I pointed at both of them. "Figure out what Genevieve wants, talk to Ramsey, and let the word out that we're offering this as a new service."

They smiled at each other, then turned to walk away.

"Wait," I called before they got far. "We need to come up with a pricing structure. If this is going to take your time, we need to figure out how much time and make sure you're paid for it by the project. Then we need to account for the cost of plants and what would likely be replacement costs. I would work something up based on the sizes of the containers we would use."

"You want us to do that?" Carson asked.

I smiled. "I do. I will help, absolutely, but you two seem

really excited about this. You can sit at the table where I do consultations and start to come up with ideas for a little while. You're here another hour?"

"Yes, sir," Gail said.

"I don't expect a full proposal today, but I don't want you working on something like this off-hours when you aren't getting paid. This is something that will add money to the business, so it needs to be supported by the business."

"Thank you, sir," Carson said.

"You both make me feel old." The door jingled with the arrival of a customer. "If it gets busy, I'll let you know, but otherwise, start coming up with plans. We'll try to get this started in the next few weeks, if you both think that'll work."

"Yes, sir," they said together.

I chuckled and shook my head, waving them to the back while I greeted the new customer.

CARSON AND GAIL'S proposal was good. Damn good. They thought of things I hadn't in just an hour. I told them both to keep track of any hours they worked on it when they weren't at Blossom & Grow, but encouraged them not to work off-hours. They needed to enjoy life, too.

But me? Blossom & Grow was my life at the moment, so I spent a few hours after I closed considering all the things I would need to do to make this venture successful.

I sat on the couch with a beer and the notebook Gail and Carson started their work in and thought over everything that would go into it. There was time, supplies, and transportation, obviously. But there was also marketing and setup. In some cases, we would have to set up the planters at the location. If I found standard containers, we could bill by the size, but not everyone would want the same thing. The theater would need tall and skinny planters that meant less plants but more dirt and filler. A place like Ramsey's office would likely need something that fit on top of a desk or table.

I could do custom prices for everything, but that would make it harder to plan for and advertise. If I wanted to advertise. How much could I do before I ran out of time in a week?

My mind was spinning with thoughts and ideas when my phone dinged with a much needed distraction. I set the notebook down and picked up my phone, smiling when I saw a notification from Book Boyfriends Wanted.

TOOBUSY

How was your day?

DIRTYLIFE

It was good actually. How was yours?

TOOBUSY

Good. I had lunch with a friend today. It was a nice break from my normal routine.

DIRTYLIFE

It's good to shake things up once in a while. And time with friends is always a good idea.

TOOBUSY

I agree. I've been thinking a lot about you and shaking things up.

DIRTYLIFE

Is that so? In what way?

TOOBUSY

Just wondering if we're going to meet sometime.

I sucked in a breath. Before Casey, I was hoping to get a chance to meet TooBusy in person. She was always talking about work and her kid, but she made me laugh. I liked that. A lot.

DIRTYLIFE

Is that your way of asking me out?

TOOBUSY

I don't want to be too forward. I know some guys don't like that. But I think lunch could be nice.

DIRTYLIFE

Like you had with your friend today?

TOOBUSY

I work a lot, and I have my daughter, so lunch is my only free time most days.

I scrolled back through all our conversations. Daughter. Working multiple jobs. Divorced a year ago.

No. My match was Casey?

Shit.

I drew a breath. The woman I was teaching to flirt so she could find another man to sleep with was using my lessons against me.

And she clearly had no idea.

How the hell was I supposed to handle this? Did I tell her? Did I keep it to myself?

I wasn't positive it was her, but I was pretty sure. If it wasn't her, I had zero guesses. Hell, I had zero guesses before, but after meeting her, it made sense.

It had to be her.

TOOBUSY

Are you still there? I wasn't trying to make things weird. If you're not interested, I understand.

87

DIRTYLIFE

No! I'm interested.

I'm definitely interested.

I just don't have a lot of time for lunch.

A definite lie, but I couldn't tell her I owned my own business and could do whatever I wanted.

DIRTYLIFE

Are you available on Saturday?

TOOBUSY

Sorry. I have my daughter home all weekend.

DIRTYLIFE

Crap. Okay. We will figure something out eventually. Don't give up on me, okay?

TOOBUSY

I won't if you don't. But if you have plans with anyone else, I can't ask you to wait until I'm free.

DIRTYLIFE

No plans with anyone else.

At least I was telling the truth about that. The only one I had any plans with was her. Flirting lessons in person and with her as my match once I figured out how to make this work. The more I thought about it, the surer I was that TooBusy was Casey.

DIRTYLIFE

What's your favorite thing to do with your daughter?

TOOBUSY

Anything I get to do with her is nice. She's getting to the age where she's not as interested in being around me. We've always liked picking out pumpkins in the fall. We didn't do it last year, but this year, I think we're going to do it again.

DIRTYLIFE

Are you a pumpkin spice person?

TOOBUSY

LOL! No! I love pumpkin pie, but I'm not a pumpkin drink person. Give me a regular coffee with a little cream and sugar, and I'm good to go.

DIRTYLIFE

Same. But I do love a good pumpkin muffin.

TOOBUSY

I've never had one.

DIRTYLIFE

You're missing out. It'll change your life. Or pumpkin cookies. Have you ever had those?

TOOBUSY

I think you're talking nonsense. Where does one get these things?

DIRTYLIFE

Stick with me, sweetheart. I'll share all my secrets.

TOOBUSY

LOL! It sounds like you're a really good guy to know.

DIRTYLIFE

You bet I am.

I smiled at my phone, wondering if I could get her to fall for me online and in person at the same time.

Then I realized what I thought and tossed my phone onto the coffee table. It dinged, but I ignored it.

I was not going to fall for Casey. Either Casey. She wasn't looking for the same thing I was. She'd already admitted that to me in both places. I had to keep that in mind.

Or I'd end up hurt all over again.

9

CASEY

I stared at my phone and waited for DirtyLife to reply. It was a good five minutes before I realized he wasn't going to. My body flashed hot, his rejection stinging more than I should have allowed.

I thought I was flirting. I thought it was going well. I put myself out there and asked if he wanted to meet. It wasn't a blatant rejection, just a brush-off followed by an attempt to reschedule. I thought it was going well.

But he just stopped replying.

I swallowed against the tightness in my throat and stood. I shook my entire body, needing the movement and to let go. We weren't dating, or married, or anything beyond text friends. It was on me if I was making more of whatever was going on than he felt. Sure, we were on a dating app, but that didn't mean he wanted to date me.

Heat flooded me again at the thought. I felt like such a fool.

I turned my phone off to stop myself from looking at the app a million more times before I went to sleep, then focused on the rest of my night. I had an hour or two of data entry to do before

I could go to sleep. Mikayla was already in bed, and quiet thankfully. She came home over the moon excited to share she'd been chosen for a solo in her chorus concert after the musical. The solo was a good boost for her confidence, and a good sign her teacher would give her a part in the musical. I didn't think she was going to be able to sleep, so the silence was a good thing.

I powered up my computer and found the data sent to me for the day. I accessed the system and got to work on everything, letting the steady work pull my entire focus and attention.

When I keyed in the last entry, I drew a breath and stretched. I verified that every cell was filled and everything was complete, then saved the work one more time and submitted it. I never knew what kind of data I'd be working on, but it didn't matter to me. I was surprised companies still used outside sources for data entry, but I wouldn't complain about a job that paid well enough to help support me.

I did a quick check of the apartment and made sure everything was picked up for the night. Mikayla's lunchbox was packed and in the fridge for the morning, next to mine. A breakfast casserole was ready to be cooked when I got up to make my coffee. I was ready for the next day.

On my way to my room, I glared at my phone. I picked it up and decided to charge it in the kitchen instead of my bedroom. I plugged it in and walked away before it powered on and alerted me to the missed messages.

Or the ones that never came in.

My mind replayed my conversation with DirtyLife as I got ready for bed. I couldn't figure out where I went wrong, but I wasn't going to be the same person I was during my marriage. I couldn't chase after someone who didn't want me. Not again. Not ever again. I knew what that did to a relationship, and to me.

Maybe I'd hear from DirtyLife again, and maybe I wouldn't, but either way, I was not going to let it ruin my life. I'd survived worse than a rejection.

MY ALARM BROKE through the haze of the early morning. I reached for it on my nightstand and silenced it before the noise gave me a headache. I sat up in bed and stretched, knowing I needed to get up or I'd curl back into bed and never emerge. I was usually up early, but if I slept long enough to have the alarm wake me up, it was never good.

I stumbled to the kitchen to start the coffee and breakfast casserole, then headed for the shower. In less than twenty minutes, I was back in the kitchen with my first mug of coffee and debating looking at my phone.

I caved and flipped it over.

A text from Natalie was the first thing I saw.

NATALIE

I guess you weren't happy with the draft you showed us. I wish we'd known you saw us this way. It's too late to make any changes, but I'm not sure this is a good idea going forward.

Um, what?

It took a minute for my caffeine-neglected brain to put things together and understand.

Gretchen changed my story.

I pulled up the newspaper site and tapped to read the article. My article. The one my name was on, but not the one I wrote.

"Dammit," I breathed.

Mikayla stumbled her way into the kitchen. "Why are you mad?"

I looked up at her, then locked my phone and set it down. I would deal with the article and Gretchen after Mikayla went to school.

"I had an article published, and my editor changed it without telling me."

"Oh. Is breakfast ready?"

I smothered my grin and checked the oven. The cheese on top was bubbly and slightly brown. It was perfect. "We need to let it cool for a minute. Do you want to pack your backpack first?"

"Sure." She slid off her chair and dragged her feet to the fridge. I handed her the lunchbox she'd packed the night before, adding two ice packs to make sure everything stayed cold enough, then she let her arm fall as though carrying it was the hardest thing she'd ever done.

Kids are funny.

I sipped my coffee and checked the time. I cut into the casserole, steam escaping from the slice I made. It would have been better to wait another five minutes, but we didn't have time. I dished up a piece for Mikayla and told her to blow on it. I cut one for myself and sat at the table as she touched the tip of her tongue to the edge.

"It's hot."

"I know. Food don't cook cold."

She snorted. The silly phrase was one we'd been telling her forever. One that always made her laugh.

I cut my casserole into chunks to let the heat out from as much of it as possible, and we finally ate our breakfast without scorching our mouths.

My fingers itched to grab my phone and read the entire article, but I resisted. I wanted to be present for Mikayla. It was important to me that she knew I was there for her. Always.

"Have you been practicing for your audition?" I asked as she emerged from the bathroom with freshly brushed teeth.

"Yeah."

"Thursday, right?"

"Yeah."

"Okay. Home on the bus today?"

"Yeah." She grabbed her backpack.

"Bye. Have a good day." I tugged her in for a forced hug.

"Bye."

I closed the door behind her as her footsteps echoed down the stairs. I locked the door, then moved toward the window to watch her get on the bus.

Five minutes later, Mikayla was headed to school, and I was reading the article I didn't write.

And seething.

The article made it seem as though Natalie had been flirting with Landon the entire time. Omar sounded like he wasn't interested in anything that had to do with planning the wedding. They both came across as shallow and mean, coming just short of accusing them of not really wanting to get married and only doing so for publicity.

What the fucking hell?

I wanted to talk to Natalie face-to-face, but first, I needed to understand what in the world happened to the article I submitted. I hurried out of the apartment, hellbent on getting answers from Gretchen and not caring if she had an issue with it.

I stormed into the newsroom, my face hot. Mike saw me coming and grinned before he caught the look on my face. He turned and went the other way.

Gretchen's door was closed, so I pounded on it before

letting myself in without caring if she was busy or not. "Excuse you. I didn't say you could enter."

"And I didn't say you could twist every word I wrote into something it was never intended to be."

"I told you to bring me something with an angle. You brought me fluff that stank of hero worship."

"It was a good article."

"No, it wasn't. It was a mediocre retelling of two people doing the world's most boring thing. Who cares about the flowers they chose? No one." She glared at me like a pest who needed to shoo.

"The people in this town aren't looking for scandals. They don't want to trash each other. There's too much nastiness in the world, and if they can find a feel-good story about people they know and respect, they're going to enjoy it. You made that article into something it wasn't."

Gretchen narrowed her eyes at me. She held my gaze for several minutes, no doubt waiting for me to back down.

I wasn't going to.

"Fine. Tell me what I printed that wasn't correct." She opened the paper to the article on page two. She smoothed the pages back and started reading.

"Natalie Edwards, director of Mountain View Retreat, laughs at the teasing look in the eye of Landon Boyd. Landon, not Natalie's future husband, knows everything there is to know about flowers. Landon owns Blossom & Grow, and the associated greenhouse and fields, and he can tell you the difference between a flower that'll profess your undying love and one that'll say we're just friends."

Gretchen looked up at me. I gritted my teeth.

"Anything incorrect so far?"

"No," I seethed.

"Okay, the next paragraph? Where you talked about their

interaction. About Natalie wanting things to be simple but not actually being simple. Was that wrong?"

I closed my eyes and sighed. "Technically, no. But—"

"What about Omar wanting her to choose what she wanted? Did he have an opinion that you didn't mention?"

"It's not that."

"Oh, it's not? So the article was accurate. I thought you came in here with your ass on fire acting like there was some gross error included in print."

"It was the way you made it all sound. Natalie wasn't flirting with Landon."

Gretchen's brows shot high. "I definitely did not write that she was. Where does it say that?"

"It doesn't specifically say that, but—"

"But nothing, Casey. You're grasping at straws here. You wanted to write these articles, and now you're mad that I made them more compelling. This is a business. This isn't your little book club."

My eyes widened. "What does that mean?"

"It means you're getting too close to these women. Your job as a journalist is to report what you see. You can't let others influence your position on a topic. And that's what's happening here."

"No, it's not. I'm writing a story about two people who are in love. People who are celebrating their happiness with the town. And instead of you wanting it to be a joyous thing, you want to twist it."

"Didn't you get divorced a year ago?"

I pulled up short. "I… I did. Why?"

"Why are you so big on love? From what I've heard, you got your teeth knocked out by it. Why are you sugarcoating this love story?"

"I'm not sugarcoating anything. I'm telling the truth. Natalie and Omar love each other. They are sharing the parts of their lives that they want to share with the people of this town. They love MacKellar Cove, and they want to—"

"No one cares, Casey. No. One. Cares. People want to witness the misery of others because it allows them the chance to feel better about their own pitiful lives. We don't want to see joy. We want despair."

"I don't. Why would you want that?"

She scoffed. "Get out of my office."

"Natalie is done," I said, not moving.

"What?"

"She texted me this morning. She said the article you published wasn't what we agreed on. It wasn't what she expected, and she isn't willing to work with me going forward."

Gretchen leaned forward, her eyes boring into me. "You have to convince her to change her mind."

"Why? I can't go to her and promise that this won't happen again. That the article I write won't be changed after I turn it in."

Gretchen sneered. "You showed her the article before you submitted it?"

"I did. I didn't think there was a reason not to. I wasn't aware that what I wrote wasn't what would be published."

"Did you do the same before you published your articles about Mr. Levine?"

"Mr. Levine was an underhanded manipulator who was lying and left this paper vulnerable to lawsuits. The only reason Mayor Knight didn't sue was because of me. Because I wrote the article about Mr. Levine and his involvement in the articles about Omar."

"Do you think that wins you something? That you used your relationship then and you're doing it now, so you should get something for it?"

"I am not! I was asked to write an article about Omar.

Everyone who knew him knew the articles were lies, but Erik printed them anyway. I am not to blame for any of this, but you're going down the same path Erik did, twisting things and making up stories that you think will sell papers. It doesn't work like that here."

Gretchen pursed her lips so tight they turned white. "Fine."

"Fine, what?"

"I won't change anything in your next article. And we'll see how things go from there."

"I can't go to Natalie and say you're going to leave one article alone but not the rest."

"You want full control. That's not how this works."

"Then, I expect any changes to be run by me at least twenty-four hours before going to print so I have time to show them to Natalie."

"Then your articles need to be in a full day earlier from now on."

"Fine, I can do that."

"Good."

"Good."

Gretchen glared at me, then snarled. "Now get out of my office."

I stood and walked out, leaving the door open because I knew it annoyed her.

That was not the way things were supposed to be. If someone's name was on the byline, the article was theirs. If Gretchen wanted to make all those changes, she should have put her own damn name on it.

"That was a pretty interesting article you wrote," Mike said as I approached his desk. "I didn't think you had it in you."

"I didn't write it."

"What?" He examined me closely. "What do you mean?"

I glanced back at Gretchen's office. "She changed everything I wrote."

"She did what?" Mike cupped my elbow and guided me into his cubicle space.

I shrugged him off. "She told me you were going to write the articles if I didn't find an angle. I wanted to write something about the wedding, about Natalie and Omar, but she didn't want that. She wants dirt."

Mike snorted. "There's no dirt on either of them. They're good people."

"You didn't help her with the changes to my article?" I was a little surprised to hear that.

"No. Hell no. I like Omar. He's a good man. Mayor Levine was a piece of crap. He liked to manipulate everything. My sister works at town hall and told me some of the things Levine did when he was still here. I was pissed when those articles came out last year about Omar because I thought he was just as big of an asshole, but I was happy to see your articles exposing Levine."

"Thanks, Mike. I... Gretchen doesn't understand how things work here. I know you like to push the line and expose people, but that's not how I work."

"I expose people who need to be exposed. I might push a little harder to find the information I need, but I don't chase after things that don't need to be chased after."

I thought about what he said and realized he was right. He wasn't telling lies. He was sharing things others didn't know but needed to. "Thanks, Mike. I think you're right."

"What are you going to do about the rest of your articles?"

"She agreed not to change anything and to give me twenty-four hours' notice before going to print so I can talk to Natalie."

"Smart."

"I hope. But now I need to convince Natalie to give me another chance."

"She saw your article before Gretchen got her hands on it, huh?"

I nodded. "Yep. And she's not happy about the changes."

"Good. Maybe it'll teach Gretchen a little about how things work around here. We're not all out to get each other. This isn't a place where everyone hates each other."

"I hope she understands one day. Or I'll leave. I won't work for someone who only wants to destroy everyone around."

Mike's dark brows shot up. A smile lifted his lips. "You let me know if it comes to that. I'll walk with you."

"Yeah?"

He nodded.

"Thanks, Mike. I appreciate it."

"Good luck with Natalie."

"Thanks. I'm definitely going to need it."

"She's not so bad. She'll understand."

"I hope so." Hope was all I had.

$\mathcal{A}$melia refused to let me see Natalie. She was the one who met me at the door, arms crossed and lips pursed, letting me know I was not welcome inside the community center.

"Will you tell her I stopped by?" I asked, hoping it would be better than nothing.

"That's all you want me to tell her?"

"I would like the chance to apologize to her in person and explain the entire situation."

"What's the situation?" Amelia asked.

"My editor twisted the entire article. Did you read it?"

Amelia snorted.

"Yeah, I figured you would. I showed Natalie my article. She said I didn't have to, but I felt like it was the right thing to do since we both knew Gretchen wanted dirt on Natalie and Omar. I didn't know she would change it."

"And you really think that's a good enough excuse?"

I shook my head. "No. There is no excuse. I just came from a meeting with Gretchen. She admitted she changed it, but she refused to print a retraction. She claimed everything was accurate, and technically it was, it was just done in a way that misrepresented Natalie and Omar."

"That's for damn sure," Amelia muttered.

"I have gotten her to agree to leave future articles alone, and if she's going to make changes, to share them twenty-four hours in advance so I have time to review them with Natalie."

"I thought Natalie said she didn't want to continue with these," Amelia said, raising her eyebrows and daring me to lie.

"She did. And I respect her decision based on what happened. However, I'm hoping she'll give me another chance. I like Natalie and Omar. I have a tremendous amount of respect for both of them. I want these articles to represent them and MacKellar Cove. Gretchen doesn't understand what that means, but she's promised she will not touch my next article."

"And after that?" Amelia asked.

"I asked the same thing. That's how I got her to agree to advance notice. But she said if the next article doesn't get the same traffic, or more, she is likely to change things."

Amelia glanced to the side. Her gaze locked on something, or someone, before she nodded. "Then I guess we better make sure the next article is a good one."

I nodded. "I will. If Natalie will agree."

As a reply, the security door clicked open.

I looked at Amelia for verification, and she nodded. I opened the door and stepped inside, seeing Natalie right inside the door.

"I am so sorry," I told her. "I had no idea those changes were going to be made until after you'd texted me. As soon as my daughter went to school, I read the article, then went right over to Gretchen. She never should have done that to you."

"No, she shouldn't. But I appreciate you standing up for me like you did."

"I'm not the only one who disagrees with what Gretchen did. If she continues like this, I will quit. And one of my colleagues said the same."

"You can't quit your job because of me," Natalie gasped.

"I can and I will because this isn't right. And I'm not going to be a part of destroying lives for the sake of selling newspapers. If something needs to be exposed, I'm on board with that. Fake news and twisted stories are not why I wanted to study journalism. I know MacKellar Cove isn't the hotbed of activity that a city is, but I like that about this place. It's a good place to raise my daughter, and a good place to live. I don't want to change that to suit one person who is bored."

Natalie chuckled softly. "I agree. And thank you. I was hurt when I read the article this morning. I never intended to make it seem like I was flirting with Landon, and Omar is very invested in this wedding."

I took a step forward and grabbed her hand. "I know. I agree. The article I sent you is the same one I submitted. I loved the way the two of you were together. I was married for a long time, and we were never that way. It was... You two really love each other."

"We do," Natalie said. "And I'll agree to keep going, but—"

I grinned immediately, until she let that *but* hang in the air.

"But I want you to come to book club."

"This weekend?" I squeaked.

Natalie shook her head. "Every weekend at least until the wedding."

"I'm a single mom. My ex isn't... I can't rely on him."

"There are a lot of moms in the group. And if I remember correctly, Melody's daughter is your daughter's best friend."

I nodded. "Yes, but I don't like asking Ramsey to watch Mikayla every week."

"Then Omar will."

"What?"

Natalie shrugged. "Omar will stay with her. If you're okay with him being around her."

"No. I mean, yes, I'm fine with Omar being around her, but I can't ask him to do that."

"I'm offering, which means he is."

Amelia snorted. Natalie grinned.

"I..."

"You're trying to make excuses, but I want you there. I like you, Casey. That's why I was so upset by this. I was surprised you would change the article after how kind it was to us. Your coming to book club will give me a chance to get to know you better, and it'll be good for everyone else to know you. My guess is they're all a little upset, too."

I winced. She wasn't wrong.

"Come Sunday. Please."

I relented. "Okay."

"Yay. Thank you."

"Thank you for understanding about Gretchen. I would never make it sound like you and Omar were like that."

"Thanks. But I guess we have to work a little harder to get something she'll like for next week. What do you say you come to my bachelorette party tomorrow night?"

"What?"

Natalie grinned. "It'll definitely spice things up. We rented out MacKellar Theater and we're going to be rowdy and crazy. Amelia is coming."

"I have my light-up penis beads ready to go," Amelia said with a grin and a wink.

Natalie chuckled. "Say you'll come. Daisy will provide the beads."

"Are you joking?"

Natalie shook her head. "Not even a little. Party starts at seven. We're going to have food and drinks and take over the adults-only theater. I have no idea what movies Daisy has planned, but she's been collecting all kinds of things that are going to have my face bright red all night."

"Lots of penises." Amelia laughed.

"Um, I'm not sure. It's a school night, so my daughter is home."

"Finley and Trent have already offered to have any of the kids who need a place to stay to come to their house. Andre and Daniel are going to be drivers for everyone so people can drink without worrying about driving home afterward. Everyone from book club is coming, and I think it'll be a really good setup for your next article. Locals get crazy."

I snorted at her less than stellar headline but knew she was right. It was definitely the kind of thing Gretchen would want in the paper. As long as I could find a way to do it that was both PG and a little scandalous.

"Let me talk to Melody. If she's going, I'll see if Mikayla can stay with her."

"She's going, but yes, talk to her. Let me know. You can ride with Sofia or Joelle since they both live in your building, and we'll get you home at the end of the night."

I contemplated my options and nodded. "Let me check with her right now, if that's okay?"

"Of course."

I stepped away to call Melody, knowing it wasn't private, but it was slightly less rude than standing in front of Natalie and Amelia and talking to someone else.

"Hey, Case. How are you?"

"I'm okay. Listen, I'm talking to Natalie right now, and she invited me to her bachelorette party tomorrow night. Are you going?"

"I am." Melody's voice was hesitant.

"The article wasn't me. I explained it all to Natalie. Gretchen changed it after I turned it in and didn't tell me."

"Oh, shit. Really? I was wondering what the hell happened."

"Yeah. Natalie thought it would be good for me to go to the party and use that for my next article. Something that might appeal to Gretchen. I'll explain everything later, but if I go, Mikayla—"

"Can always stay here. I told you that before. Amber will love a weeknight sleepover."

"So will Mikayla, but I hate asking you guys."

"And Ramsey already told you he's happy to have her here anytime. It's totally fine. And it'll be good for you to be around everyone and explain."

"I know. Natalie is also insisting I come to book club every week."

Melody chuckled. "Good for her. I knew I liked her."

I snorted.

"Mikayla can come here for those, too. Don't think twice about it. Please."

"Thanks, Mel."

"Any time. Hi to Natalie and Amelia."

"I'll tell them. Talk soon."

"Bye, hun."

"Bye."

"She said yes?" Natalie asked, even though she knew the answer.

"She did."

"Good. Then you're out of excuses. I've already let Sofia and Joelle know to grab you before they come tomorrow night."

I chuckled. "Thanks, Natalie. I'm looking forward to it."

"So am I. Only a few more weeks until I'm a married

woman, and I'm going to enjoy all the festivities leading up to it. And then I'm going to enjoy being married to the man I love."

"You deserve it," Amelia said. "It's so good to see you this happy."

"Thanks. I never thought I'd find someone who loved me for who I am, but Omar is everything I ever hoped for and more."

"He's perfect for you." Amelia hugged Natalie, and they pulled me into their little circle.

I laughed, feeling the tightness in my chest. I never knew love like Natalie had with Omar. I probably never would. And that was hard to accept.

But it was my choice. I was not looking for heartbreak again. Ever.

MIKAYLA WAS THRILLED to have a chance to sleep over at Amber's house on a school night. I was not so thrilled with it, but I lost the battle. Melody decided to ride back to my place with me so I had my car at home and she didn't have a car, and at six-thirty, we knocked on Sofia's door.

"Hi!" Sofia said, letting us in. "It's so good to see you guys!"

I worried about the reception I would get after the article, but Melody assured me it would be fine. Sofia's welcome made me think maybe Melody was right.

"How are you?" I asked her.

"Good. We're almost ready. Daniel is going to drop the three of us off, then I think he's going to Trent's. Ramsey is taking the girls there for a little while, right?" Sofia asked Melody.

Melody nodded. "Yep. I think all the guys and kids are going there for dinner."

"Daisy sounds really excited about tonight. Do you have any idea what she's planned?" Sofia asked.

Melody smirked. "I might know a few things." Melody owned a party planning company that planned and outfitted supplies for parties for young kids.

"Are you expanding your business?" I asked her.

Melody snorted. "God no. I love a good penis joke, but with Amber at home, I am not going to stock a million penises in my house."

"I walked in at the wrong time for that comment," Daniel said from behind Sofia. Daniel was really Trey Ryan, but he went by his middle name in MacKellar Cove. He was a rock-star turned songwriter who fell in love with Sofia one summer and never left town. He was always a nice guy when I spoke to him, but the occasions were few and far between. To admit I was starstruck by him was an understatement.

"Do you remember Casey?" Sofia asked, nodding to me as we all moved into the hallway.

"The reporter, right?" he asked.

I winced. "Yeah." His tone was less than friendly.

"Sofia said your editor changed that article about Natalie and Omar. Such bullshit."

"It was. She doesn't understand life here."

"It's an adjustment for sure, but a good one if someone is willing to let go of the toxic bullshit that exists in the world. It's nice to be somewhere that people actually want to be your friend for the right reasons." Daniel threw his arm around Sofia's shoulder and kissed her temple.

"You didn't come here with those same thoughts, though. It took a little while to wear you down," Sofia said. She led the way to the door and outside into the cool evening air.

"True. But love makes everything look better. Maybe she

needs a little romance in her life." Daniel smirked as he unlocked his vehicle.

"She probably does, but I'm not about to tell her that," I said.

Daniel snorted. "Fair enough."

Melody and I sat in the backseat of Daniel's SUV. The drive to MacKellar Theater was quick and full of speculation about what we were in for at the bachelorette party.

"Is Omar having a bachelor party?" I asked.

"Saturday night," Daniel answered. "A bunch of the couples have kids, so Natalie and Omar split up the days so there were people available to watch the kids. Since Natalie wanted to go to the theater, the only option was a weeknight since they have public movies on the weekends."

"That's really thoughtful of them," I said.

"You know how they are. They're good people," Melody said.

"The best. Proof is me sitting here after what happened." I scowled at the thought of the article.

"We're putting that all in the past and going to enjoy tonight." Sofia leaned across the console as Daniel shifted into park. She gave him a kiss, one he pulled her back into after she tried to slip away.

Melody and I climbed out, leaving them to say goodbye alone. Melody looped her arm through mine and led the way to the door. A curtain was hung over the entrance on the inside, declaring that the theater was closed for a private party. Melody grinned widely.

"And so it begins," she said as she opened the door.

I walked inside, the sound of voices meeting my ears through the thick curtains that blocked the view from the street. I pulled the curtain back and laughed.

There were penises everywhere. Inflatable ones hung from the ceiling. String lights decorated the walls. Everyone wore penis glasses and light-up necklaces. Natalie wore a giant penis hat with an arrow declaring her the bride-to-be.

"Oh. My. God," Sofia said, appearing next to me. "This is the best thing ever."

Melody grabbed my arm and pulled me into the chaos. "Let's go find some penises."

I snorted and let her drag me along.

"Hey! You're here! Necklace?" Daisy offered each of us, draping light-up penis necklaces around our necks without waiting for a reply. The necklaces blinked slowly at us.

"Are they judging us?" Sofia asked.

"I was wondering the same thing!" Melody said.

"Right? You can speed them up by… pressing the buttons," Daisy said.

"This is going to be so much fun," Sofia said. Piper called her name from across the room, and Sofia walked away to hug her bestie.

"Natalie is going to be so excited to see you both. She's already started drinking. What do you guys want?" Daisy snorted. "I started drinking with her. You have to get a penis glass."

The candy counter was completely transformed. All the candy was removed, and in its place was a variety of penis-shaped decor. On top was a collection of penis candy and treats.

"It's all filled with something," Daisy said, barely containing her laughter. "Valentina is a true master."

"Did I hear my name?" Valentina said. She was the baker at Cove Bakery, the best bakery for a hundred miles, if I had a vote. She was talented and creative, but this was next level.

"How in the world did you do all this?" Melody asked Valentina.

"It was so much fun. Brantley was not happy to be my taste-tester, but he got over it." Valentina snickered.

"You had him eating penis candy, didn't you?" Melody asked.

"Of course! I had to know if the flavors would hold up in the smaller sizes." Valentina smirked.

"You're so bad. Did he believe that lie?" Melody asked.

"He was rewarded for his sacrifice," Valentina said with a wink.

"Nice." Melody chuckled. "Which one is your favorite?"

"They're all good. We have dark chocolate with sea salt and caramel, milk chocolate with cherry, and white chocolate with ganache inside. Of course, you have to see the cake." Valentina pointed to a massive penis cake taking center stage on a table against the opposite wall.

"Oh, that's amazing," Melody said, leading me to it.

I stared at the gigantic dick-shaped cake and couldn't hold back my laughter. "This is the best party I've ever been to."

"Woohoo!" Natalie said, hearing my comment and joining us.

Everyone else echoed her cheer.

"I'm so excited for my massive penis," Natalie said. She threw her arm around my shoulders. "I'm so drunk. But please don't write that."

"I promise you, we're going to get the fun and the excitement of the night, not the details."

"Perfect. Now, let's get you a penis!" Natalie shouted, eliciting cheers from everyone else there.

I had to laugh. It was going to be a fun night.

11

*P*enis necklace. Penis drink. Penis ice cubes in the drink. Penis snacks, penis pizzas, penis cake. I was married for a decade and hadn't ever been around so much penis in my life.

It was kind of fun.

"I was really disappointed we couldn't throw penis confetti everywhere, but Xavier was afraid some would be left behind," Melody said as we sat down with our slices of penis pizza.

"Yeah, that would be bad," I agreed. "It would have been pretty great, though. I didn't know this many penis things existed."

Melody snorted. "Right? It's wild the stuff that's available for bachelorette parties. Daisy and I had way too much fun. The penis curtain was my favorite."

I shook my head. The doorway to the movie theater was covered with a curtain of penises that hung like streamers from the doorway. Upright penises, of course. White and navy, like their wedding colors. All the tables had matching penis decorations strung around the edge. And more penises on coasters and centerpieces.

"I have to say, walking through a curtain of penises was a first for me."

"The penis drinks are pretty good. I was so happy we found these glasses and the stir sticks."

I couldn't help laughing. Everything for the party had a penis on it.

"More drinks!" Willow said, returning to our table with Elise right behind her.

Willow was Melody's sister and closest friend. They had a falling out a few years ago, but things improved and they were close again. Elise and Willow hit it off when they realized they shared the same dirty sense of humor.

"So, who's getting laid tonight?" Elise asked not at all quietly.

Cheers went up from half the guests. A whistle followed, punctuated by the steady bass pounding from the speakers as *Magic Mike* played on the theater screen.

"If I wasn't planning on it before, watching this movie is making me ready to run home now," Willow said with a saucy wink.

"Right?" Elise stared at the screen as the main characters executed body rolls that did not seem like any real human could perform. "This is the next best thing to a strip club. I think Daisy is a genius. And you for helping put all this together." Elise hugged Melody.

"It was fun. The movie is a great option. Natalie said she wanted something low-key and relaxed. Daisy had all the ideas. I just helped her pull it off." Melody took a sip of the drinks Willow and Elise brought us.

I followed suit, letting the sweetness of the liquor settle in my stomach. I was more than a little tipsy. I was supposed to be working, but I was having fun. The party was a huge celebration of friendship and love, and I was honored Natalie invited me.

The party continued as the men on the screen practiced all their gravity-defying moves, and I enjoyed all the penis perfection and cock concoctions.

"Oh, shit," I breathed as I stood to go to the bathroom.

"You're trashed." Melody caught my arm and laughed. "How many of those did you have?" She nodded at my empty drink.

I shrugged. "A few, I guess. I just haven't stood up in a while."

"Are you going to be okay?"

I waved her off and headed for the penis curtain to find the bathroom. A giant blue penis was on the men's bathroom door, and a giant pink penis with an engagement ring was on the women's bathroom door. I chuckled as I pushed the door open.

"Casey! I'm so happy you're here. Are you having fun? I'm having fun." Natalie was even drunker than I was. She threw her arms around me and nearly sent us both to the floor.

"Whoa," I said, laughing with her as I caught us with a hand against the counter.

"Whoops. I'm sorry. I think I had a little too much to drink."

"Are you okay?"

"Yep. I am having a lot of fun. I like seeing everyone and having us all together, you know? This is how life should be. Happy and fun and full of dicks." She slapped a hand over her mouth. "One dick. I don't want other dicks. Just Omar's. Did I tell you about the time I fell and grabbed his dick? I was so embarrassed, but even soft, it was a nice dick." She grinned at me. "I like his dick."

I snorted. "That's good since you're going to be enjoying it for the rest of your life."

"Oh, I will. I never liked dick that much. I mean, I never tried anything else, but I didn't have a lot of boyfriends before Omar. He's the best one ever. He likes me and all my crazy. He says I make him happy."

"That's a really important part of a marriage."

"It is. Is that why your marriage didn't last? I don't want that to happen to me. Can you tell me what I should avoid?" Her eyes went wide like she was waiting for me to distill the greatest secret of all time.

I leaned in, the alcohol in my system making me giggle. "Avoid bad dicks."

Natalie nodded, all serious. "Okay. I will. What else?"

I shrugged. "I don't know. My marriage didn't last because we didn't like each other that much. He never made me laugh. Landon makes me laugh. I want that in my next relationship. If I ever have another one. I tried flirting with my match, but he shut me down. I don't think I'm ever going to have sex again."

"You should take a giant penis home. Not to have sex with, but just so you have a penis with you. Ooh, maybe you should take some of the small ones, too. Then you can keep one in your bag and one in your bathroom. You can be surrounded by penises!"

"Um, what is going on in here?" Daisy asked, sounding far too sober for my drunk sensibilities.

"We're talking about bad dicks and no sex," Natalie said, like that explained everything.

"What does that mean?" Daisy asked.

"It means Casey is never having sex again because her husband had a bad dick." Natalie looked at me and nodded.

Daisy slid me a look. "The movie is almost over. Do you want to finish watching it?"

"Yes! I love *Magic Mike*. Do you think I can get Omar to dance like that for me? He can be my stripper. I don't want the waxed and greased guys rubbing all over me, but Omar would be nice to rub all over me. I think we should ask him…"

Natalie's voice faded as Daisy led her out of the bathroom. The door slid closed behind them, and I remembered why I was in there.

I rushed to a stall and closed the door. I sat down and relaxed, letting my spinning brain settle again. When I stood, the bathroom door opened again. I flushed and opened the stall door to find Valentina and Goldie walking in.

"Hi!" I said to them.

"Hey. Are you drunk?" Goldie asked.

I nodded. "I am. I don't have a lot of chances to drink anymore, and it hit me harder than I thought. Is it obvious?"

"Everyone is drunk. Except Haley, who's nursing, and Daisy, who's making sure everyone is okay. You have a ride home, right?" Valentina asked.

I nodded again, my head getting wobbly with the move. "Sofia and Daniel drove me here. I live in their building."

"Good. I'm glad you were able to come. We both know how hard divorce can be, and life as a single mom. Are you okay?" Goldie asked.

"Why are you nice to me? After that article came out?" I asked her.

"Natalie told everyone what happened. I've been there with bosses who do everything possible to ruin your career. It sucks. And you don't deserve to be blamed for it," Goldie said.

"We don't judge people based on one thing either. We know you're a friend to Natalie. She really wanted you here," Valentina added.

"I am a friend to her. I like both Natalie and Omar. A lot. I want their love to inspire others. It inspires me."

"They are pretty great," Goldie agreed.

I washed my hands and left while the two of them locked stall doors. I went back to the theater and resumed my seat, finding a fresh pair of drinks in front of my seat.

"Last round, so I got us both two. We're not driving," Melody held up one glass for us to toast. "Cheers."

"Thanks for hanging with me this whole time. I'm sure you had other people you wanted to talk to," I told her, taking a healthy sip of my drink.

"We're friends, Casey. You didn't hold me back from anyone else. I had fun. And I heard you told Natalie to avoid bad dicks. What was that all about?"

I snorted and relayed my conversation with Natalie in the bathroom. Melody laughed and toasted with me again. "To good dicks only."

"To good dicks!"

"Hurray!" everyone else said, hearing our toast.

Melody and I finished our drinks as the movie finished playing. Daisy asked for help getting Natalie to the door, then poured her into Omar's SUV with a laugh.

"Did you guys leave any liquor in town for us?" Omar teased Daisy.

Daisy shook her head. "Nope. We drank it all!" Daisy laughed and waved as they left.

Melody asked Daisy if she needed help cleaning up, and all of us pitched in to de-dick the movie theater. Daisy brought out bins to store most of the supplies, telling people to keep anything they wanted.

She handed me a dick centerpiece and a penis shot glass. "Natalie wanted you to have these. I'm not asking questions."

I snorted and accepted the gifts. "Thank you. It's the only dick I'm going to get anytime soon, so I'll enjoy."

Daisy threw her head back and laughed. "Then you need more dicks. You have your necklace." She nodded to the light-up necklaces we all wore. "And your glass, straw, and ice cube." Everyone had their own for the night, and we were all taking them home. "Ooh! Coaster?" Daisy handed one over, then grabbed an inflatable. "This too. And the string of dicks."

"Sounds like my dating life," I muttered.

Daisy snorted. "That's… Sorry. That was funny."

"Unfortunately true."

"What's true?" a voice asked from right behind me. A voice I was beginning to know well. Landon.

"Casey is taking home a string of dicks. She said it's like her dating life."

"Ouch," he said, a smirk teasing the corners of his lips.

"I don't mean you," I assured him.

"Well, that's good to know." He held my gaze for a long moment. "Are you ready to go?"

"Go where?"

He chuckled. "I'm helping with rides. Andre dragged me out tonight and then coerced me into driving a bunch of drunk women home after a night…" He trailed off as he looked around. "With a bunch of dicks."

I snorted. "Yes, but none of them were real."

"That's a shame."

I opened my mouth to say something. I don't know what I was going to say. My gaze slammed into his, and all thoughts fled my brain. All thoughts except that I wanted his dick.

Landon chuckled. "Maybe when you're not drunk."

I slapped a hand over my mouth. "Did I say that out loud?"

"I think that means it's time to get you home."

I nodded and let him lead me outside into the cold night. It was dark, most of the town sound asleep already.

Landon's hand was warm on my back as he guided me to his SUV. He opened the front door and steadied me while I balanced all my dicks and tried to hoist myself up. His hands went to my hips, his body pressed against my back.

He stilled for a minute, drawing a breath.

Heat rushed to my cheeks as I realized he was working to gain enough strength to lift my oversized body into the vehicle.

"You smell good," he whispered into my hair.

"What?"

"You smell like blackberries and lilac." He shivered against me, and I felt something thick against my backside that wasn't there a minute ago.

"Oh."

"I'm sorry. I shouldn't…" He hoisted me up into the seat and slammed the door before I had a chance to think about exactly what was happening.

I stared as he walked around the front of the vehicle. He stopped next to his door, head down and lips moving like he was giving himself a pep talk.

He lifted his head and locked eyes with me.

The breath swept out of my lungs so fast it made me dizzy. The lust in his eyes… Was it lust? I'd never had a man look at me like he was.

He yanked open the door and climbed in next to me, tearing his gaze from mine and gripping the steering wheel so tight his knuckles turned white. "I know this isn't part of our deal. I'm sorry I crossed a line."

"What line did you cross?" *And can you cross is a little farther?*

"You wanted to know how to flirt with someone else, not me. We're not… You're not looking for anything beyond sex. I get it. I won't cross that line again and put my hands on you."

"I liked your hands on me," I whispered.

He sucked in a sharp breath. "Casey."

The word was pained, like it was taking something from him to groan my name.

Laughter cut through the air as others came out of the theater. Landon cranked up the SUV and pulled away from the curb without another word.

It was only a few seconds before he was parking in front of my building. A few more before he was opening my door.

"Are you coming in?" I blurted.

He chuckled. "I would love to, but I think you need some sleep."

"I'm fine."

"You fell asleep on the drive here."

"No, I didn't. It's like five minutes away."

"And yet, you were sleeping."

"I guess I'm drunker than I realized."

"Which is why I'm going to walk you to your apartment and leave you with all your dicks."

I looked down at all the dicks in my hands and knew without a doubt in the world that I would rather leave all of them behind and play with his.

But I couldn't say that to him.

I twisted my mouth to keep the words inside and nodded.

He helped me slide from the seat and collected the penises I dropped on the sidewalk. We shuffled my collection so I could get my keys and unlock the front door.

Landon followed me quietly up the stairs to my apartment. His footsteps were soft on the carpeted stairs, but I could feel his presence right behind me. He was close enough to catch me if I stumbled, or if I swayed against his body.

I was tempted, but I didn't want to risk hurting us both.

We made it to my door, and he leaned against the wall as I unlocked the door. I reached in and flipped the light on. "Do you want to come in for a minute?"

He stared into my eyes, neither of us moving or breathing for several long beats, then he nodded.

I walked inside, holding the door for him to follow. He grabbed it and let it close quietly, mindful of my neighbors. I went to the kitchen to deposit my dicks on the table.

Landon followed, setting his part of my cock collection down.

I snorted a laugh.

"What are you laughing at?"

"There's never been even one dick in this apartment since I moved in. Now there's a few dozen."

He chuckled with me, the soft puff of his breath on my neck dragging my gaze up to his.

Again, I got lost in his eyes. Gold circled his widening pupil, giving a brightness to his dark brown eyes. I leaned toward him, drawn in by an invisible force I wasn't even aware was moving me.

He groaned and closed the distance between us, his lips slamming down on mine and stealing all breath and thought and sanity from me.

I sighed against his lips, smiling at the feel of him against me. His erection grew between us, and I wrapped my arms around his waist, holding him close to me.

He kissed my lips with quiet leisure, tasting each of my lips with the firm press of his. His tongue peeked out to slick over my lower lip, and I groaned and licked my tongue along his.

He shivered and drew me closer with a quick inhale. His arms banded around my back, hauling me against my new favorite dick.

I chuckled at the thought, and he withdrew.

"Not the reaction I was hoping for."

"I was just thinking you have my new favorite dick."

He snorted. "All these options and you have a favorite?"

I nodded. "Without a doubt."

His breath left him in a shaky rush. "I should go."

"Why?"

He smiled and tucked my hair behind my ear. His fingers lingered on my jaw, making me shiver. "Because I really want to stay."

"That makes no sense. If you want to stay, you should stay."

"Not when you're drunk, Casey. I don't want you to regret anything tomorrow, and if I'm here, you might."

"I won't."

"Then tomorrow you can tell me."

I pouted, but even as my body ached for him, I knew he was right. It was the alcohol that made me bold enough to say the things I'd said to him.

"Lock the door behind me. And drink some water before you go to bed. Maybe take some pain meds."

I nodded. "I will. Reegan was a fool to let you go."

He paused with his hand on the doorknob. "Good night, Casey."

"Good night, Landon."

He kissed my forehead, and then he was gone.

12

LANDON

I played her parting words in my head my entire drive home. *Reegan was a fool to let you go.* Except I was the one who finally said the words that ended things. I was the one who let her go.

I parked behind my shop and sat in the silence as my vehicle cooled, the engine popping softly. Ending things with Reegan never felt foolish to me. Not when I knew we weren't meant to be together. She'd become a comfortable part of my life, a part I didn't want to go without. But kissing Casey…

I'd never been so turned on by a simple kiss before. Not even when I was a kid and didn't know what the words meant or what a kiss could lead to. Being around Casey was a whole new kind of experience. One I wanted to repeat as often as possible.

Our sleepy town was quiet as I made my way inside and up to my apartment. I grabbed a glass and filled it with water, then headed for a cold shower. Casey's favorite dick still had a big head after her declaration.

I tossed my clothes in the hamper and stepped into the shower, wincing at the cold water. I closed my eyes and ducked my head under the water, knowing I wouldn't be able to go to sleep until I alleviated the pressure building. My brain was insistent on replaying the evening until the cold shower felt like a steam room.

I slapped the handle to warm the water and reached for my dick. One stroke and I was groaning. Another and I was bucking against my hand.

"Fuck."

I stroked harder, faster, squeezing with every slam of my fist on my dick. My other hand hit the wall. Water pounded on my back, sliding down my chest and adding a slickness to my fist.

"Holy… fuck."

I couldn't stroke myself fast enough. Casey looking up at me with a collection of cocks in her lap, eyes sleepy. Casey telling me I have her favorite dick. Casey falling over my display and looking cute as shit with her pink cheeks. Casey walking into my shop dressed like a professional and rocking my damn world when she asked me for flirting lessons.

And that kiss.

"Yes. Fuck!" I came hard as I thought about our kiss. Her tongue peeking out to taste mine. Would she get her tongue involved when she sucked my dick? Would she use her hands? Would she moan with me?

I nearly collapsed as I imagined Casey on her knees in the shower with me. She had no idea what she did to me. How desirable she was. How fucking sexy she was.

I dragged in my breath and fought back the bone-deep need to sleep. After a few seconds, I turned off the shower and got out, knowing if I didn't get to bed fast, my mind would drag her back to the front and I'd never get any sleep.

Five minutes later, I was in bed, naked, and wishing I wasn't alone.

I DIDN'T HEAR anything from Casey for three days. I sent her a few texts, asking if she wanted to get together for lunch again, but she never replied.

I tried to rationalize with myself that she was busy, but I knew that wasn't really what was going on. She was hiding from me.

Which begged the question why?

Was she ashamed of getting drunk and flirting with me? Was she regretting the kiss? Was she done with flirting lessons since she proved she knew what she was doing?

I didn't know the answer, and I didn't know anyone to ask. Not that I would. Probably. Maybe.

Fine, I was dying to ask someone, but how pathetic was I? A grown-ass man asking my buddy if he thought a woman liked me. Nope. Not going back to high school bullshit.

Which meant I had to find a way to talk to Casey.

I felt like an asshole manipulating her, but it felt like the best option. Especially since my other thought was to show up at her apartment, but I wasn't sure how she would feel about that and the possibility that her daughter would be home.

DIRTYLIFE

Now it's my turn to apologize for being out of touch. Work has been busy lately. How are you?

I wasn't sure if she'd message back, but it wasn't long before she did.

TOOBUSY

I wasn't sure I'd hear from you again. It seemed like I scared you off asking about getting together.

DIRTYLIFE

Not scared. Work and life got more hectic than I expected. I should have reached out.

TOOBUSY

It's no big deal.

DIRTYLIFE

It is to me. I got a little wrapped up in my head and let work pull me in. It wasn't fair to you. Or me because I missed talking to you.

TOOBUSY

You're making it tough to be upset.

DIRTYLIFE

Good. Then my plan is working.

TOOBUSY

DIRTYLIFE

I deserve that. But I am sorry. And I did miss talking to you. How have you been the last few days?

TOOBUSY

Nothing new for me. My kid picked up a new afterschool activity. Fun for her, more work for me. But it's nice to see her enjoying something new.

DIRTYLIFE

I imagine it would be. I love kids. Hopefully one day I'll have some.

TOOBUSY

My daughter is the best thing I ever did. For all my regrets about my marriage, having her was never one of them.

DIRTYLIFE

Do you want more kids?

TOOBUSY

Once upon a time I did. But now, it's not likely. And I'm not sure I really want more.

DIRTYLIFE

Can I ask why?

TOOBUSY

Ending a relationship is hard. You know that. Being with someone you thought you'd spend your entire life with... and then not... It was harder than I expected to get to a place where I was open to dating. But getting married? Having more kids? Building a life with someone? I know it's what you're looking for, but I'm just not. I don't think I can do it again.

Reading her words... It was a punch to the gut. Not because she wanted something different than me, but because I knew what Casey had to offer. Not just sex, but the kind of woman I was coming to learn she was. Smart, funny, interesting. Yeah, she twisted me up inside and out, but even if she ended up with someone else, the lucky son of a bitch would have a woman who loved with her entire self.

She was scared, but that didn't diminish who she was. I saw her light. I saw the way she looked at Natalie and Omar when they were staring at each other and oblivious to the world. She wanted the same thing. She wanted to be loved the way Omar loved Natalie.

TOOBUSY

I figured that was why you stopped talking to me. You realized we wanted different things and couldn't see the point of continuing whatever this is.

DIRTYLIFE

That's not it. I like talking to you. A lot. And I don't know where this is going with us, but that doesn't mean we can't enjoy it along the way.

TOOBUSY

Is it worth it if we both know we want different things?

I wasn't ready to end our conversations. Not online and not in person. Why was she so quick to?

DIRTYLIFE

How about this? We set a date to meet in a few weeks. We keep talking until then, get to know each other, and if either of us doesn't want to meet in person, no hard feelings.

TOOBUSY

Are you trying to Sleepless in Seattle me?

DIRTYLIFE

I don't know what that means.

TOOBUSY

It's a movie. God, you're making me feel old that you don't know the movie. These two people agree to meet on Valentine's Day at the top of the Empire State Building.

DIRTYLIFE

That's a bit of a drive, but if you really want to do that, I can make it work. We might need to make it longer than just lunch, though.

TOOBUSY

I'm not saying that. Just… Never mind. Okay. I'll agree. When do you want to meet?

Natalie and Omar's wedding was in three weeks, so it had to be after that.

DIRTYLIFE

Three weeks from this coming Tuesday. Lunch. You pick the place.

TOOBUSY

Do you know O'Kelley's in MacKellar Cove?

DIRTYLIFE

I do.

TOOBUSY

Noon? Three weeks from Tuesday.

DIRTYLIFE

I will meet you there.

TOOBUSY

If I don't scare you off by then.

DIRTYLIFE

Not going to happen.

TOOBUSY

Such confidence.

DIRTYLIFE

LOL! Maybe I just know when I've found something worthwhile. What are you up to this weekend? Anything fun and exciting?

TOOBUSY

I'm working. My daughter has plans today, so I have some time to get work done.

DIRTYLIFE

You really don't take time off, do you? What do you do for fun?

TOOBUSY

I don't have a lot of that anymore.

DIRTYLIFE

Well, what would you do if fun was the only thing on your agenda for today?

TOOBUSY

I don't know. It's been so long since I've had that kind of freedom that I can't think of how I'd spend it.

DIRTYLIFE

That's your homework for the next time we talk.

TOOBUSY

You're giving me homework?

DIRTYLIFE

I need to know what to plan for our dates after three weeks from Tuesday.

TOOBUSY

I seem to have a knack for turning men off, so if you do show up that day, I have no doubt it'll be the last time we see each other.

DIRTYLIFE

I have no doubt at all that I will be begging you for another date.

TOOBUSY

If you say so.

DIRTYLIFE

I know so.

TOOBUSY

We'll see. But for now, I really need to work. I only have another hour before my daughter is done.

DIRTYLIFE

It was good talking to you. And I hope you find something fun to do this weekend.

TOOBUSY

Yeah.

I smiled as I signed off. Except for the part about having a knack for turning men off, it was a good chat. But that one piece of information was all I needed to know she didn't think I wanted her.

She was so wrong. Not only did I want to see her more, but I wanted to crack her wide open and find out all the secrets she hid from the world.

But first, I had to work.

ANDRE LET himself in the back door as I was locking the front one. While Casey had been dodging me, I'd been dodging Andre. I was not ready to answer all the questions I knew he would be asking. But I was clearly out of time.

"Hey," I said when he met me in the back. "I need to run up and change."

"I'll be here when you're ready." The words were subtle, but the tone was ominous.

"What?" I asked, pausing on the bottom step.

"What, what? I didn't say anything?"

"Your smirk did."

He laughed fully. "Don't blame me for being curious about you swooping in to take Casey home and never showing up again."

"It wasn't like that."

"I didn't say what it was like. You're the one filling in the blanks."

"Fuck you."

"Uh huh. Go get changed. You can tell me all about it on the way to the bachelor party."

I groaned. I let his laughter follow me up the stairs. A part of me wanted to leave him down there stewing, but I didn't want to be late to Omar's bachelor party. I changed out of my work clothes and jumped into a pair of jeans and a clean button-down shirt. I rolled the sleeves up and headed for the door again.

Andre hadn't moved. "I thought you were going to stall."

"I thought about it."

He laughed and led the way to his truck. Andre offered to drive since he was working Sunday morning and wouldn't have more than one drink. I wasn't planning on more than that either, but I didn't mind having someone to go with.

Even if he was an obnoxious pain in the ass who was going to demand more information than I wanted to share.

"So, you and Casey?" Andre asked as he pulled onto the street and drove past Blossom & Grow.

"We're getting to know each other," I said.

"Which means?"

"Which means we're talking. When she came with Omar and Natalie to finalize the flowers, we talked. I... She's interesting."

"She's also a single mom and divorced not that long ago," Andre warned.

"I'm aware of both of those things."

"And they don't bother you?"

"Why would they?"

Andre was quiet for a long minute. He stared straight ahead, his hands gripping and loosening on the steering wheel as he searched for words.

I waited him out, not willing to fill in more than I already had. When Casey asked me to teach her how to flirt, I made the decision not to tell anyone else what our arrangement was. I never spoke to her about it, but it didn't feel right to share. It was between us.

"After Reegan..." He glanced sideways at me. "After things ended, I thought you would bounce back. I expected you to start dating. You seemed stuck. Like you couldn't believe things were over. Even though you said you made that choice, it still felt like you weren't okay with it or ready for it or whatever. I guess I expected you to snap, eventually. To sleep your way through town or go on a weekend bender in another town or something. I never expected you to tie yourself to a divorced single mom."

My first thought was anger, but I slowed it down and processed what he said. "Dating is not easy. Not just in general, but specifically for me right now. Everyone in town assumes Reegan and I are going to work things out. When I go on dates, and I have, they end because no one wants to piss Reegan off."

"That's not fair to you."

"It's not. But it's what's happening right now. But not with Casey. She listened when I said things are over with Reegan. She believed me. She knows what it's like to be in the position I'm in. Fresh off a long-term relationship with all the pain that goes with that."

"So, she's like a friend?"

"I didn't say that." I couldn't stop my smile remembering our kiss. "We're spending time together."

"You really like her, don't you?"

I nodded and met my friend's questioning look. "I do."

Andre exhaled a laugh and shook his head. "Well, then I'm happy for you."

"We're not moving in together or anything."

Andre paused. "And maybe you won't, but I like that you found someone who makes you happy for right now. Maybe not forever, but you never know."

I nodded. "Yeah."

Andre got out of his truck, leaving me to process the conversation.

I'd just convinced Casey to give me a chance. I wasn't

going to screw it up by deciding the end of our relationship before we'd even started one.

I followed Andre into O'Kelley's and to the back where Hudson had roped off a section for Omar's bachelor party. Omar insisted he didn't want a big thing, but he wanted a chance to sit and talk and enjoy time with friends.

My guess was that he knew if we were at O'Kelley's, no one would hire strippers.

Omar greeted us, offering drinks and making sure we knew all the food was taken care of.

"Congrats, man," I told Omar. "Almost here."

"I can't wait. Three more weeks until I get to call her my wife." Omar's grin stretched across his face and radiated joy.

"You're a lucky man," I said.

"I am. I am."

"What advice do you have for the last single man in MacKellar Cove?"

Omar snorted. "I hear you might not be as single as you claim. Didn't you and Casey leave the bachelorette party together?"

"Ah, I gave her a ride home. But that's it."

"You don't sound so sure about that," Omar said.

"I'm not going to say that's all I was hoping would happen. But she was drinking, and I wasn't going to cross a line without knowing she was on board with it."

"I get that. For what it's worth, I think the world of Casey. Natalie was hurt when that article came out, but Casey swears it was all her editor, and I believe her. She's a good person. Really sees the good in others."

"I think so, too."

"Then I wish you luck. Her ex was a real piece of work, from what I heard. Casey needs someone who will treat her the way she deserves."

"I appreciate the vote of confidence."

"I mean it, Landon. You're a good man."

Hudson called Omar's name from the other side of the area.

Omar waved, then faced me. "Don't give up on her. Some women are a little harder to get to know. Natalie was one of them, but worth it. I think Casey is the same."

"So do I."

13

Seeing the aftermath of the bachelorette party left me thinking the bachelor party was tame. Not that I was complaining. I wasn't looking to stare at strippers with a bunch of married or involved men and have to take one for the team. I'd been the non-single guy enough times to know that was what ended up happening. It was not for me.

Most of the conversation revolved around marriage, with the men who'd taken the plunge dishing out their advice.

"Communication is the most important thing. As someone who almost screwed everything up and lost Blake, make sure you talk to each other," Ian said.

"I agree with that one," Ramsey said, nodding along.

"Make sure you tell her how much you want her," James said, earning a laugh.

"No, he's right," Rowan defended his fellow police officer. "It's not just about sex or getting her into bed. When I tell Willow she's the only one for me and I don't know how I got so lucky to spend my life with her, she knows there's no one else. She knows she's loved completely, no matter how crazy she gets or what she comes up with. We all need that sometimes."

James nodded, clapping Rowan on the back in agreement.

"Treat her like a queen," Knox said. "And do your part at home. Especially if you have kids. Haley has been killing herself at work and at home. She doesn't like to walk away, but when I take the baby and force her to take a bath or sleep or something that gives her a break, she feels more like herself afterward."

"I second that one," Sebastian said.

"Enjoy every moment," Hudson said quietly, capturing the attention of everyone. He shook his head and pressed his lips together before continuing. "There will be times when she makes you crazy, and not in a good way. When she frustrates the shit out of you. Enjoy the good and the bad. Not just because you don't know when you're going to run out of moments, but because those arguments, fights, disagreements… those are going to lead to a new depth in your relationship. They'll make it better because you both know you can say anything you need to say and it won't destroy what you have."

I swallowed the thickness in my throat, fighting my emotions with his declaration. Judging by the silence around me, I wasn't the only one feeling the impact of his words.

"Thanks, man," Omar said, hugging Hudson and slapping his back. "You're right."

Hudson nodded, hugging Omar back. They shared a smile as they pulled back, all of us echoing the same thoughts with quiet nods and smiles of our own.

I didn't share any advice since I wasn't in a relationship and no one wants to hear from the single guy at a bachelor party, but I took in all their words. One day I'd need them.

The drinking resumed, and the mood lightened after the

advice was shared. James talked Ramsey into a game of darts, then complained when Ramsey won. Andre asked Knox about his new baby, which brought out the phone.

I looked over Andre's shoulder at Knox and Haley's baby girl, Amanda. The pink bundle was small and squishy and made me jealous as fuck.

I wanted that. Not Knox's baby, but a family of my own. Someone to share my life with. Kids and a future and a life that wasn't on hold until I found someone who wanted the same thing.

I excused myself as the two of them talked and left the party area, needing a break from all the happiness and joy I was on the outside of. I was happy for all of them. They all deserved the happiness they'd found, but where the hell was my happiness? Where was my joy? Where was my happy ending?

I asked the bartender for a beer and sat on a stool on the far side of the bar. Two women sat next to me. One of them smiled at me. They weren't familiar, but the other one whispered something to her friend. Something that sounded suspiciously like Reegan's name.

I wanted to yell at them that I was single. That Reegan was old news. That we weren't getting back together. Now or ever. But I didn't have the energy.

The women were both beautiful, but neither of them stirred any desire in me. They weren't curvy single moms with too many jobs and no desire to get involved with me, or anyone.

I laughed to myself without any humor in it. I spent three years with a woman who didn't want the same things I did and ended my relationship with her because of it, and a year later, I was in the same situation, wanting a woman who had no interest in the things I wanted.

What was wrong with me?

"What are you doing over here?" Andre asked, taking the vacated seat next to me.

"Getting a beer."

"There's beer back there with everyone else."

I nodded and sipped my drink.

"What's going on?"

I leveled him with a look.

"Reegan?"

"Fucking hell. No. I thought I made it clear things are over with Reegan. I swear to fuck if you blame my mood on Reegan again, I'm not talking to you."

"Promise?" Andre smirked.

"Fuck you."

"Casey?"

I shrugged. "She doesn't want to get married again. Or have more kids."

"Whoa, seriously? You're moving fast if you've already proposed to her."

"I haven't proposed. Fucking hell. We talk."

Andre narrowed his eyes. "You talk? Like on dates or online?"

I avoided his knowing gaze. "Both?"

"Fuck. You matched with her? How do you know it's her?"

"I figured it out."

"And she knows it's you?"

I shook my head. "I don't think so."

"You have to tell her."

"No. Not yet."

"You know it's going to go badly if you keep it from her."

"I'm willing to take that risk."

"Are you? Because if she finds out you knew and lied to her about it for weeks, she might not forgive you for it."

"It'll be fine."

"So you're using that connection to find out more about her? Is that how you know she doesn't want to get married?"

"No, she told me that in person."

Andre snorted. "Sounds like you're off to a great start with her."

I chuckled. "Something like that."

After a minute, Andre asked, "Why are you getting involved with Casey if you want different things?"

I exhaled a laugh. "Fuck if I know."

Andre studied me carefully. "You ended things with Reegan because she didn't want kids, right?"

"Yeah."

"What's different about Casey?"

"What do you mean?"

"I assume you and Reegan talked about kids or no kids long before she refused to move in with you. I know that was the final thing and made you realize you weren't on the same page."

"Yeah?"

"There was something that kept you together as long as you were."

I scrubbed a hand down my face. "A lot of things, yeah." I loved her was a big one, but at the end, that wasn't enough. By the end, I was holding my breath. I told myself at the time it was hope, but what I was hoping for wasn't what I thought I was hoping for. When Reegan refused to move in with me, I was relieved.

And I was an asshole for it.

"You are going to end up in the same place with Casey," Andre said. "She doesn't want more kids or to get married, so what's different?"

I opened my mouth to tell him everything was different, but he was right. Nothing was different.

"I'm not trying to piss you off. If you like her, go for it, but I don't want to see you hurt again."

"I'll be fine."

"I know you will be, but I love you, man. You're like a brother to me."

"A younger brother," I quipped.

Andre snorted. "A brother I would have beat up a lot when we were kids."

"You could try," I said with a smirk.

"Fucking hell, I'm trying to be serious here." He chuckled.

"I know. And thanks. I don't know what it is about Casey. She makes me smile. She has this strength in her that she doesn't seem to see but is so obvious when I look at her. She has no idea how sexy she is, and it makes me fucking crazy. I mean, she told me—" I cut myself off before I told him she said I had her favorite dick.

"You already have secrets and inside jokes. It's been a long time since I've seen you look like that when talking about a woman." Andre clapped me on the back. "I get it. I don't want you to get hurt, but I get it."

"You get what?" I asked, wondering what the hell he was talking about.

He chuckled and stood. "You'll figure it out, eventually. I'm going back to the party. You coming?"

"Figure what out?" I asked, trailing behind him. "What the hell are you talking about?"

Andre just laughed and led the way back to the others, knowing I would drop it once we were surrounded.

I WAS NOT in love with Casey. It took me far longer to figure it out than I wanted to admit, but it finally hit me that was what Andre assumed.

I barely knew her. Love wasn't... It wasn't possible. Maybe one day, but not yet. Not when we were pretending.

But if she was going to continue ignoring me and avoiding me, I wasn't sure I still had a date to Omar and Natalie's wedding. And I needed that answer before I said anything to anyone about it.

Five days of silence told me I had no choice but to show up at her apartment, which was why on Monday morning, before I opened the store, I was standing in front of Casey's building. Lucky for me, it was also Andre's building, and I wasn't above using my connections to get access to the woman I was not in love with.

I texted Andre to buzz me in but not to expect me at his door. He sent back a thumbs up and the door in front of me buzzed. I smiled as I yanked it open and let myself into the building.

Taking Casey home from the bachelorette party gave me the advantage of knowing which apartment was hers. The building was almost as quiet as that night, but the stirrings of people getting ready to leave for the day told me it was not the same.

I stood outside her door and raised my hand to knock, stopping when I heard her voice inside. Shit. I forgot she had a kid. A young kid who was still at home. Unless Casey was talking to herself.

Nope. There was a second voice. And both voices were getting closer to the door.

The door opened, but neither of them noticed me as they were talking to each other.

"Rehearsal is done at four, right?" Casey asked.

"Yes. All week." Her daughter had the same brown hair as Casey but shorter and with more curl in it. She came up to Casey's chest when they hugged.

They turned as one and both startled when they saw me.

"Landon," Casey exclaimed. "What are you doing here?"

"Who's he?" The teenage attitude came through in just two words and almost made me laugh.

"This is my friend, Landon. Landon, this is my daughter, Mikayla. Who is going to miss the bus if she doesn't get moving."

Mikayla rolled her eyes and moved past me.

"Nice to meet you," I said to her.

"You, too," she said, dutifully, as if she couldn't bring herself to not reply.

I turned to Casey and watched her as she worried her bottom lip and stared after her daughter until she disappeared down the stairs.

"Why are you here? And how did you get in?"

"Andre lives in this building. I asked him to buzz me in."

"He doesn't live on this floor."

"I know. But I'm not here to see him."

She crossed her arms over her chest. "What does that mean?"

"You haven't been returning my texts."

"I've been busy," she said without meeting my gaze.

I cupped her jaw and eased it up until I could look her in the eye. "I don't believe you."

"Really? I'm a single mom who works three jobs. I am always too busy. I barely have enough time to shower, let alone text you constantly."

"We both know that's not the reason you haven't texted me back in five days, Casey."

Her brows shot up. "We do, huh? Then enlighten me. Why am I not texting you back?"

"Because you think kissing me was a mistake."

"You're the one who ran out of here."

"I wouldn't say I ran, but I left because I was afraid you would regret it if I didn't."

"So, what? Do you want a medal for being right?"

"No. I want you to talk to me. I want you to kiss me again. I want you to tell me you still want me."

"What?" she breathed.

A door opened across the hall, and she forced a smile for her neighbor.

"Morning, Casey."

"Hi, Ron. Have a good day."

"You, too. Everything okay?"

She nodded. "All good. Thanks."

Ron gave me a look that was more protective than a random neighbor should be giving another man.

I wanted to growl at him. To puff out my chest. To show him I was the bigger man and he needed to back the fuck off.

"Let's talk inside," Casey whispered.

And all I did was smirk and follow her into her apartment. With Ron heading to work.

Yeah, I was an asshole. And maybe Andre wasn't completely wrong. But it wasn't love. It was lust. It was desire. It was all the chemical and biological things that drew two people together.

"We're not having sex," Casey said, leaning against the now closed door.

"Ever?" I gasped.

She huffed a laugh. "I meant right now, but I'm not promising anything in the future either."

"Listen, I'm not here for that. We… We have an agreement. You said you wanted me to help you learn to flirt. And I wanted a date for the wedding. If there's chemistry between us, there's nothing wrong with that."

"There is if we don't want the same things."

"I will never force you into anything, Casey. And yes, I want kids. I want to get married. I want to settle down one day and have someone I wake up to in the morning and fall asleep with every night. But that doesn't mean I'm not willing to enjoy the next few weeks with you."

She drew a breath, held it, then blew it out slowly. "I'll make you a new deal. Same deal, but with a deadline. After the wedding, we go our separate ways."

My chest hurt with her suggestion. My body tightened. I felt like I'd been kicked. But I refused to let her see it. "No more avoiding me. We meet at least twice a week. And we make sure we are believable as a couple at the wedding."

"What does that mean?"

"It means you're going to have to kiss me again. And dance with me. And let me touch you and act like you're enjoying it." I eased closer to her as I spoke. When I was within reach of her, I took her hand.

She trembled at my touch. "Landon."

I didn't hesitate. I tugged her against me, slamming my lips over hers.

She responded to my kiss instantly, sucking in a breath and letting it out with a sigh. Her hand went to my shirt and grabbed hold of me.

I cupped her jaw with my other hand and licked my way inside her mouth. I brought our joined hands behind her back and held her against me, devouring her the way I wanted to the other night.

She whimpered. She didn't fight my kiss or try to control it. I could tell she was enjoying herself, but she wasn't showing me what she wanted, what she liked.

I craved that information. I wanted to know everything about her. What turned her on, what made her retreat. Her favorite joke and her favorite food. I wanted it all.

An alarm went off somewhere to my left, and I let her pull away from me.

She rushed to the kitchen and silenced the alarm. "I'm sorry. I have to go to work this morning."

"You don't have to apologize to me for living your life."

She smiled. "I told you I'm busy."

"I know you are. Do we have a deal? Lunch twice a week, at least. Or whatever else you want to do. If that's afternoon coffee or dinner or gathering more dick collections."

She snorted a laugh.

"Where did you put all of that?" There wasn't a dick in sight. Except the one trying to get out of my pants.

"They're in my room. In my closet, where Mikayla won't see them all."

"Makes sense. And I'm sorry for showing up with her here. I didn't think."

Casey shook her head. "It's okay. She's pretty absorbed in her world. She's probably already forgotten you were here."

"I hope so. She's not going to the wedding?"

"No. I'm technically going for work, so I never planned to take her, but Finley and Trent offered their house for a sleepover for all the kids. Trent has a house manager who lives there, and the older high school kids are going to be in charge of all the younger kids."

"That's a pretty good deal."

Casey nodded. "It is. This community is pretty exceptional."

"So are you," I whispered.

She smiled and ducked her head. Her cheeks turned red.

I made a mental note to pay her more compliments. She needed to know how amazing she was.

"Um, I need to go. I'm sorry."

"Understood. Do you want to have lunch today?"

She shook her head. "I can't today. After my meeting this morning, I'm cleaning houses the rest of the day until I get Mikayla from school."

"Tomorrow?"

She hesitated, then nodded. "I can do tomorrow."

"Good. I'll text you later, and we can decide on a time and place." I stepped closer to her and kissed her softly. "Have a good day."

"You, too," she breathed.

I smiled and let myself out of her apartment. Back on track.

14

CASEY

I had every expectation that Gretchen would demand changes to my article about Natalie's bachelorette party, and zero expectations that Landon would show up at my door when I didn't text him back.

I was wrong on both counts.

Not only did Gretchen not want to change a thing in my article, she actually praised me for it, saying it was some of my best work.

She did not need to find out I was drunk for most of the party and definitely did not need to know I wrote half the article the same night, after Landon kissed me and left me wanting way more than a kiss.

I deleted those parts of the article, but when I read them the morning after, I knew I couldn't face him again. Until he showed up at my door and made me feel like kissing him was not only not a mistake but it was a gift. The man could kiss. I thought my drunk brain was wrong when it said he was exceptional, but nope. He was exceptional.

One more thing that made me wonder why in the world Reegan let him go.

149

And made me jealous of whatever woman didn't.

Too bad it couldn't be me. But I wasn't looking for a new husband. Or to start over as a mom. My old dreams were gone, and even Landon's echoing of them wouldn't get me to change my mind.

Right after Mikayla left for the bus Tuesday morning, I looked up my article, holding my breath as I read every word to make sure Gretchen didn't change it without telling me again.

The women of MacKellar Cove know how to throw a party. This reporter was lucky enough to get an invitation to Natalie Edwards' bachelorette party, and it is not a night I will soon forget. Friendship and love were on full display, along with a selection of carefully curated adult treats. From the cake to the decorations, there was no doubt the night was destined to be a lot of fun.

I smiled. Every word was mine, and every word was perfect. Natalie was thrilled with the article, and I couldn't wait to get started on the next one. I wanted to capture the vibe of the reception and was showcasing the photographer, band, and DJ. They were the people who would set the tone for the reception and be the pieces Natalie and Omar would remember forever.

I was on my own to meet with the vendors. Natalie and Omar were working every day to make sure they had a full two weeks off for the wedding, and the band, DJ, and photographer had weddings booked solid over the weekend. I had a meeting scheduled with the photographer for Tuesday morning and one with the band for Wednesday, but the DJ was proving harder to connect with. I'd left him a message the week before asking to schedule a time to talk, but he never got back to me.

The phone rang twice, then a man picked up.

"This is Adam."

"Hi, Adam. This is Casey White with the MacKellar Cove Gazette. I've been trying to reach you to set up a time to meet. I'm working on an article about Natalie Edwards and Omar Knight's wedding and know you would be a great addition to it. Are you available sometime this week so we could talk?"

"No."

"Oh. Um, okay, maybe we could speak over the phone?"

"Not happening."

"Is there a reason you aren't willing to speak to me?"

"I don't know you. And I don't owe you an explanation."

"You don't, but—"

The phone was silent. I looked, and he hung up.

"Dammit." I didn't want to bother Natalie with the issue I was having getting in touch with her DJ, but if I couldn't get him to speak to me, I was either going to have to change the article or reach out to Natalie.

I didn't like either option.

I did some research on other things I could write the article about, other vendors who would help to set the tone for the reception, but I was stumped. Without the music, a wedding would just be a bunch of people talking. The band was great, but they were playing during the cocktail hour and dinner. The DJ would be the one who got everyone on the dance floor. He would play the music Natalie and Omar chose. He would make the night one to remember.

But he didn't want to talk to me.

I was still trying to figure out other options when I left to meet Landon for lunch. He wanted to go to Just Tacos, and since it was one of my favorite places, I agreed easily.

He was already at a table when I walked in. He stood and

slid his phone into his pocket, walking to me like he couldn't keep himself from my side.

"Hi," he said, leaning down to kiss my cheek.

"Hi." My face flamed. The other diners watched us, probably wondering what in the world he was doing with me.

"I wanted to wait for you to order. Do you know what you want?"

You? My cheeks burned hotter with that thought.

"I like the way you think," he whispered, forgoing my cheek and kissing me on the lips. He pulled back quickly and grinned at me. "We'll save that thought for another time."

"Did I say that out loud?"

He chuckled and grabbed my hand. "Your face did."

"You don't know what I was thinking."

He squeezed my hand. "No, but I know I have your favorite."

"Oh my God," I groaned. "I hoped you'd forgotten about that."

He tapped his temple. "Never. That's locked in here for life."

I closed my eyes and shook my head, wishing that were enough to erase my embarrassment.

"You have no idea how big of a turn-on that statement was," he whispered against my ear. "I haven't been able to stop thinking about it. Or taking matters into my own hands because of it."

My breath puffed out of me. I looked at him, my gaze slamming into his. His pupils were dilated. There was no hint of teasing in his eyes. "You..."

"Absolutely, Casey."

"Oh."

"Does that make you uncomfortable? I didn't intend that."

I shook my head, wishing I could cross my legs or take

matters into my own hands. "Not uncomfortable in the way you're asking."

He chuckled. "That's good to know."

"What can I get for you guys today?" the woman behind the counter asked.

"I'll take three soft tacos, grilled chicken, loaded. Water to drink. And chips and salsa. Do you want queso?"

I nodded.

"We'll do queso, too, please."

"Are you together?" the woman asked as she finished keying in his order.

"No," I said.

"Yes," Landon said louder. "Casey, order."

The commanding tone of his voice made me shiver. I swallowed roughly, then ordered three loaded beef and bean tacos and a water.

"Can I get a name for the order?"

"Landon," he said, tapping his phone to pay for our meal. "Thank you."

"Enjoy."

Landon pulled me away from the counter and back to the table he was at when I arrived. "Next time we meet for lunch, we need to go somewhere more private so I can kiss you how I want to."

"Your flirting is next level, you know that? I knew you were good, but this is…"

"Not flirting for the sake of flirting, Casey. I told you the first rule is you have to mean it."

"I don't think I know what to do with that."

"With what?"

"With you saying you mean it. I'm way older than you, and we want different things."

"And that means I can't be attracted to you?"

"No, I just…"

"First, I don't think you're that much older than me. You might not be older than me at all. I'm thirty-five. Can I ask how old you are?"

"I just turned thirty-eight."

"Less than three years. That means we would have been in high school at the same time. If I was older than you, you wouldn't think twice about a few years between us, so why is it an issue that you're a little older?"

"I… I thought you were a lot younger."

"Ouch."

I laughed with him. "I didn't mean it like that."

"No, no, it's fine. You're telling me I'm old. I get it."

I shook my head. "I'm older than you, so what does that make me?"

"Perfect."

I snorted. "Nowhere close."

He reached for my hand. "You're beautiful and sexy and smart and talented and a great mother and independent and you have a laugh that makes my heart stop and you make me want to spend as much time with you as I can talk you into."

My cheeks got hotter and hotter with each word he said. I didn't know how to take compliments at all, but he had this way of speaking to me as if he couldn't imagine not telling me these things. I bit my lip and lowered my chin to hide from him.

His name rang out over the sound of the other diners, and he winked at me before he went to collect our lunch. I exhaled a slow breath and tried to calm my overactive desire for the man I had no right to want.

Even though I really, really wanted him.

Landon set the trays on the table and made sure we had everything we ordered before I unwrapped my first taco.

"Your article was really good," he said as I bit into my taco.

"You read it?" I asked around my food.

He nodded, his eyes narrowing as if he couldn't believe I asked. "Of course. I like to know what's going on in town, but I also enjoy your words. You're really talented, Casey."

"Thanks. Too bad not everyone feels the same way."

"What do you mean?"

I shook my head. "Nothing. I'm just complaining."

"And I want to know what's going on with you. Who doesn't feel the same way about your writing?"

"I don't know if he has ever read anything I've written, but I'm trying to get a meeting with the DJ Natalie and Omar hired. He's been avoiding my calls, and when he answered today, he told me he won't talk to me. I don't know why."

"Do you want me to call him?"

"You know Adam?"

Landon pulled out his phone and tapped the screen. "I'm the one who suggested him. He's worked a few weddings I've done the flowers for and heard great things about him. We've recommended each other a few times. There aren't a ton of vendors in the Thousand Islands. It's all small towns up and down the area. Adam is talented. And he's local. He lives about twenty minutes north with his husband and two kids."

"I feel bad asking you to get involved."

"I don't mind at all. Let's eat, and I'll call him before you leave me for the day."

"You have to get back to work, too."

He chuckled. "I do, but I'd rather spend the afternoon with you."

My cheeks warmed again. I smiled as I took another bite of my taco. "So, what's my next lesson? I don't think the first one worked."

"What do you mean?"

"I'm on that dating app. Book Boyfriends Wanted?"

"I'm familiar with it," he said, sounding less than thrilled.

"I'm sorry. Is it… I shouldn't."

"Shouldn't what?"

"I shouldn't be talking to you about other men."

"I won't lie and say I'm totally on board with you seeing other men, but after the wedding, I agreed to walk away if that's what you want. We started this because you wanted to learn how to flirt."

I nibbled my lip and debated how much to tell him about DirtyLife.

"Just say it, Casey. You met someone else?"

"Yes and no. We've been talking for a while. Since before you and I started talking."

"Is he the one you were thinking about flirting with when you asked me to teach you?"

I nodded. "Yeah. He's easy to talk to, but mostly we complain about our exes and how hard it is to move on. But after your last lesson, I tried to ask him out. He said he wasn't available to meet for lunch because of work."

"Which isn't unheard of," he said.

"I know, but it felt like he wasn't telling me the truth."

"What do you mean?"

I shrugged. "I don't know. I just felt like there was a reason he didn't want to meet."

"So you're not talking anymore?"

"We are. We didn't for a few days, but he reached out and said he wanted to meet. We agreed to talk for a few weeks, and we're going to meet after the wedding. I figured that was okay. Is that okay?"

"We will be done with lessons," Landon said with a smile I could tell was forced. "I will bow out gracefully."

"I'm not intending to hurt you."

"I know. And it's fine. You need to figure out what makes you happy. And if this guy is the one who makes you happy, I can't tell you not to meet him."

"Thanks. But I need more lessons. Since it was not so easy to get him to agree to meet, I know I'm going to need to do better when we actually get together."

"Flirting online can be tough. In person, you can use more than just words."

"True."

"I guess your next lesson needs to be flirting without saying a word." He wiggled his eyebrows.

I laughed. "You're being ridiculous."

"Maybe I just like to hear you laugh."

Damn, he was good. My entire body flashed with heat. "I can understand that."

"Good. What would you do to make me laugh?"

"Strip?"

He choked on his water. "That would definitely not make me laugh. I'd be speechless, not laughing."

"Men are simple creatures."

He nodded. "Yes, we are, but I'm not speechless every time I see a naked woman."

"I don't know what I would do to make you laugh."

"That's okay. Everyone is different. I suggested that since you said you want laughter in your next relationship. Relationships and flirting aren't just about sex or chemistry. They're about finding things that keep you together. Of course, you know that. Sorry."

"No, you're right. My ex and I didn't have enough things that kept us together. We had chemistry at first, but we got married because I ended up pregnant. We didn't go into it with that plan. We never had that plan. We decided to get married because of Mikayla, not because we couldn't imagine not being together. We were never like Natalie and Omar."

Landon nodded but didn't say anything.

"Is that... I didn't mean to get into my failed marriage. I'm sorry."

"Don't apologize for your past. I wasn't thinking about that. I was… I had the same thought about Omar and Natalie. Reegan and I were never like that either. By the end, we were comfortable. We spent time together. She'd show up at my place, and I'd go to hers. We had routines. But watching Natalie and Omar is showing me a completely different side of relationships that I've never experienced."

"Same."

"But I want to. One day. I want that."

I ached to agree. To say I was hoping for it, too. But I couldn't. The idea of opening myself up, to being that vulnerable with another person, and watching them walk out the door… It would break me for good.

"Anyway," Landon said when I didn't agree, "I'll give Adam a call and see if he can meet with you this week. I need to get back to work, but I'll let you know what he says." Landon stood and carried his tray to the trash. He dumped his trash and kept going, walking outside and leaving me to finish my lunch alone.

Not that I blamed him for being upset. But I couldn't change the way I felt. No matter how much I wished I could.

15

Landon texted me as I was waiting to pick Mikayla up to let me know Adam was willing to meet with me. He shared Adam's contact information, leaving it up to me to schedule the meeting.

I thanked him, but it didn't seem like enough. My stomach twisted. I didn't like being at odds with Landon. It made no sense, but knowing he was upset had me feeling like something was wrong.

Since I had a little time before Mikayla was supposed to be done, I called Adam to set up a meeting. He was more agreeable after learning I knew Landon, confirming we did know each other, and we agreed to meet two days later to talk about the wedding.

Mikayla got in a few seconds after I hung up with Adam. She was bustling with energy and excitement about the upcoming musical.

"It's so cool. I get to sing, and Amber is dancing. The show is going to be so much fun. You're going to go, right?"

"Of course. I wouldn't miss it." I pulled out of the lot and headed toward home.

"Do you think Dad is going to come?"

Fuck. Her soft question speared me. We both knew the answer to her question, but I couldn't shred her hope. I was sick of being the bad guy. Of shielding her from his shitty behavior. If he didn't want to show up for her, he needed to be the one who said it. "Why don't you call and ask him? Make sure he knows the dates. We can share the ticket information with him when we get it if he can make it."

"Yeah?"

"Yeah, sweetie. Of course. Call him now." I handed over my phone.

"The guy who was at our apartment yesterday? Was his name Landon?"

My heart lurched. "Yeah, why?"

"He sent you a text. Do you want me to read it?"

"No! I mean, I'll read it later and text him back."

"Who is he?"

"He's a friend. We're going to Natalie and Omar's wedding together."

"Oh. Okay." She tapped the screen and held the phone to her ear.

I tried not to panic while she called Kyle. I wanted to pull over and read the text from Landon, but I had to focus on Mikayla.

"He didn't answer," she breathed.

"Did you want to leave a message?"

"No. He won't come anyway. Why should I bother?"

Shit. It wasn't fair to her. Kyle had just as much to do with my getting pregnant as I did. We agreed we would always be there for our daughter. I expected him to hold up his end of things. "I'll reach out to him again and make sure he has the dates. Maybe he was busy and couldn't answer the phone."

She grumbled something that I took as agreement, then crossed her arms and sank in her seat. She was quiet until we got home, then grabbed her stuff and dragged her feet to the door.

Inside, Mikayla went to her room without a word. My heart ached for her. It wasn't fair to her that her father was a selfish prick who only cared about himself. I stared after my kid, then called her father with the intention of telling him exactly what I thought of him.

"Why do you keep calling me?" Kyle asked as he answered the phone. "I'm busy."

"Mikayla was calling you," I said. "She wanted to talk to her father."

"I have a lot going on. Can you just tell me what she wanted?"

"She's in the school musical. She wants you to come see her."

"I don't think I can."

"I didn't even tell you when it is," I hissed. I checked to make sure she hadn't come out of her room and moved to the kitchen so she wouldn't hear me.

"Fine, when is it?"

"It's next month. The weekend before Thanksgiving. Thursday, Friday, Saturday evenings, and Sunday afternoon."

"I'm not going to be able to make it."

"What the hell is wrong with you? She's your daughter. She wants you there. She wants a relationship with you. Why can't you give that to her?"

"What do you want from me, Case? I was never a good father. She likes you better."

"Maybe that's because you never tried. If you put in even a tiny bit of effort, it would be very different."

"I doubt it."

"What am I supposed to tell her?"

"Whatever you want."

"Kyle, don't be like this. Kyle!"

The phone was silent.

"Dammit," I snarled.

"He's not coming, is he?" Mikayla asked from behind me.

I spun and knew she'd heard most of my conversation with him. "Mik, I…"

"It's okay. I know he doesn't really care. I just thought…"

"I'm sorry, sweetie. I don't have anymore excuses for your dad. He should be here. He should be around for you. And it's about him that he's not. It's not you."

"Okay."

"I mean it, Mik. You have done nothing wrong. It's all on him."

"I just… I don't know."

"I know. What do you say we go out to eat tonight?"

"I thought you didn't like doing that." She eyed me suspiciously.

"I don't, but it's a special night. You're working hard on the musical, and you deserve a night to relax."

"What about homework?"

"How much do you have?"

"Not much."

"Let's go. Maybe we'll get some flowers before we come home, too. Something to brighten this place up."

"Lilies?"

I chuckled. "Sure."

"Can we go there first?"

"If you want."

"Yeah!"

"Let's go."

Mikayla was smiling as we walked out the door. Bribery wasn't my favorite thing, but desperate times and all that.

I wasn't sure what made me suggest flowers, but seeing her light up about them made my heart warm.

I parked in front of Blossom & Grow and followed

Mikayla to the front door of the shop. She went straight to the refrigerated case on the right.

"Welcome to Blossom & Grow. I'll be right up to help you," Landon called out from somewhere out of sight.

"Thank you!" Mikayla replied.

I chuckled and followed her to the case, seeing Landon's skills in every bunch of flowers. He didn't just cut them and stuff them in there, he made them all beautiful. He mixed colors and textures, creating pieces of art with each bundle.

"How can I help you ladies today?" Landon asked from behind us. "Casey? Hi. Um…" He trailed off and focused on Mikayla.

"This is my daughter, Mikayla. You didn't really meet yesterday. Mikayla, this is my friend, Landon."

"That you're going to the wedding with?" Mikayla asked.

I nodded. "He is."

I didn't miss the smile that crossed Landon's face knowing I'd told Mikayla about him, but he wiped it away before she saw it. "It's nice to meet you, Mikayla."

"You, too. My mom said we could get some flowers. Do you have any lilies? They're my favorite."

"I do. They are over here. Do you have a certain kind of lily you prefer?"

Mikayla followed Landon to the other side of the store, leaving me to trail behind them as they discussed all things lily. I didn't know Mikayla liked lilies, let alone knew anything about them, but she was having an entire conversation with Landon about lilies.

"Mom, can we get this one?" Mikayla asked.

Landon met my gaze, an appraising look in his eyes. "I'd love you to have this. My treat."

"I can't let you do that. This is your business, your livelihood."

"And I'd love to know you have something beautiful in

your home. You've been saying you wanted flowers for weeks and haven't taken anything home."

"I keep forgetting when I come in here," I admitted, my cheeks warming.

"Then please take these. They are my treat." He grabbed the bouquet and carried it to the front as if I'd agreed.

"I didn't agree to it."

"No, but you will."

"How do you know that?"

He nodded behind me, and I remembered my daughter was there, watching us.

"Is that your favorite?" I asked Mikayla.

She nodded, her eyes flickering from me to Landon.

"Okay. Thank you," I told Landon.

"You're welcome."

"You should come to dinner with us," Mikayla said while Landon and I were staring at each other.

"What?" I blurted.

"Sure," he said at the same time.

I looked over at him, my eyes wide. He shrugged.

"I'm about to close for the day. I was locking up out back when you came in. But I don't have to if you'd rather I didn't."

I had no option but to say yes. If I said no, I was a jerk. But I couldn't exactly enjoy flirting lessons with him when my kid was right there.

But I could enjoy his company, which I had been doing far too much lately.

"You should come with us," I finally said.

His grin was one of victory and gratitude. "Let me finish locking up and I'll be right back."

I nodded, watching him walk away.

"I like him, Mom."

"Me, too. He's very nice."

"Where are we going to eat?"

Shit. Paying for Mikayla and me was already a tight stretch of my budget. Adding Landon in was going to make things even harder, but there was no way I'd ask him to pay for his own dinner.

I ran through our usual places and struggled to think of somewhere we could afford.

"All right, ladies. Where are we headed?" Landon asked, joining us once more.

"We haven't decided yet," Mikayla said. "We don't go out to eat a lot. Where would you recommend?"

"My favorite place is Will Work For Burgers, but I can also be talked into Gino's without any work at all."

"I've never been to either," Mikayla said.

"No way," Landon gasped, glancing at me as he ushered us toward the front. "Burgers or Italian? My treat since I'm invading your night out."

"You already gave us flowers. I can't ask you to buy dinner, too."

"You're not asking, Casey. I'm happy to do it. I don't get to have dinner with two amazing women most nights."

"Just on some?" Mikayla asked with a smirk.

"Mikayla!"

Landon tipped his head back and laughed hard. "I like you. You've got fire. A bit like your mother."

Mikayla shook her head. "She's a mom. She doesn't have that."

"Oh, your mother has fire. Did she tell you the first time she came into Blossom & Grow she knocked over a display and almost took out another one?"

"How is that fire?"

Landon considered her question for a second, then shrugged. "I don't know, but it definitely had an impact."

Mikayla snorted. "Old people are weird."

"Mikayla! You don't tell people they're old."

"Why not? Adults are old."

I sighed heavily, but Landon chuckled.

"We are old compared to you. But there are still a few things we can teach you."

"Like what?"

I unlocked my SUV, pointing it out to Landon. He opened the front door for Mikayla, making a show of helping her in. She laughed, her cheeks turning red as she relished his attention.

Landon sat behind Mikayla, his gaze locked on the side of my face.

I started the vehicle and turned to look at him. "Where are we going?"

"That's up to you ladies. Burgers are quicker if there's something you need to get home for, but I'm up for either. I have no plans for the rest of the night."

"Italian?" Mikayla suggested.

"I thought you said you have homework."

Her face scrunched up. "I was hoping you forgot about that."

"We'll do Italian next time. Will Work For Burgers is good. They have all kinds. There's something like six different cheeses and a dozen toppings. They have stuffed burgers, standard burgers, double burgers, even a triple. How hungry are you, Mikayla?"

She giggled. "I'm pretty hungry."

"Uh oh. I might have underestimated how much the two of you can eat. We might have to go back for more money," Landon teased.

"Or you can do the dishes," Mikayla joked.

I chuckled, wondering when I had last heard Mikayla like that. She was a good kid, kind and quiet at times. She never joked around with Kyle like she was with Landon. She did with me sometimes, and it was my favorite thing ever. To hear her have the same comfort with Landon made me appreciate him that much more.

The two of them bantered back and forth as I drove. It didn't take long to get to Will Work For Burgers. The three of us walked in, and Landon asked for a table for three.

Mikayla wanted to sit next to Landon, so he ended up across from me at the table. The server took our drink orders, then left us to look over the menu. Every time I looked up, my gaze landed on him.

He looked way too handsome for a man who was supposed to be my friend and who wasn't looking for the same things I was. His eyes crinkled at the edges when he laughed at something Mikayla said. His lips were constantly curled up in a smile. His hands held his menu carefully, like it was something precious instead of a menu that would be handled by a dozen more people before the end of the day.

The server came back and took our food orders, then left the three of us alone.

"How is rehearsal going?" Landon asked Mikayla.

"It's so much fun."

"Good. I was in a few school productions growing up."

"You were?"

Landon nodded. "I was. I was the star of the chorus in my third grade musical, I was a monkey in fourth grade, and I was a tree in fifth grade."

Mikayla snorted a laugh. "You know all about showbiz then."

Landon kept his face neutral. "I do. It started to get to me. I was a terror going into sixth grade." He shook his head sadly. "Fame was a real problem for me, and my parents said I needed to take a step back and remember who I was."

"That was probably the right move. You can't let it go to your head."

"Definitely not. It makes you hard to be around if you get too cocky."

Mikayla laughed again. "I can see that happening for you."

"Mikayla!" I interjected.

She clapped a hand over her mouth. "Sorry."

Landon shook his head. "Nothing to apologize for. We're just joking around. I know that." He looked at me. "I think she has your sense of humor."

My cheeks heated. I nodded. "She does. But usually she doesn't let it out around other adults."

"I'm honored to be someone you feel comfortable around," Landon told Mikayla.

"I didn't mean to offend you."

"No offense at all. I promise. I have a tendency to relive my elementary school fame, and it's good to have someone around to remind me not to go overboard."

Mikayla giggled. "You need to watch that."

Landon smiled. "Definitely. Tell me more about you, Mikayla. What else are you into?"

Mikayla opened up to Landon in a way I'd never seen before. They went from one topic to another, talking about school and friends and even boys her friends had crushes on. She turned bright red when Landon asked if she had a boyfriend. She said she did not have a boyfriend, but there was a boy she liked.

I'd never gotten all that information out of her.

Our food came, and we dug in, declaring the burgers the best we'd ever had.

Landon stole a fry from Mikayla's plate, and she stole one of his in retaliation. He cut off a piece of his burger for her to try and offered a bite to me. He held out the burger to me, his gaze locked on mine while I leaned forward to take a bite.

His pupils dilated. His nostrils flared. He shifted in his seat.

What was this man doing to me? I hadn't been able to get him out of my mind all day, and when I had a chance, I spent the evening with him and my kid. Like we were a family.

Mikayla asked if we could go out for ice cream after our burgers, and we ended up in line with other families at The Creamery. Mikayla saw a friend from school and went to talk to them while Landon and I held our place in line.

"I'm buying ice cream," I told Landon.

"If you insist," he said. He was quiet for a minute while I stared at the sign listing all the options. "It was really nice to meet Mikayla."

"She's a good kid."

"She has a great mom."

I smiled at him. "Thanks. She had a rough afternoon."

"What happened?"

"My ex. She wanted him to come to see her in the musical, and he said he can't."

Landon's eyes went wide. "He told her he's not coming?"

I shrugged. "He told me. She called him, and he didn't answer. I called him back, and he said he's busy. Before I told him when the show is."

"What an ass."

"Yep."

"You both deserve better."

"Thanks."

He was quiet for a minute as we moved closer to the window to order. "I'm sorry I ran out of lunch today."

I forced a smile. "It's okay."

He shook his head. "It's not, though. I knew what this was when we started talking. It's not fair of me to change the rules now."

"What do you mean?"

He waited until I looked at him. The desire in his gaze was the same I'd seen from him more than once. It was a look that made me want more from him. That made me want to know what things could be like with him.

It scared the hell out of me.

"I like spending time with you. I want to do it more often. Not just lunches where I teach you how to flirt with other men, but dates where you flirt with me."

"Landon," I breathed.

"I know. You don't feel the same. I just—"

"I... do. I..."

"You do?"

I shrugged. "I—"

"Mom, Carrie's family said we could sit with them. She's in the musical with me. Is that cool?" Mikayla asked, interrupting the conversation I was afraid to have.

I forced a smile and nodded. "Of course. Do you know what ice cream you want?"

"Yeah."

"It's our turn. Go tell her." I glanced at Landon, catching the smile lingering on his lips.

He whispered, "We'll finish this conversation later."

And I know he felt me shiver against him.

I was in trouble with this man. So much trouble.

LANDON

I was going to embarrass myself when I stood up. Sitting next to Casey as she licked her ice cream cone was doing things to me that should not be happening when I was sitting at a table with two teenagers and other parents. But fuck me, Casey was making me want to be that ice cream cone.

She had no idea I wanted her as much as I did. But hearing she felt even a little bit of the same thing had me grinning like an idiot and unable to stop staring at her.

Mikayla and her friend were sitting at the end of the table and talking about their musical. Casey was holding down a conversation with the girl's mom. The dad was watching over his girls like if he looked away something bad would happen. He had a hand on his wife's knee, and a smile that said she was his entire world.

I wanted that. A woman I could touch in public and not think twice about what anyone else thought. I was pretty sure Casey would not handle it well if I put my hand on her thigh. Although she was going to have to be okay with it at the wedding.

Which meant I needed to find a way to control my reaction to her. Because sporting a hard-on for the entire wedding was not a good look.

"You own the flower shop, right?" the dad asked me as we were finishing up our ice cream. I couldn't remember his name.

"I do. Blossom & Grow."

"I was trying to place you. I always get her flowers from you." He nodded his head toward his wife.

"And they're beautiful," she said with a broad grin.

I smiled. "I'm happy to hear you enjoy them."

"The only thing I don't enjoy is that he usually brings me flowers when he screws up somehow. Can you fix that?" the wife asked.

I chuckled with them. "I don't think I have that ability, but clearly the flowers help you to forgive him."

She looked at her husband adoringly. "Yeah, they help."

"Mom, I have homework to finish," Carrie said, drawing the attention of the adults.

"So do I," Mikayla said.

"If everyone is done, we can go," Casey said, checking with the other mom.

"We're good," Carrie's mom said. "It was so good to see you guys."

The two moms shared a hug, and the dad shook my hand. "Nice to meet you."

"You, too," I told him. "Hopefully I won't see you too soon."

He laughed. "Doubtful."

"Maybe you'll see him because he's being nice," the mom said, sliding her arm around her husband's waist.

He looped his arm over her shoulders. "I think I need to do that. Surprise her."

"It would be a surprise."

I laughed and told the dad to call me. The three of them headed in the opposite direction to their car, and I followed Mikayla and Casey to Casey's. "That was fun."

"Yeah. You should come to dinner with us every night," Mikayla said.

Casey's laugh was strained. "Landon has his own life, honey. I don't think that's going to be an option."

"Maybe we can do something every week, though," I suggested, not caring that it might get me in trouble with Casey. I wanted to spend more time with her, and if that meant Mikayla hanging around us, I wasn't opposed to it.

"I'm not sure we can work that out. Between work and the musical, we're pretty busy," Casey said.

"But you have to eat. Maybe I can pick up a pizza and come over sometimes. It would be nice to see more of both of you."

Casey slid me a look that suggested I stop talking.

"Yeah, Mom, we should do that," Mikayla said.

Casey forced a smile for her daughter. "We'll see."

Mikayla's shoulders sank, which told me that meant *no* in Casey language.

"Get in, honey," Casey told her, standing next to the car.

I stayed with Casey, knowing I was about to get a lecture. She waited until Mikayla was in the car before she turned to me.

"I can't afford to take her out every week, and I can't ask you to pay for us all the time."

"We don't have to go out. I can cook for you. Or you can cook for me."

She chuckled.

"You said you wanted to spend more time with me. Did you change your mind, or are you worried about Mikayla?"

She drew a breath and glanced at the car. "Kyle is not a

great dad. He's not there for her. He hasn't really ever been. She can't handle another man walking away from her."

I moved closer to her. "What about you?"

"I'm fine," she said, stiffening her shoulders and standing up straighter, as if to prove to herself she could stand on her own two feet.

"I know you are. But you don't have to be so strong all the time. You could let me in. Lean on me a little."

She shook her head. "I can't. Not when I know you could disappear at any minute."

"I'm not going anywhere."

"I'm not a good bet, Landon. I know that. I'm a divorced single mom with money problems and nothing to offer you."

"You have everything I want right now, Casey. All I want is you."

She shook her head, the fading sunlight catching tears on her lashes. "I don't know how much of myself I can offer. Between work and my daughter... I have to be there for Mikayla. I'm all she has. That's why I'm not looking for a relationship. We want different things."

"We don't need to make any decisions right now. We agreed to get to know each other. We're going to the wedding together. Don't end this now, Casey."

"I'm not. I don't want to. But I can't have you around Mikayla."

"You were the one who came to my store today. Who introduced us."

"I know. And I shouldn't have."

"I'm glad you did."

She smiled up at me. "She really likes you."

"The feeling is mutual. She's a great kid. Funny and a little sassy and smart."

Casey laughed softly. "She was never like that with Kyle."

"Like what?"

"Sassy. He would snap if she was like that."

"That's not fair. A kid should be allowed to express themselves at home. Especially at home."

She nodded. "I think the same thing."

"So where do we go from here?"

"I don't know."

"I want to see you again. With or without Mikayla. Both would be my choice."

"You're not like anyone else I know."

"I hope that's a good thing."

She looked me in the eye and said, "So do I."

CASEY DROPPED me off at home, then waved as she drove away. Mikayla waved, too, and I wondered when I'd see her again. Casey had to do what was right for her daughter, but I hated that Mikayla was not a priority for her father. It wasn't fair to the kid.

I waited about thirty minutes, then sent Casey a text asking when we could get together to finish our conversation from earlier.

I work all day tomorrow.

What about the next day?

I have the meeting with Adam in the morning.

After that?

I need to start writing my article.

Come here to write.

To your shop?

Yeah. You can sit in the back where we met with Omar and Natalie. If it's too busy, you can go up to my apartment. We can have lunch together.

Okay.

I open at ten, but come earlier if you want. Park behind the shop so your car isn't on the street and let yourself in the back door.

Are you sure?

Yes.

Okay. I'll see you then.

Looking forward to it.

I smiled at my phone. Casey in my space. In my home and in my shop. It was a step. A big one from what I could tell about Casey.

I spent the rest of the evening cleaning up my apartment and making sure she wouldn't run screaming. My boots were all downstairs in the shop since they were dirty, but with my job, it was inevitable I would track dirt upstairs.

When I finally went to bed, I dreamed about Casey there with me and woke up with my hand around my dick. I groaned and hurried to the shower to alleviate the pressure, moaning her name as I came hard.

The woman was driving me crazy. It had been more than a year since I had sex, and until I met Casey, I didn't miss it. I was fine in my celibacy. But with her around, I was finding it difficult to keep her out of my bedroom, even if it was only in my head.

Knowing she'd be there in a day had me distracted and horny all day. I went through the motions, handling everything, but I was happy to see the day end and a new one begin. One that would give me more time with Casey.

I was up at eight and got ready for my day. I didn't know what time her meeting with Adam was, so I wanted to make sure I was ready no matter when she showed up. At nine, I was finishing my coffee in the shop when there was a knock on the backdoor followed by someone trying to open the door.

My pulse kicked up as I hurried to it, hopeful it was Casey.

"Sorry. It's early. I should have waited until later," she said when I opened the door.

"I told you to come."

"I know, but you said you open at ten."

I grabbed her arm and pulled her inside so I could close the door behind her. I crowded her against it and inhaled her scent.

She sucked in a breath. "Hi."

"Hi." I ducked my head, getting closer to her with every breath. Her lips turned up before my lips met hers.

Her bag hit the floor next to our feet, then her hands were in my hair.

Desire pumped through my blood, my cock hard in seconds. I pressed against her, letting her feel what she did to me, and cupped her ass, dragging her against my erection.

She whimpered against my lips, and I withdrew, only to have her chase my kiss.

I chuckled and sealed my lips over hers again, prying her mouth open with my tongue.

She scratched her nails over my scalp, and I groaned. "Casey."

"Don't stop," she begged.

I slid my hands to her thighs and lifted her off her feet,

slamming her back against the door and holding her in place with my body against her front.

"Holy shit," she breathed.

"Are you okay?"

"I don't even know. How can you hold me up?"

I grinned at her. "Beautiful, I carry around bags of dirt for a living. I'll carry you to my bed if you let me."

"You will?"

"When you're ready."

"I'm ready. Let's go."

I pulled back and looked closely at her. "Are you sure about that?"

"I wanted you the night of the bachelorette party. I wanted you when you took us for dinner and ice cream. I wanted you the day I was in here and knocked down your display. Trust me when I say I want you, Landon."

I kissed her hard, needing to feel the passion between us. I craved her, unlike anyone I'd ever known. I would stop if she said to, but it would hurt.

I made sure she was secure in my hold, then pushed away from the door and carried her to the stairs up to my apartment.

She pulled back from our kiss as I took the first step. "You don't have to carry me up."

"There's no more blood in my brain because of the way you looked at me when I said I'd carry you to my bed. Between how much I want you and the adrenaline coursing through me, I'm not stopping until you're unable to walk."

"Then hurry up because I might combust right here."

"Hold on, beautiful."

She gripped me tighter with her arms and legs, and I raced up the stairs with one hand on her ass and the other on the handrail. I opened my apartment door and stalked across the small space to my bedroom, kicking the doors closed on my way, just in case anyone showed up.

Casey didn't let go of me as I lowered her to the bed, dragging me down on top of her. I kissed her again, passion driving my every move.

"Don't go slow," she whispered.

"Couldn't if I wanted to, but you need to tell me you want this. You want me. I don't want you to regret this."

"I'll regret it if you're not inside me within two minutes."

I smirked and kissed her with slow, thick plunges of my tongue into her mouth and a rock of my hips against her center.

She whimpered and twisted to get me to hit where she wanted me.

"Two minutes isn't nearly long enough for me."

"Why not?"

"Because I want to feel you come at least twice before I slide your favorite dick inside you."

She snorted a laugh. "I'm never living that down!"

"Nope. But today you get an introduction."

She grinned, a look of pure pleasure on her face. "Let's get to it then."

I pushed up off her and stripped off my shirt. She sat up and ran her short nails over my chest. I reached for the button of my jeans, but she slapped my hands away and slipped the button free. She dragged the zipper down, the sound loud in the otherwise quiet room.

She pushed at my jeans and helped them slide to the floor. I kicked them away, then reached for her, grabbed the edge of her top and tugged it up and off before she had a chance to react. She squeaked and wrapped her arms around herself.

"None of that. I want to see you."

"Does it have to be so bright in here?"

"The better to see you with."

She chuckled. "Are you a wolf?"

I shook my head. "Just a man who knows what he likes. And you're gorgeous, Casey. Let me see all of you."

"There's a lot of me."

"Quit stalling and let me see you."

She sighed and moved her hands, letting me see her belly. "I have a lot of stretch marks."

"You had a baby. That's expected. You are stunning." I licked my lips, imagining what she would taste like.

"You make me feel like it."

I looked at her face, studying her closely. "I mean it, Case. This isn't empty flirting. This is me telling you I find you incredibly attractive, and I'm using all my energy to not scare you by pouncing on you."

"I'd rather you pounced."

"You would?"

She nodded. "If you can hold back…" She shrugged.

"Well, fuck, beautiful. If that's what you want…" I trailed off as I moved toward her, no longer playing or teasing or waiting. She was mine, and I was going to show her how badly I wanted her.

I kissed her hard, grabbing her breast in my hand and sliding my thumb over her nipple. I pinched the taut bud and twisted it just enough to make her gasp. I leaned her back on the bed and reached for her pants, removing them before I settled on top of her.

I pinned her to the mattress with my body, pinning her legs between mine and holding her hands tight in my fist. I licked and kissed her until she writhed beneath me, then I moved to the side and slid a hand down her stomach to the edge of her panties. I didn't hesitate before delving beneath, finding her slick flesh plump and ready for me.

"Fuck, Casey, you're so wet."

"It's been a while."

"For me, too," I admitted. "I haven't wanted anyone like I want you. Not ever."

"Not even—"

I cut her words off with a hard kiss and a bite of her lower lip. "We're not talking about exes in bed. You're mine right now, and I'm yours. There's no one else here with us when we're in bed. Agree?"

She bit her lip and nodded.

"Good. Now let me hear you come, Casey." I plunged a finger into her tight channel and pressed down hard on her clit.

She moaned and rocked her hips against my hand. "It's going to take me a minute."

"I'm not going anywhere. Tell me what you like. How do you make yourself come?"

"Usually on my clit."

I slid my finger out of her and dragged her slickness up to her clit, then pressed two fingers into her. "Do you want to come like this?"

"Yeah… yes."

"Can I take off the rest of your clothes?"

"Yes."

She helped me by pushing her panties down, then sitting up to unclasp her bra. My hand went back to her center, and I eased a third finger into her to make space for my cock in a minute.

"You feel good."

"You're so wet, Casey. I can't wait to feel you on my cock."

"I want that."

"Soon, beautiful. Come on my fingers first."

She moaned.

"Oh, you like that." I rubbed my calloused thumb over her clit again, and she moaned louder. "You really like that."

"Friction… is good. So good."

"Hell, yeah, it is." I rubbed her clit faster and pushed my fingers deeper into her until I felt her body respond and tighten around my fingers. "Come for me, Casey. No one's here. You can be as loud as you want."

"Oh, fuck, that's so fucking good." She bit her lip.

I kissed her, sucking her lip between my teeth. "Come, Casey."

She cried out her orgasm, her body dripping. I wanted to keep going, to hear her again, but I knew I'd lose it before I got inside her if I waited for another one.

I took her hand and set it on her body, then removed mine. "I need a condom. Don't stop."

She looked at me but didn't do anything.

I shoved my briefs down and stepped out of them, then grabbed a condom from the drawer next to my bed. I turned to look at her as I tore it open and found her watching me, her fingers not moving.

"I don't... I've never masturbated in front of someone before."

"Well fuck. We're going to have to get to that. How about you put this on me?" I offered her the condom.

She took it from my hand and sat up. She rolled it on quickly, squeezing my dick before she laid back down.

"Hard or slow?"

"Fuck me hard, Landon. Please."

I grabbed her ankles and tugged her to the edge of the bed. She squealed with the move, then moaned. I slid my hands up her legs to her center and exposed her clit to my gaze. "Fuck, you're beautiful."

She didn't say anything, so I lined up at her entrance.

"Are you ready?"

"Please."

I slammed into her, my balls hitting her body as I sank all

the way inside. I stilled, worried I was going to come before I could move.

She squeezed her channel around me, and I cursed.

I withdrew, then slammed back home.

"Landon. Yes." Her whispered words hit me square in the chest.

I grabbed her hand and held onto her as I pounded into her body, feeling like I was having an out-of-body experience.

"Holy shit," I breathed.

"Yes. More. Fuck."

I couldn't slow down or ease up or take a breath. I swore I was going to pass out. But if I stopped, things I couldn't start thinking would sink in. So I kept going, slamming my body against hers, changing the angle until she moaned, then pounding more, harder, faster like she asked.

Then she shouted, the words a blur as her core locked down on my dick and refused to let it go.

I followed her over the edge, trapped and owned and hopelessly lost to the woman who told me I had her favorite dick.

17

CASEY

What in the hell was that? Sex wasn't like that. It wasn't supposed to make me feel like I was going to cry. Sex was just…

Hell, I didn't know.

As soon as Mikayla got on the bus, I packed up my stuff. I wanted to go to Landon, but I felt crazy rushing over to see him. I hadn't been able to stop thinking about him, and I wanted sex. Bad. With him.

So I asked for it. But I never expected it to be like that.

It was one more thing that told me Reegan was crazy to have ever let him go.

"Wow," he breathed.

"Same," I said.

He chuckled. "I should let you up."

"You don't have to hurry."

He let me feel his weight again, then kissed me sweetly, no tongue, like we had all the time in the world. Then he got up.

He offered me a hand to help me to my feet, then pointed to the bathroom so I could go first.

I closed the door, feeling like it was crossing a line to leave it open, and quickly used the bathroom. I washed my hands and remembered that my clothes were not in the bathroom with me. Which left me to open the door in all my plus-size glory for him to see.

"Stop hiding from me," Landon said from the other side of the door.

I chuckled. "You're not supposed to be able to read my mind." I opened the door slowly.

He waited, arms crossed and brows raised, for me to step out. He hadn't bothered to get dressed yet, and I watched as his dick grew in size and pointed at me. "I'm really happy you came over early."

I chuckled and pushed past him to get my clothes. I wrinkled my nose, hating that my clothes smelled like sex.

"What's wrong?"

"I probably should have thought ahead to bring a change of clothes."

"Did I ruin them?"

"No, they just smell like sex."

"Want to borrow something? Or wash anything?"

"I..." How big of a line was I stepping over? "I should just run home and change."

"Here." He opened a drawer and tossed me a pair of sweatpants, then opened another drawer and handed me a tee. "Wear those for now. Stay up here until you have to go. I'll toss your stuff in the wash. It won't take long. Any special instructions?"

I shook my head. "No, but you don't have to do that."

"Well, I am the one who couldn't resist you."

"I came here hoping for that reaction."

A slow, sexy smirk lifted his lips.

"Oh, stop," I said with a laugh. "You know I want you."

"I do now. You're coming back here after your meeting, right?"

"I was thinking about it. You said I could work here. If you don't mind. Sometimes I struggle to focus when I'm home with all the other things I need to do."

"You are welcome here anytime you want to be here."

I rolled my eyes. "Because you want more sex."

He shook his head and moved close to me. "No, Casey, because I like having you in my home. I like knowing my sheets are going to smell like you. My sweats are going to be right up against your naked body. My couch is going to have you on it. I like seeing you in my space and, yeah, I like fucking you in my bed, but it's a lot more than that."

"Okay," I breathed, because what the hell else could I say to that?

I stepped into his sweatpants, surprised when they were big on me, then I tugged his shirt over my head, again noting how big it was. He got dressed in clean clothes, then took everything we were both wearing to the laundry room next to his kitchen and started the wash.

"You said you have to open at ten?"

He nodded. "I do, but Gail and Carson will be here…" He checked the clock. "Soon."

"I didn't realize that."

"All good. They have keys."

A door slammed downstairs, and we looked at each other.

"Stay up here and get some work done. I'll be back up in twenty minutes to put the clothes in the dryer."

"I can do that."

"Nope. You have work to do. You don't need to let my home distract you."

"What if I want to snoop?"

He chuckled. "Then by all means, get as distracted as

you'd like." He leaned over me and kissed me softly again. "I'll be back up here soon."

I smiled and watched him walk to the door. He winked before he closed it, then left me alone in his apartment.

The tears that lingered during sex raced back to my eyes, blurring my vision. What was wrong with me? I'd been having sex for more than half my life. I never got emotional about it. Not my first time, or when I found out I was pregnant, or even when Kyle and I got married and celebrated our wedding night.

But that wasn't just sex. Whatever just happened with Landon was magical. It was… the kind of thing they talked about at book club. Sex with someone who knew you and whom you knew. I thought I'd experienced that with Kyle. We were married for years. We knew each other. But sex with him was never more than an act.

I thought the women at book club were full of shit. I thought they were saying things to feel better about their marriages. But if that was what they were talking about…

I was in trouble. I was in so much trouble. That was the kind of sex I could get addicted to. Landon was the kind of man I could get addicted to.

"Nope. Not happening," I told myself, shaking off the thoughts and looking around for my bag.

Only to remember it was downstairs by the door where Landon kissed away all rational thought.

"Shit."

He was coming back up soon, and hopefully he noticed my bag and would bring it with him. Until then, I… could snoop.

I chuckled to myself and realized I had no desire to go through his things. I trusted him. He told me whatever I asked him, and I knew he wasn't lying to me.

I laid back on his couch and closed my eyes, letting the silence surround me and settle in. I wasn't used to quiet since Mikayla was born, and living in an apartment was louder with neighbors who shared walls. Listening to the silence gave me a kind of peace I didn't realize I was missing until I focused on it.

My entire body relaxed. My shoulders eased. Tension seeped from my body. Between the amazing orgasms and the quiet, I wasn't sure I'd ever want to leave his apartment.

Footsteps on the stairs outside the door had my eyes opening before the door did. Landon let himself in, my bag in his hand. "I just noticed this. Sorry. I didn't mean to interrupt you."

I smiled. "I was enjoying how quiet it is here."

He exhaled a laugh. "Usually the silence makes me crazy. I always have the TV or music on."

"It's so loud at my apartment that it's hard to focus sometimes. I would get so much work done if it was as quiet as it is here."

"Then come back. Work here whenever you want."

I was already shaking my head. "No. I couldn't do that. It's not fair to you."

"Says who? I'm downstairs. I won't bother you. No one will. I come up here for lunch most of the time, but no one else does. Except Andre once in a while, but less now that he's with Joelle."

"I don't know."

"Think about it. See how much you get done and see if you want to come back. You are always welcome."

"Thank you."

"I'm going to check the laundry, then get out of your way again."

I nodded, wanting to ask him to stay more than I should. I could not fall for this man.

He changed the laundry and said everything would be done in forty-five minutes, then kissed me and disappeared again.

I listened for his footsteps going down the stairs, then grabbed my laptop and got to work.

The next thing I knew, Landon was opening the door, and my article was fully outlined.

"How is it going?"

"I'm almost done," I admitted. "I've never written this much in such a short period of time."

"I think my place is magical."

"You're magical," I said without thinking.

He chuckled. "Good to know you think so."

My cheeks heated.

"What time is your meeting?"

I checked the time and stood. "I should get going."

"After you change," Landon said, looking down at his sweats.

"Ooh, yes. Thank you. I can wash these before I give them back to you."

He shook his head. "And miss out on having your scent on them? Nope. I'm good."

I chuckled, my cheeks burning.

"Are you coming back after for lunch?"

I nodded. "If that's okay."

"Absolutely." He crossed the room to me and pulled me against his body. "I like having you here."

He kissed me slowly, his fingers finding my bare skin and his tongue slicking over my lips. I licked his tongue, and he groaned, sucking my tongue into his mouth.

It wasn't long before I was panting and slick between my thighs.

He pulled back with a curse. "I am going to lose my mind with you. I know you need to go, but when you come back for lunch, I hope you can work really fast so I have time to make you come again."

"You're not afraid to say what you're thinking, are you?"

He smoothed my hair back from my face. "Not usually. Is that a problem? I want you to know where you stand with me. It was… It was the reason things ended with Reegan. We weren't on the same page. I know you're not looking for the same thing I am, but I'm not going to lie to you about what I want or make you think I've changed my mind about anything. I want you, Casey. I want to hear you come and feel you and taste you and enjoy your body. I want to make you laugh and dance at the wedding with you and have fun as long as you're feeling the same things."

"Okay."

He smiled, his eyes crinkling and lighting up. "Good. Then get changed and go before I convince you to cancel."

I chuckled, knowing it wouldn't take much for him to convince me, but I had to focus on the article. The series was good money, and having a regular column, even if it was temporary, was significant for me.

"Gail and Carson are downstairs, but they won't say anything about you being here if they see you. The backdoor is unlocked, so you can go out that way and get to your car, then come back in and come right up here if you want."

"Okay. Thanks."

"And if you want people to know you're here, come out front and kiss me like I belong to you."

I laughed, but he just winked before he let himself out of the apartment again.

I changed back into my professional clothes, leaving Landon's sweats on his bed. I chewed on my lip and debated going to the front, but I was running late and didn't want Adam to wait for me.

Ninety minutes later, after a more than pleasant conversation with Adam, and with the rest of my article forming in my mind, I walked through the back door and kept going to the front of Blossom & Grow.

Landon was behind the counter, cashing out a customer. He thanked the man for coming in, then noticed me and grinned. "How did the interview go?"

I walked over to him and nodded. "It was really good. And it never would have happened without your help. Thank you." I lifted onto my toes, reaching for his shoulders as I did to pull him into a kiss.

He turned toward me and met my kiss halfway, hands landing on my hips and holding me against him.

I pulled back just enough to meet his gaze and saw the delight I was feeling reflected back at me.

"Thank you," he whispered against my ear.

"The whole town will know soon."

He chuckled. "After lunch the other day, we got them started. Are you okay with that?"

I nodded and pulled back from him. "I'm going to head upstairs to work on my article. Do you want me to start something for lunch?"

"It's all taken care of," he said cryptically.

"Okay. I'll see you soon."

He winked at me, then turned his attention back to the customers.

I pressed my fingers to my lips as I walked up the stairs to his apartment. If we were going to make the wedding date believable, people had to know. They were definitely going to know now.

LANDON and I fell into a routine over the next week. After Mikayla got on the bus, I went to Landon's. We ran up to his apartment before his employees showed up, then I worked on my article until I had to go to another meeting or job.

On Sunday, I was finally feeling comfortable about going to book club. Four weeks in a row was new for me, but I found I really enjoyed my time with the ladies of MacKellar Cove. Melody said they weren't going to have book club the following weekend because of the wedding, and I knew I was going to miss the time with women I'd started to think of as friends.

Then I walked in. A cold sweat washed over me. Reegan was sitting next to Blake.

"Hi!" Reegan said to Melody and I, getting up to hug us both.

"Hi!" Melody and I replied, hugging Reegan.

I flashed Melody a *help me* look, and she took over.

"We don't usually see you here. How are you? What have you been up to?" Melody asked, taking the seat next to Reegan and monopolizing the conversation.

"Finley kept asking me to come, but I always felt a little weird socializing with my boss," Reegan said with a chuckle.

"Which I told her was silly," Finley said.

Reegan was the nanny for Finley's son through the summer since George was a year old. It was also how I knew Reegan. Finley and Trent invited all the kids over to hang out for the summer. Mikayla went with Amber a few times over the summer so I didn't have to pay for her to be in camp every week.

"You finally agreed with her?" Melody asked.

Reegan shook her head. "No, but since George is going to kindergarten next fall, Finley and Trent are planning to take most of the summer off to spend time with him, and then he's going to be in summer camp so he can be with friends."

"That makes sense," Melody said to Finley. "Amber never did summer camp every day, but she always loved when she went. It's good for them to have a structure."

Finley nodded. "That's what we've been thinking. But we feel bad ending our agreement with Reegan. George adores her."

"He's so good. The feeling is mutual," Reegan said. "And I'm not worried about the summer. I might travel or teach summer school or find another family who needs a nanny. I'm keeping my options open right now."

"We still feel bad. Trent said he'd find a job for you if you need something."

Reegan shook her head. "No. I'd never ask him to do that. I don't need a summer job. I liked working for you guys, and it was nice to stay busy."

"We are going to miss you," Finley said. "You'll have to come over and see us sometime."

"I will do that."

"As long as she's not off enjoying her life somewhere far from MacKellar Cove," Willow said. "You said traveling? Where would you go?"

I glanced at Willow and noticed her wink at me.

I looked around the room and noticed everyone was focused on Reegan. As the night continued, they all asked her more and more questions, keeping the focus on her.

Whenever there was a lull in the conversation, someone else jumped in with a new topic.

None of them asked about Landon and me, even though I was sure they'd all heard how much time I was spending there in the last two weeks. Melody asked me about it on the way over, but said she didn't want me to share anything until we were all together.

No one asked anything. Because they were protecting me. From Reegan?

Guilt twisted my gut as I listened to her talk about her life. Landon said things were definitely over, but why would he pick me over her? Why would he want to spend time with me when a woman like her was available?

I had to know the answer.

18

LANDON

I was watching TV and nursing a beer when there was a knock on the door downstairs. I paused, wondering if I was hearing things, but no. Someone was definitely knocking on the door.

I checked my phone but didn't have any messages. I had cameras around the property, and a quick check showed Casey outside my door.

"What the hell?" I asked myself as I raced down the stairs. I yanked open the door and almost took a punch to the face as she reached to pound on the door again.

"Why are you spending time with me?" she asked without saying hello.

"What?"

"Why are you spending time with me? Why would you pick me, even for a little while?"

"Where is this coming from?"

"Why are you avoiding the question?"

"I'm not avoiding the question. I'm confused by the question."

She was not going to let me avoid answering.

I didn't really have an answer. What option did I have but to admit that? "I don't think I have one specific reason. I am enjoying spending time together."

"But why? Why would you pick me when Reegan is still single?"

I took a step back, shocked at the confidence in her statement. The absolute conviction that there was no reason I would choose to spend time with her over Reegan.

"You said you two broke up because you wanted different things. So do we. What's different?"

"We already had this conversation. I told you I was blindsided by Reegan. She let me believe we were moving in the same direction, until she signed a new lease on her apartment and refused to move in with me. Why are you bringing this up?"

Casey paced back and forth outside the door, her feet dragging on the gravel. "She was at book club tonight. Normally, they aren't afraid to grill each other on every detail of their lives. They asked me all about us when you drove me home after the bachelorette party. Wanted to know what was going on with us. Then again when we kissed in public. But this week, they didn't say a word."

"Maybe they didn't have anything new to ask about."

"No. No, that wasn't it." She shook her head and kept pacing. "They were protecting me from her. Keeping each other from saying anything about us being together because she was there. Is she still in love with you?"

"No. Absolutely not," I said.

"Then why would they avoid talking about us?"

"I don't know, Casey, but what I do know is I don't care what anyone else thinks. I care about what you think. What's going on with you. I thought we were in agreement. We are spending time together. Enjoying each other. Having fun. And we'll worry about where it's leading another time."

"It's not leading anywhere. It can't. Not when you and Reegan—"

I shut her up with a hard press of my lips against hers. She fought me, trying to get away, but I didn't let her. I needed to feel her against me. Feel her lips on mine, the softening of her body against me, the clutch of her fingers in my hair.

When she sagged against me and whimpered into my mouth, I cupped her hips and lifted her. She wrapped her legs around my hips as I stalked through the shop to the consultation room. The table was the perfect height for her ass, for me to press against her warm heat.

She moaned against me and held on tight when I tried to step back.

I pressed into her once more, grinding my erection against her core.

She bit my lip, then slicked her tongue over it, tightening her legs around my hips.

If she wanted it like that, I'd happily give it to her. I shoved her back onto the table and crawled on top of her, knowing the table would support us.

She arched against me, grabbing at my clothes.

I pulled back and shoved my clothes off, staring at her as she struggled to do the same. We didn't speak, but when I rolled a condom on, she bit her lower lip.

I reached for her and tugged her back to the edge of the table. My lips crashed down on hers. We fought each other, teeth clashing and tongues battling. I teased her folds, making sure she was ready for me.

She was soaked, her body drawing me in with one stroke. I pressed three fingers into her. She tightened around me, moaning as I worked her entrance.

I withdrew my fingers and brought them to my mouth.

She trembled against me as I sucked her come off.

"Next time I get it from you."

"Fuck me, Landon."

I slammed into her before she finished the request.

She came instantly, crying out and squeezing my dick hard.

I stilled inside her, letting her adjust to me. As soon as her body let up on its grip, I eased out and pounded into her again.

The table shifted with our strokes. She wrapped her legs around my hips, keeping me tight to her body. I leaned over her, needing the leverage to drive her crazy. To drive us both crazy.

"Oh, fuck. Yes."

"This. You want to know why I'm spending time with you. It's this. It's knowing you feel this good on my dick when you come. It's knowing I can talk to you and you're right here with me. It's making you laugh and seeing your humor and feeling like I can do anything. It's you, Casey. It's all you. You're amazing."

"Landon!" she cried as she came hard, her core quivering around my dick and dragging me with her over the edge.

"Oh, fuck, Casey," I growled as I came harder than I ever have before. My legs turned to jelly, wanting to give out, but I locked my knees and managed to stay upright.

She held on to me, not letting me go until our bodies had cooled and I was in danger of slipping out of her. "I didn't come here for that," she whispered as she eased her thighs.

I bit my lip to tell her I wished she had instead of coming to accuse me of not wanting her enough. If she knew how much time she occupied in my mind, she'd run screaming.

"I should head home."

I brushed the hair back from her face and ignored her obvious desire to get the hell out of there. "I'm happy you came over. But I need you to hear something."

"Okay."

"I'm not with Reegan because I don't want to be with Reegan. We were together long enough that we both knew what it was like for us to be together. I wasn't willing to give up what I've always wanted, and neither was she. But we never had the conversations we needed to have. We were on different paths, and we both knew it, but neither of us knew how to end things. We are done. We are both happy we are done. It was the right thing for us. And whatever this is between us has nothing to do with her."

"Okay."

"I like you, Casey. I enjoy spending time with you. I've really enjoyed having sex. But before that, I enjoyed you. Not because of Reegan or in spite of her or anything to do with her. All because of you."

She nodded, her lips turning up at the edges. "Thank you."

I kissed her again, then finally stepped back. I caught my cock and removed the condom while Casey searched for her clothes. When we were both dressed, I walked her to the door. "I'm sorry I took you the way I did. I hope I didn't hurt you."

She chuckled. "It was pretty hot, actually. I think I'm going to be sore, but in such a good way."

I laughed and pulled her into my arms, unable to let her walk away without one more kiss. "Be careful going home."

"I will. Sorry I interrupted your night."

"You can interrupt it whenever you want. Am I going to see you tomorrow?"

"If that's okay."

"Always. I'm looking forward to it."

"Good night, Landon."

"Good night, Casey."

CASEY TEXTED me late the next morning to let me know her meeting at the paper went long and she wouldn't be able to come over before her afternoon job. I asked if she wanted to meet for lunch.

I was in trouble. I was having a hard time going longer than a day without seeing her.

She texted back that she could meet for a quick lunch, and we agreed to meet at Just Tacos since it was fast.

Casey wasn't there when I arrived, but I knew her order, so I went ahead and got food for both of us. Casey walked in right as our order was called and grabbed her cup to get a drink.

I carried the tray back to the table and was stopped by a customer who had been buying flowers from me for years. He asked how I was doing and said hello. I returned the greeting, not expecting it to be more than that, but he wasn't done.

"Is that your sister?" Eric asked.

I chuckled. "No, she's not my sister."

"What are you doing with her?"

"We're having lunch."

"Does Reegan know you're having lunch with another woman? Because I don't think she'd be too happy to see it."

"We're just friends," Casey said, overhearing Eric's inappropriate question.

Eric gave her a look, then met his wife outside on the curb.

"Why did you tell him that?"

Casey shook her head. "I don't want to get into an argument with someone about what we are."

"But you're okay getting into an argument with me about it?"

"We know what we are."

"Do we? What would you call what we are?"

"Dating?"

"You don't sound so convinced."

"I don't know. I just…"

"The wedding is this weekend, Casey. What do you think people are going to say when we show up together? When I spin you around the dance floor? When I kiss the hell out of you and sneak out early with you?"

Her cheeks turned redder with each of my questions. "I… I'm not used to this. My ex never put his hands on me in public. People barely knew we were married."

"Is that what you want me to be like?"

"No." She snorted. "No. I hated it. But it's what I'm used to."

"Okay, then let's come to an agreement right now. You're going to stop worrying about what we are, if I'm wishing you were Reegan, and what everyone else is thinking about us. Okay?"

"What is your side of the deal?"

"I'm going to think of new ways to make you come," I whispered.

Her cheeks flashed bright red. "Landon."

"What?"

"You can't say things like that to me."

"Why not?"

She squirmed in her seat.

"Does it turn you on?"

"Maybe."

"I think it does. And I think you're going to think about me later tonight. You're going to slide your hand into your panties and make yourself come. You're going to wish I was there with you to lick you until you scream, then stretch you out and come with you."

"Jesus," she exhaled.

"If it makes you feel better, I'm going to replay this

conversation later, too. I'm going to shoot all over my shower walls as I imagine you touching yourself."

"You will?"

"I do all the time."

"No, you don't."

I laughed mirthlessly. "Yeah, I do. Since before we started flirting lessons."

Her mouth fell open.

"I like a woman who can make me laugh."

She grinned, her cheeks turning pink again.

"I can't wait until the wedding. Until I have you all to myself for an entire night."

"What?"

"I thought you said Mikayla was spending the night at the MacKellars."

"She is, but I… I didn't know you wanted us to spend the night together."

"We don't have to if you have a better offer."

She shook her head. "No better offer."

"Good. Then will you be mine for the night?"

She nibbled her lip, her eyes dancing with excitement. "Yes."

I smiled, feeling like it was a victory. Casey in my bed all night long. Hell yes.

TWO DAYS UNTIL THE WEDDING. The flowers were on the truck arriving at the end of the day, and I was ready to get everything put together. It was going to be a long two days, but I was ready for it.

Natalie and Omar needed bouquets, boutonnieres, and centerpieces. As long as everything came in, I would go through the order tonight, and then on Friday, I had time to get all the centerpieces done. Saturday morning, I'd create the bouquets and boutonnieres, then deliver everything to them.

I kept watching for the truck, anxious to have my hands on all the flowers I needed. The sunflowers were coming from my own garden, but the navy roses and hydrangeas and the white impatiens and lobelias were on the shipment.

"Do you need us to stay, boss?" Carson asked when it was almost time for him and Gail to head out for the day.

I shook my head, hearing the truck pull in. "It sounds like they're here."

"We can keep the shop open if you want."

I checked the time. "There's only a few more minutes. You two can go ahead. By the time the truck gets in position, I'll close up."

"Have a good night," Gail said, heading for the door with Carson right behind her.

I waved to them, then checked the rest of the stock was good for the night and locked the door.

I went out back, finding the driver climbing out of the truck.

"Got an order for you."

"Thank you."

He handed me a clipboard with everything he was delivering, and I immediately spotted an issue. "There were supposed to be two dozen navy roses, and four dozen hydrangeas, impatiens, and lobelias. And a bunch of other stuff."

The driver shrugged. "I don't know what to tell you. I just deliver them, not grow them."

"But this isn't even half of what I ordered."

"It's what they gave me."

I scanned through the rest of the order and noticed other things that weren't listed. Some was for the wedding, and some was standard stock I tried to keep on hand. None of it was good.

"Do you want me to unload what I have?" the driver asked.

I nodded. "Yeah. I need all this and more, so I'll have to call them and see what's going on."

The driver nodded and started to unload everything he had.

I studied the shipment report and pulled up the order I sent in weeks ago. I noted where they didn't match up and had everything ready to call the distributor when the driver left.

Thirty minutes later, everything was unloaded and stored in my cases in the back. I didn't have time to sort through and distribute stuff, but I did have time to make a phone call.

Except they weren't answering.

Fucking hell.

I left a message and followed up with an email detailing where my shipment was short and showing the proof of what I paid for and what was actually delivered, according to their own information.

Then, I spent the rest of the evening going through my own stock to come up with a backup plan. Because if I was going to fuck up anything, it was not going to be the mayor's wedding.

19

_I_ bolted upright on Friday morning, in a panic about the flowers. I looked around my room. Nothing was out of place. It was still dark outside. It had to have been my mind that woke me up.

I eased out of bed and took a shower to clear the fuzziness from me. I needed coffee and breakfast and another set of eyes on everything I'd come up with. Gail and Carson were working Saturday while I was dealing with everything for the wedding, which meant I was alone for the day with no one to talk through the changes I made.

For a wedding.

Without the bride's permission.

It was a fucking disaster.

The most important wedding of my career, and I was messing it up.

But I had no choice. Calling Natalie the day before her wedding to tell her I had to make major changes and there was no way to do what we agreed would only make her panic. If I'd learned anything from Omar, it was that Natalie did not deal with changes well.

I was finishing breakfast when there was a knock on the back door. I checked the clock and realized Casey would be on the other side of the door.

I hurried downstairs and opened the door, needing her calmness to help me.

She bustled inside and shivered. "It's freezing out there."

"It is?"

"Yeah, it's been raining all morning, and it's cold. You didn't have the door open. Is everything okay?"

I drew a breath and reached for her, pulling her into my arms for a hug that I needed more than I cared to admit. "I had a rough night."

"What's wrong? Are you okay?"

I nodded. "The flowers for Natalie and Omar's wedding aren't right."

"What?" She backed up to look at me, as if she thought it was a joke.

"They didn't send everything I ordered. I reached out to them last night, but no one was available to speak to me. I spent hours going through my stock and pulling what I have that I can use, but I'm not sure it's going to be enough."

"Then let's see what you have and come up with something."

I closed my eyes and nodded. "Thank you."

"Have you told Natalie yet?"

I winced and shook my head. "I wanted to have some ideas before I did. I was trying to decide if I should call her or Omar or someone else to help her not freak out."

"She needs to know, but yeah, it'll probably be easier if Omar is here with her. She told me he keeps her calm."

"Let me show you what I have, and then I'll call her."

"Do you want me to stay here with you when they come?"

I smiled at her and pulled her in for another hug. "Do you have to work today?"

She shook her head. "I'm off all day. I'm going to the rehearsal tonight, then spending the day with Natalie tomorrow while she's getting ready."

"And you're willing to give up your day off to help me?"

She smiled, with something in her gaze I hadn't noticed before. She slid her hand across my cheek. "Of course."

"Thank you." I leaned down and kissed her for the first time since she arrived. I poured all of me into the kiss, needing her to feel my gratitude in ways I couldn't express any other way. I wanted her, but more than that, I wanted her to know she meant more to me than a quick fuck or a fake date.

Which was also why I pulled back.

"If you're going to kiss me like that, maybe I'll spend all my free days with you," she teased.

"Works for me," I joked back, holding in all the things I really wanted to tell her.

"Show me what you have. Maybe we can come up with a few options and then call Natalie and Omar."

I nodded and led her to the consultation room.

We spent the next hour going over everything I had started to pull together the night before. I showed her what I'd intended from our original meeting a few weeks ago using the flowers that did arrive, then the things I was considering based on what I had.

Casey made some suggestions that I thought were excellent, and by the time I opened the store, we had a few really good choices and some options that blended everything together and would keep most guests from figuring out there was anything different.

"Do you want me to call her?" Casey offered.

I shook my head. "It's my responsibility. I'll do it. I think I'm going to call Omar first, though. See what he says. He might want to pick her up and bring her here."

"That's a good idea."

I tapped Omar's name and waited for him to answer. When he did, I could hear the smile in his voice and knew I'd be destroying it.

"Morning, Landon. How are you?"

"Um, not great, actually. There was an issue with the flowers, and I've had to make some changes."

"What issue?" Omar asked, all serious.

"Half of them didn't arrive like they were supposed to. I have enough flowers with what I have in stock, but it's going to change the overall look of everything. I want you and Natalie to approve the changes before tomorrow. I know you're both busy."

"We're actually off today, so we aren't that busy. We were going to pack for our honeymoon and relax for the day. We can be to you in fifteen minutes, if that's okay."

"Yeah, absolutely. I'll see you both then. Thanks, Omar. And I'm really sorry about this."

"Not on you. I'm sure whatever you came up with is excellent."

"I hope so. See you soon." I hung up and met Casey's curious gaze. "They'll be here in fifteen minutes."

"That's good. Then they can look at everything, and you will know how to proceed."

I drew a breath. "I couldn't have done this without you."

"Apparently, we make a good team."

"Yes, we do."

The door opened up front, pulling me away from her. She stayed in the room while I went out to help the customer.

"Morning," Justin said. He came in every other week to get flowers for his wife's grave. After thirty-two years of marriage, he lost her to cancer, but he still visited her every day and took her flowers all the time.

"How are you, Justin?"

"I'm good. Not such a great day."

I wrinkled my nose. "No, it's not. You need something that'll hold up in the weather?"

"Yeah, if you've got something like that, I'd appreciate it."

"Sure. Let's take a look. I had to pull a few things out thanks to a mixup with the delivery and the mayor's wedding, but I should have options. You go for pinks, reds, and green, right?"

"If you've got them. It can be tough this time of year to find those bright colors."

"I think we can find a few things." I went to the case and pulled out a few options for Justin. Pink zinnias and poppies, red carnations and lilies, and green ferns all matched the colors Justin liked to bring to his wife. I grabbed the bins with each of them and set them out so he could choose a few.

"Those pink ones are beautiful. Nancy would have loved those." He pointed to the poppies.

"They're great flowers. Do you want a bunch of those or to mix a few things in?"

"I like these red ones, but I'm not sure how they look together." He caressed the lily petals.

"Let's try this," I said, taking a few of the poppies, adding two lilies, then separating them with ferns. I went back to the case and grabbed some tiny white roses to break up the colors even more and showed him the bouquet.

He reached for it, his gaze locked on the flowers. "Every time I come in here, I watch you do that, and I still have no idea how you pull it all together. That's beautiful. Nancy would be so proud to have these with her."

I smiled at the man and carried the bouquet to the counter so I could wrap it up well. "I love what I do," I told Justin as I worked. "Flowers don't get mad at you. They just want someone to love them."

"Kind of like people, huh?" Justin said.

I chuckled. "Very true."

The front door opened, and Omar and Natalie rushed inside.

"What happened?" Natalie asked.

"Casey is in the back. You can go right back and talk to her. I'll be there in a minute."

Natalie didn't let me finish before she headed to the back. Omar paused and gave me a grateful smile. "Sorry."

I shook my head. "I get it. But I think we have some good options."

"Thanks, Landon."

I nodded and let him follow Natalie to the back.

"Here to find some new stuff?" Justin asked, handing over his credit card.

"Yeah. I had to let them know everything I ordered didn't come in."

"You seem pretty relaxed about it."

I snorted. "I wasn't a few hours ago."

"But something changed. I'm guessing it's that Casey you said is back there."

My body warmed at his suggestion.

"You've been different the last few weeks. I thought you were finally getting over your ex, but it sounds like maybe you've been getting under this Casey woman."

"Justin," I breathed, laughing at his crude comment.

"Oh, I'm an old man who has kids and grandkids. I know how things work. And I know you're happier with this woman than you were with the last one. More days than not, I'd come in and you were scowling. The last few weeks, you've been all smiles. She's good for you, Landon. It's nice to see it."

"Thanks, Justin."

"Hold on to her."

I sighed. "I'm going to try."

"Good. Enjoy this rainy day. I'm going to see the one who always makes me smile."

I grinned. "Let me know how these flowers work out."

"You know I will. See you in a few weeks."

I waved as Justin shuffled to the door, then went to face the bride.

Natalie and Omar were sitting with Casey when I walked in, all three of them smiling.

"This looks better than I expected," I said.

Natalie jumped up and hugged me. "Thank you. Casey said you worked on this last night and this morning. I wouldn't have noticed the changes if you hadn't called us."

"I didn't want to spring it on you the day of your wedding. I hated to do that today, but I didn't think it was fair."

"Omar said you placed the order, and they didn't deliver what you asked for. It's not on you."

"Yeah, but it is. They've done this before, though not this bad, so I knew it was a possibility. Usually I get notice in advance."

"Places can just not send what you ordered?" Omar asked.

I shrugged. "If the flowers don't exist, they can't create them. There are greenhouses that stock most retail stores, but sometimes plants don't work out the way we hope. It's why I've been working to expand my greenhouse. The more I can grow here, the less I need to order in."

"And you have enough business for that?" Omar asked.

I chuckled. "I'm getting there. My two employees are exceptional, and they've drummed up some new business for me with local places that want to have potted plants in their offices. Between the walk-ins, the regulars, and the businesses, I'm going to sell out everything in the greenhouse this year. We'd go bigger if I had more space."

"Wow. Good for you. That's amazing. And if you need anything from me, please let me know."

I chuckled. "Your wedding is enough. I'm getting more business from others getting married in the area who thought they had to go farther away for their wedding flowers. It's good to have the mayor, and the local paper, spotlighting my business."

"You deserve to be highlighted," Casey said.

"Thank you."

"When did you two get together?" Natalie asked.

"And that's our cue to go. See you both tomorrow. Casey, see you later tonight. Thanks again to both of you," Omar said, dragging Natalie to the door.

Casey and I followed them out, laughing at Natalie arguing and Omar not letting her go before they were outside. He stopped and kissed her in the rain until she stopped fighting him, then they disappeared from view.

Casey laughed. "They loved what you came up with."

"It sounds like they loved what you came up with."

She shrugged. "We make a good team."

"Yes, we do. Thank you for your help. I was panicking today, and when you showed up, I knew it would all work out."

"Now, we need to put everything together so it's ready for tomorrow."

"Thank you. So much."

"You're welcome. But now you have one more thing you need to teach me."

My body flashed hot, and my dick hardened. "You're a tease."

She chuckled and looked back at me over her shoulder. "Who said I'm teasing?"

I groaned and followed her, wishing I was laying her out on the table instead of the flowers.

WITH CASEY'S HELP, I finished all of the centerpieces on Friday before she left to get ready for the rehearsal. I hated that I wouldn't see her again until the wedding, but I loved that I was going to have her all to myself for the night.

Saturday morning, I loaded up the truck with everything for the wedding and headed to Mountain View Retreat. Natalie's summer camp was open for weddings and other town events throughout the year. The location was what brought Natalie and Omar together when it was donated and she took it over to use for the camp.

Natalie used Blossom & Grow plants outside the camp and around the office, and seeing the place lit up and decorated for the reception was a full circle moment.

There were people working in the gathering hall, getting things put together for later. I found who appeared to be in charge and asked if I could set out centerpieces. She volunteered to help, and we had the truck unloaded and everything done in record time.

My next stop was Daisy's house, where all the women were getting ready.

"Did you go to the Retreat?" Natalie asked.

I nodded. "I did. And everything looks amazing. The flowers are all set up, and it looks like they're ready for the day."

"Good. Thank you. I can't believe this is all happening," Natalie whispered, almost to herself. "I never thought I'd get married, and now I'm marrying the freaking mayor."

"You're not marrying the mayor," Casey said, moving in front of Natalie and taking her hands. "You're marrying the man who loves you. The man you can't wait to spend the rest of your life with. The man who likes you and all your crazy."

Natalie laughed. "I can't believe you remember that. I was so drunk."

"You were, but you were also happy. You asked me what makes a good marriage. What to avoid. Why mine didn't last. Do you remember what I said?"

"Avoid bad dicks," Natalie said.

I snorted a laugh.

Casey slid me a look. "Yes. And make each other laugh. Find out what the other needs and be the one who gives it to them. Open yourselves up to each other. A marriage isn't about today, or about who you each are in this moment. It's about the rest of your lives. It's about finding someone who is always there for you, who knows what you need before you do. A marriage is more than one day. It's a lifetime of shared secrets and stolen moments and finding joy when life is crazy and you're not sure where the joy is coming from. Find joy in each other."

Natalie nodded, rolling her lips in. "Thank you, Casey." Natalie hugged Casey hard.

Daisy sniffed, dabbing under her eyes. "Your ex is an idiot."

Casey laughed. "No, he's not. We weren't right for each other. We got married for the wrong reasons for us."

"Maybe next time you'll get married for the right reasons," Natalie said.

"Maybe I will," Casey said, her gaze straying to me.

My lips turned up without conscious thought. She wasn't saying no. She wasn't rejecting the idea. And she was looking at me.

The woman I loved was thinking about marriage, talking about forever, and looking at me.

Maybe teaching her how to flirt was the second best thing I ever could have done.

Right after falling in love with her.

20

I went home after dropping off the flowers to Omar and reassuring him that Natalie was as excited about getting married as he was. He looked like the happiest man on earth. He sure was the luckiest. The woman he loved felt the same way and was going to be his in a few hours.

Damn, I wanted that.

Gail and Carson were handling the store, so I went right upstairs to get ready. I had my suit already picked out and laid out on the bed. I scrubbed a hand over my stubbled jaw and decided to shave before I took a shower.

With my face clean and smooth, I jumped in the shower and hurried through the rest of my routine. I checked my reflection before I headed downstairs, hoping the charcoal suit was good enough for the wedding.

A whistle pierced the air when I stopped at the bottom of the stairs. I looked up and saw Carson waving at me.

"Looking good, boss. I've never seen you in a suit."

I laughed. "Usually I'm covered in dirt."

"Same," Carson said. "Yo! Come see the boss all cleaned up."

Gail appeared a second later and whistled low. "You're looking nice, boss." She looked at Carson. "Can I say that without it being weird?"

"You tell me when I look nice for a date," Carson said.

"True. I didn't mean any offense, boss," Gail said.

"None taken. By either of you. I appreciate it. I'm a little nervous about tonight." I don't know why I admitted that to them.

"It's all good. Casey is hot, and she's totally into you," Carson said.

"What he said," Gail agreed.

"You two haven't seen us together."

"She's been hanging out here for weeks, boss. Women don't do that unless they really like you," Gail explained.

"And it's MacKellar Cove. Everyone knows everyone here. We know who she is," Carson said.

I drew a breath. "Do you think she's going to like the suit?"

Gail moved closer and swatted at my hand as I tugged on the tie. "If you stop messing with it she will. Or better yet, mess it up on the ride and ask her to fix it for you."

I snorted, but she wasn't joking.

"It's like zipping up her dress. It's hot to show you're a little vulnerable and willing to open up to her about it. Women like that."

"Yeah?"

Gail nodded. "Absolutely. Have fun tonight, boss. We figure the store will be pretty quiet, but we'll be here until close and make sure everything is good before we leave."

"Thanks. I really appreciate you two working here."

"And we appreciate the jobs. Seriously."

I nodded, then headed out the back door.

Casey and I didn't talk about arriving together for the wedding since she was going to be with Natalie all day, but I wanted to make sure she had a ride.

> Leaving for the wedding now. Where's your car?

> I'm actually home right now. When they started pictures, I headed out.

> Can I come pick you up? Then you don't have to worry about driving?

> That would be great.

> I'll see you in five minutes. I can wait if you aren't ready.

> I'll be ready.

> See you soon.

I tucked my phone away and pulled out of the lot behind the shop. My hands were shaking. I was so damn nervous.

A spot was open right in front of her building. I parked and started to get out when the front door opened.

Casey walked out in a dark red dress that hung to her ankles. The sleeves were short with a square neckline that showcased the upper swell of her breasts. The dress was tight below her breasts and flowed to below her hips where the fabric gathered and gave it dimension, then another gathering around her knees.

The dress left me speechless. It hinted at a flirty side but was modest enough for a wedding. The color was stunning on her, especially with the delicate silver jewelry and strappy heels she wore with it.

"You don't like it?" she asked when I didn't move.

I shook my head, snapping out of my trance and moving

around to where she stood on the sidewalk. I hooked my arm around her back and yanked her tight to me, then paused with my lips an inch from hers. "Can I kiss you?"

"Why would you think you have to ask?"

"Makeup. I don't want to mess it up and have you annoyed with me."

"Makeup can be fixed."

I didn't wait for her to say more. I sealed my lips over hers and showed her just how much I liked her dress. I spread my hand wide on her back, enjoying the exposed skin on her upper back with a matching cut to the front. I was going to have my hands on her all night.

"Does that mean you do like the dress?"

"I fucking love this dress."

She grinned against my lips. "I feel the same about this suit."

I took a step back. "Yeah? It's okay?"

"Oh, yeah."

"What about the tie? I'm not used to them and keep tugging on it."

Casey stepped closer to me and pulled the knot, straightening the tie I'd yanked off center. She smoothed her hand down my tie and held on to the end. "You look really nice."

"Thank you. Are you ready? Wait, I thought you were going to bring a bag to stay with me."

"I wasn't sure you still wanted that," she said, avoiding my gaze.

I tilted her chin up with one finger. "Yes, I do. I'm not going to force you, but I would really enjoy having you in my bed all night long tonight."

"Okay. Let me go grab it."

"Do you want me to come with you?"

She snickered. "We'll never make it to the wedding. I'll be right back."

"I'm going to take that to mean you're not going to be able to keep your hands off me all night."

She grinned as she opened the door, her gaze traveling down my body.

It was going to be a good night.

CASEY and I sat toward the back of the crowd for the wedding. She held my hand and dabbed her eyes and laughed when Natalie almost ran up the aisle as soon as she saw Omar.

The wedding was beautiful, and the two of them were so happy it was hard not to get emotional. I wanted the same thing for myself. I wanted to build a future with Casey.

After the wedding, everyone headed over to Mountain View Retreat while the wedding party took pictures. Casey held my hand as we walked inside and squeezed hard when she saw all the tables.

"Wow. This is amazing," she gushed. "You're incredibly talented."

"Thank you. I couldn't have done it all if it weren't for you."

She smiled up at me and slid her arms around my neck. "I'm not so sure about that. I've seen the way you pull things together. You have an incredible eye for what you do."

"I really love it."

She grinned, holding my gaze.

The desire to tell her how I felt was strong. It was going to happen if I wasn't careful, so I broke our link and asked if she wanted to find our table.

"Yeah, let's see who we're with. Hopefully people we like."

We were at a table with Andre and Joelle and two couples we didn't know. One woman said she was Omar's assistant at town hall, and the other said she didn't work for Omar but was a coworker at town hall. Not long after we introduced ourselves, Natalie and Omar were being announced.

They went right into the first dance as husband and wife. I caught Casey staring wistfully in their direction.

"Are you okay?"

She nodded. "I missed a lot of traditions when I got married. We went to the courthouse and skipped the reception and honeymoon part of things."

"Like you told Natalie yesterday, the wedding is just one day. It's the marriage that matters."

Casey snorted. "And we both know how that turned out. Maybe I should have told her to make the most of her wedding because the marriage might suck."

"I don't think that's going to be a problem for those two."

Omar dipped Natalie low as the final notes of the song played and kissed her until Natalie's cheeks were red and the entire crowd was cheering.

"No, I don't think so either," Casey said with a sigh.

"Do you want a drink?" I asked her.

"Sure. Wine or something."

I nodded and asked Andre if he wanted to go with me to get drinks.

"You two are pretty close. I didn't realize it was serious," Andre said when we were a little away from the table.

"I don't think she's there yet."

"But you are?"

I nodded. "Yeah. And I'm not sure how it's going to end up. She keeps telling me she doesn't want to get married again or have more kids or want anything beyond just sex."

"You're sleeping with her?" Andre blurted.

"Tell the whole place, would you?"

"Sorry. I didn't know. Sorry."

"It's fine. I never felt like this with… anyone else. It's like we understand each other on a different level."

Andre nodded. "I get that."

"I just have to convince her I'm serious about us."

"Does she know you're her match yet?"

I shook my head. "No, but she hasn't been talking to that me much lately."

"What do you think that means?"

"I'm hoping it means she's content with me in person and isn't looking for another guy online."

He tapped his beer bottle against mine. "Here's hoping."

WE ATE A DELICIOUS DINNER, then the DJ started playing music for everyone to dance. It took a little persuading to get Casey onto the dance floor, but once she was there, she stayed. She danced with the women, and she danced with me.

It was hours into the reception, and things were quieting down when a slower song came on. Casey draped her arms around my neck and leaned against me.

"Hi," she whispered.

"Hi. Are you having fun?"

She nodded. "I am. I didn't think I'd enjoy it this much, but Natalie and Omar have definitely made tonight fun for everyone."

"They have."

"I think they're getting ready to escape."

"Yeah?"

Casey nodded to where Natalie and Omar were gathering their things.

"They are. That's sneaky."

"It's smart. It'll take them an hour to get out of here if they don't just leave."

"They have important things to get to."

She raised her eyebrows at me. "Important things?"

"The rest of their lives."

"You're a romantic, aren't you?"

I nodded and slid my hand over her neck. "I am. I create bouquets and provide flowers for weddings and am surrounded by it all the time. I love what I do, but I'm definitely a romantic."

"I find that very sexy."

"Oh, you do?"

"Yes, I do."

"As sexy as this suit?" I asked, kissing my way across her jaw.

She hummed. "That's a tough choice. Can they tie?"

"Of course. As long as you're still talking about me."

She laughed and tilted her head to the side. "I'm definitely talking about you. And I'm about ready to follow Natalie and Omar out the door."

"I'm ready when you are."

"There are a few things you said we have to do tonight."

"So many things I can't wait to do to you."

"I think it's time for us to go."

"I'm right behind you."

She laughed and led me to our table. She picked up her purse, then led the way to my truck.

I held her hand on the drive back to my place. She grabbed her bag from the back when I parked, and we made our way inside.

"This dress has been driving me crazy all night," I told her as I followed her up the stairs to my apartment.

"I could tell. You haven't stopped touching me. It's had me wet all day."

I groaned. "I think I need proof of that."

"Maybe you should let us inside first."

I pressed myself against her back, reaching around her to unlock the door. We stumbled inside, grabbing each other as I kicked the door closed and hauled her against me.

She dropped her bag on the floor and pulled me to the bedroom with my tie wrapped around her hand. In the room, she let go of me and stepped back.

"I think we need to go to more weddings. I really like you in that suit."

"So you said. I can't disagree, though. That dress is killing me."

"Wait until you see what's under it."

I moved toward her, needing her with a desperation I hadn't felt before.

She turned her back to me and glanced over her shoulder at me. "Will you unzip me?"

I kissed her neck and grasped the pull. Slowly, I unzipped her dress, exposing her back to my hungry gaze. Black lace stretched across her back, and matching black lace hugged her ass. I bent and kissed her bare skin, licking my way up her spine.

"You make me feel so beautiful."

"Because you are."

She chuckled. "Thank you." She turned and let the dress fall to the floor in a pool of fabric, leaving her in only her black lace bra and panties.

"Jesus," I hissed. "You're fucking gorgeous."

"And as much as I love this suit, I'd rather see it on the floor."

I snorted. I reached for the tie, but she swatted my hands away again.

She looked up at me from beneath dark lashes, holding my gaze while she pulled my tie loose. She let the fabric flutter to the floor, then worked my buttons free one-by-one. She pushed the shirt off my shoulders and brought her hands to my pants.

I swallowed all the things I wanted to say to her and let her finish undressing me. I stood before her completely naked, my cock pointing at her and demanding she wear the same thing.

She moved to the bed and sat on the edge, reaching back to unhook her bra. Her breasts spilled free, resting on her plump belly.

I dropped to my knees in front of her and brought one nipple to my mouth, teasing the peak with my teeth and licking my way around her areola. She moaned and held my head in place, pressing herself into my mouth when I switched sides.

I released her nipples and kissed my way down her belly, watching her as she watched me. When I stopped at her panties, she laid back on the bed. Her hips rose as I tugged the delicate lace from her body.

She trembled under my appraisal, her core leaking.

"You're so fucking beautiful," I whispered, kissing her thigh. "I am so lucky you're here with me."

She exhaled a laugh. "I think I'm the lucky one."

"No talking down about yourself. Not with me around. You are beautiful, Casey. You make me…" I swallowed hard. "You turn me on so much."

She hesitated, her gaze meeting mine. She nibbled her lip. "Me, too."

I kissed her thigh again, then worked my way over to her center. I looked up at her, locking my eyes on hers as I brought my lips to her core.

"Oh, yes," she whispered, her eyes closing.

"Look at me, Casey. I want you to see how much I enjoy your body."

She opened her eyes and looked at me.

I licked her core, groaning at the taste of her on my tongue. "So fucking good."

"Holy fuck," she breathed.

I pressed two fingers into her, finding her soaked and swollen. I added a third finger and gave her clit a kiss.

"Landon," she moaned, her hips rocking against my face.

I released her and licked over her clit, pumping my fingers quickly into her. I stared at her face, her gaze on mine, as I devoured her. A sweep, then a kiss. I sucked hard, then eased my tongue to caress her clit.

She moved with me, responding to everything I did to her. Her muscles clenched and her eyes slid closed, and I let her fall over the edge with her clit sucked hard in my mouth and my fingers slamming deep into her.

"Oh, fuck. Landon. Yes. Landon. Oh, yes!" She screamed and cried and grabbed my head as she came, ramming my face against her body.

I fucking loved it. Watching her lose her shit, seeing her come hard, with my name on her tongue and her clit on mine, was everything to me. She was everything.

And with my face buried between her legs, I said the words I ached to say, knowing she couldn't hear them and run.

21

CASEY

My orgasm rolled through me, carrying me to a place I had never been. A place with a man who made me want the things I'd given up on a long time ago. A place where a future wasn't so scary because we were doing it together.

I let all my hopes and dreams out in my scream as I came hard against Landon's lips. Tears welled up in my eyes and spilled down my cheeks. How did a man I'd only known a few weeks make me feel like he held the key to everything I'd wanted my entire life?

Landon's tongue eased, licking me clean before he withdrew from between my legs. He kissed my inner thighs, then worked his way up my body.

I wiped my eyes, hoping to hide my reaction from him, but the man didn't miss anything.

"What did I do?" he breathed, his entire body hovering over mine.

I shook my head. "Nothing. You didn't do anything. I promise."

"You're crying. Something happened. What's wrong, Casey? Please talk to me."

"I just… It was good. So good it brought tears to my eyes. You're amazing, and you make me feel like anything is possible."

"Anything is possible." He lowered onto me just enough for me to feel his skin not his weight. He kissed me gently, his lips brushing mine for a few seconds before he pulled back. "Are you sure that's all it was?"

I nodded, keeping the things I wished I could tell him inside. Maybe one day I'd tell him I loved him. Maybe one day I would feel safe saying those words. But not yet.

"Do you want to stop?"

"No," I blurted.

He exhaled a laugh. "Well, okay. I guess I don't have to beg because you are."

I chuckled. "I will if I need to. I want to feel you inside me, Landon." I wrapped my arms around his neck and tugged him onto me. "I want to feel your weight on me."

He let himself sink onto me and kissed me. His tongue teased my lips and snuck inside for a second before he retreated. He kissed his way to my ear and whispered, "I loved feeling you come on my tongue."

"It was…" I swallowed roughly, my emotions fighting to the surface again. "You're amazing."

"We're pretty amazing together." He bit my earlobe, tugging with his teeth, then ran his tongue along the shell and nibbled his way across my jaw. He rolled off me long enough to grab a condom and sheath himself, then he was pressing into me with no resistance from my core.

I sighed as he filled me, stretching my body in that delicious way that told me it wasn't just a toy but a live man inside me. My core trembled with awareness, my body feeling alive and awake and so fucking turned on it was insane.

And then Landon moved. Good Lord, the man had skills. He rotated his hips and shifted his angle, and I was helpless against him. Not that I wanted to fight. Oh, no, I wanted to surrender. I wanted to give all of myself to this man. To have all of him. To never doubt how he felt about me.

I swallowed back the fear that rose up as quickly as my orgasm and let my basic instincts take over. My core tightened around him as I came hard. My words were a jumbled mess of nothing, my feelings much the same.

He pounded into me, my orgasm triggering his. He grabbed my hand as if I were the only thing that could ground him.

I looked up at him and found him staring at me.

"Casey," he groaned as he shook, his shoulders bowing up tight against his ears, his muscles tensing, then he let go.

He held my gaze as he erupted inside me. His mouth opened, his jaw slack.

I reached my free hand for his face, dragging my nails across his jaw before I cupped his cheek.

His entire body trembled before he collapsed onto me.

I held him, my legs and arms around him. He breathed into me, sweat dripping from his body onto mine. His lips moved against my neck, like he was whispering, but I couldn't hear him say anything.

He stopped shaking a few minutes later and pushed himself off me enough to meet my gaze. "Thank you for being my date."

I chuckled. "Thank you for teaching me how to flirt. Although I'm not sure I'm any better than I used to be."

"You never needed lessons, Casey. All you needed to do was be yourself, and men would fall all over themselves for you."

I snorted. "Not in my experience."

"Maybe you just never knew the right one."

My breath hitched. "Maybe."

He smiled and kissed my nose, then rolled off me. He offered me a hand to help me up, then let me use the bathroom first. When I came out, he smiled and took his turn.

I wasn't sure what I was supposed to do. Was I supposed to sit on the couch? Get into his bed? Ask to go home? Would he think I was being clingy if I stayed, even though he asked me to?

"What are you thinking right now?"

I turned and found him leaning against the bathroom doorframe. He was completely naked, his cock half-hard, surrounded by a nest of dark hair. He was completely confident in his body, but that was no shock when I looked at him. He was lean and muscled. Any woman would call herself lucky to have his attention.

And it was all on me.

"I don't know what you want me to do, and I don't want to overstay my welcome."

He pushed off the doorframe and stalked toward me.

I resisted the urge to run away from him.

His smirk said he noticed I fought my urge, and he was happy I did. "You are never going to overstay your welcome because I want you here all the time. I asked you to pack a bag and stay. If you want to go home, I will take you, but I love having you here. I want you here."

"Okay."

He kissed me. "Okay. Do you need a drink? I was going to get some water."

I nodded. "Sounds good."

"Then I want you again. If you're up for it."

I grinned. "I think I could be persuaded."

He kissed me hard, his tongue slipping between my lips.

He tasted like mouthwash instead of me. "I wasn't sure how you felt about tasting yourself on me."

"I wasn't either, but I think I liked it."

He smoothed the hair back from my face. "Then I'll have to get some more of you on my tongue before the night is over."

I chuckled, my core clenching at the casual dirty conversation. Moisture seeped between my thighs. "I will not argue."

"Good. First water. Then you on my counter."

"Landon!"

"I saw the way you trembled. I might need a few minutes to recover, but clearly you don't."

My breath got stuck in my throat. The man was going to make me break all my rules. And I was going to love every minute of it.

I WAS awake before Landon the next morning. Years of getting up super early with a kid forced me to be a morning person. When I was married, I loved it. Being up before Kyle and Mikayla was the time of day I had to myself, sometimes the only time.

But watching Landon sleep had me wishing I could stay in bed longer with him. I wanted to see him open his eyes, see the look on his face when I was right there.

Which was part of why I slid out of his bed even though it wasn't even six and made my way to the kitchen. My cheeks heated as I leaned against the counter he'd perched me on and licked me until I screamed his name and made a mess of his counter. He produced a condom and silenced my guilt by fucking me until we were both screaming and the counter was soaked from our sweat and come and kisses.

He cleaned the counter while I used the bathroom, then joined me in his bed. We talked for hours, kissing and getting to know more about each other than how quickly we could make the other come, and finally fell asleep with our arms and legs tangled.

I was letting myself fall for him. I didn't expect it or plan for it, but I couldn't stop it either. He was sweet and sexy and funny. I enjoyed being around him. And if I was being honest with myself, we wanted the same things.

I wanted a family. A husband. More kids. A life in MacKellar Cove. All the things my friends had. Everything Natalie and Omar shared.

The only thing holding me back was fear. Fear that whomever I picked next would end up like Kyle. Fear that we would barely speak by the end. Fear that he would feel trapped.

Fear that I would feel trapped.

I'd never regret having Mikayla, but I regretted going along with what others expected. I knew Kyle and I weren't right for each other, but saying no when he asked if we should get married scared me more than saying yes.

My stomach tightened, making me feel sick.

Landon wasn't the same. The situation wasn't the same. I wasn't pregnant, and he wasn't proposing. Hell, I didn't even think he felt the same as I did. He was having fun, and he said he liked me, but it wasn't a forever kind of thing.

And I couldn't worry about if it could be. I had a busy day, and an even busier week. I needed to get Mikayla, make sure she was ready for the week, and get started on my article. Gretchen wanted it first thing Monday morning, and while it was almost done, I still had work to do.

I started the coffee and grabbed my phone. I made notes about the wedding and added in pieces I knew would complete the picture. Gretchen kept asking about drama, but she hadn't changed any of my articles since the first one. If she was going to change one, this would be the one. She knew Natalie and Omar were gone on their honeymoon and that I couldn't get Natalie's approval for changes.

But that didn't mean Gretchen wouldn't push for any.

My stomach rolled again. I had no interest in creating drama. Especially for two people who had been through enough.

The coffee gurgled to a stop, and I grabbed a cup, curling up on the couch to fill in pieces of my story.

Two hours later, Landon stirred. I heard the sheets move, then his hand slapped the mattress. His feet hit the floor and moved toward the living room, then he emerged.

"You're still here," he said, his voice rough from sleep, and his cock hard from the same. "I thought you'd left."

"Did you want me to?"

He shook his head and walked over to me, dropping onto the couch next to me and pulling me into his arms roughly. He kissed the top of my head, then sucked in a shaky breath as he held me.

"Are you okay?"

He nodded and pulled back. He forced a smile. "All good. Thank you for staying. I take it you're a morning person."

I nodded. "Unfortunately. I was always the one who got up with Mikayla when she was little, and I made sure everything was ready for everyone to get out of the house. It's just habit now to be up early."

"Even though we were up late last night?"

"Yep. I wish I could sleep in, but I never do."

"You could have woken me up. I would have tried to wear you out." He waggled his brows and grinned.

I laughed. "Next time."

Surprise flashed across his face before he schooled it into a simple grin. "Next time."

"I made coffee."

"What else did you do this morning?"

"Work. I'm figuring out my article about the wedding. I am exposing Natalie as the woman in that picture from two years ago with Omar."

"Wait, what? Why are you doing that?"

"Natalie told me to. My editor wants dirt, and Natalie said I should write about it. They explained what happened and how that night started their relationship. We thought it would be a good bookend to their story. The ugly beginning and the beautiful end of their romance."

"That's poetic."

I laughed. "Yeah. I thought the same thing. I need to turn it in tomorrow, but I have to get Mikayla sometime this morning, so I was getting stuff done while you were sleeping."

"What time do you need me to take you home?"

I shrugged, not wanting to go but knowing I needed to. "Probably soon. If that's okay."

"Of course. Whatever works for you. I'll get a cup of coffee and get dressed."

"You could hold off on that second part for a little longer." I raised my eyebrows at him.

"Why, Ms. White, are you propositioning me?"

"Only if you say yes."

"Always, Casey. I'm always going to say yes to you."

I grinned, then whooped when he scooped me up and carried me to his bed.

Everything else could wait.

I SUBMITTED my article as soon as Mikayla was on the bus Monday morning. When I arrived for the morning meeting,

Gretchen said she'd received it and would be in touch after she read it.

I was not looking forward to her feedback. I was proud of the article. It was good. It told Natalie and Omar's whole story and wrapped up their wedding series. I sent a copy to Natalie, but I hoped she was enjoying her honeymoon too much to read it. For my own peace of mind, I also sent it to Amelia and Daisy, knowing Natalie's boss and best friend would be looking out for Natalie's best interests while she was enjoying her new married life.

The meeting wasn't long, but I had a house to clean afterward and no time to see Landon for lunch. With Mikayla's musical rehearsal, I picked up a second house for the day, making my day even tighter.

When I was finished with both, I had less than thirty minutes before I needed to pick Mikayla up. I debated going to see Landon or stopping at the grocery store, but I had no groceries in my house, so that option won out even though I really wanted to see Landon.

I grabbed a small cart and made my way through the aisles, looking for quick options since our evenings were busier as the musical drew closer. Rehearsals were going to be longer, and Mikayla would be starving. I picked out a few extra school-approved, allergy-friendly snacks she could pack to take with her, and a few easy dinner options I could make ahead of time and we could have for a few days.

I was almost to the end of my trip when I spotted the one woman I did not want to run into. Ever.

Reegan.

"Hi Casey. How are you?" she asked with a tentative smile.

Freshly fucked and feeling fantastic thanks to your ex. And by the way, why in the hell were you crazy enough to let him go? Thanks, but what were you thinking?

"I'm… I'm good, Reegan. How are you?"

"Good. I, um, it looked like you and Landon were having fun at the wedding."

Shit. My stomach knotted again. It was supposed to be casual. We were flirting, not falling in love. I couldn't help how I felt, but it was wrong of me to stand in the way of two people who were supposed to be together.

Even if Landon insisted it was over.

"I'm sorry. We… He said you two were over. I wasn't trying to step on your toes."

Reegan laughed softly. "Landon… We are over. We have been for a long time. A part of me will always love him, but not the same way you two love each other."

"That's not… We don't…"

"I know what Landon looks like when he's in love. You don't have to convince me it's not true, Casey. I'm not upset. I'm really happy for the two of you. We don't know each other well, but I know Landon. You're good for him. He hasn't looked that happy in a long time."

"We're just spending time together."

Reegan sighed, then smiled. "It's none of my business, Casey. I just wanted you to know I'm not going to cause trouble for you or try to steal him back or anything. Landon and I are better as friends, if that, and I want him to find his happiness. It was good to see he found it with you."

"Thanks," I whispered as she wheeled her cart away.

She turned the corner down an aisle and disappeared from my view.

Was she right? Did Landon love me?

A wave of nausea washed over me. I slapped a hand over my mouth and raced to the bathroom, abandoning my cart in the middle of the store.

I made it to the stall, emptying my stomach before I slumped against the wall.

Oh, shit.

22

I woke up on Tuesday morning to a request from Gretchen to come into the office immediately. More like a demand. But whatever. I had things to do before I could see her.

I got Mikayla on the bus, then stared at my phone for way too long. Because I had to go into the paper the day before, I didn't see Landon for lunch. He asked if I was going to meet him today, but I couldn't.

I was meeting my match for lunch.

I already have lunch plans, but I'll come see you tomorrow if you're available.

I'll be here.

I locked my phone and forced myself to go into the office. All I wanted to do was curl up on the couch, but I couldn't. I had responsibilities.

Starting with defending my article.

Gretchen was fuming by the time I arrived. She barked at

me to come to her office, clearly watching for me before I got there.

Mike flashed me a sympathetic look, and a few others eyed me curiously. I held my head high as I went to face Gretchen.

"What the hell garbage is this?" Gretchen demanded before the door was closed. "Are you trying to put this paper out of business?"

I didn't want to react, but I blanched at her tone. "I'm trying to write articles I believe the people of MacKellar Cove will enjoy."

"Not all endings are happy, but this one is. The woman our favorite mayor was seen with two years ago… She's the woman he loves, the one he's spending the rest of his life with. And they couldn't be happier together," Gretchen read from the article I submitted.

"I take it you don't like it?"

"No, I don't like it. I hate it! No one cares. No one wants all the daisies and none of the drama. I've given you the rope to create articles that people would read, Casey, and all you've done is write fluff that kisses ass. That's not what we do here."

I drew a breath and let it out slowly. My blood pressure was high, as it always was when I had to meet with Gretchen. "What is it we do? What are you asking me to do?"

"I'm asking you to write something people want to read. Everyone knows that picture was Natalie. It's old news now. You said nothing about drama at the wedding, one of them getting cold feet. Anything. We need something better than this."

"None of that happened. They were excited, happy. Their love is real."

"Then make it up." She scoffed. "I don't know what makes you think we're here to be friends with everyone, but we're not. We're here to sell newspapers. To showcase the interesting parts of this town. You're not giving me anything that fits that. You're not going to last long in this industry if you're not willing to do what it takes to capture attention."

I pushed to a stand and shrugged. "Then I guess I won't last."

"What are you talking about?" Gretchen demanded.

"I quit, Gretchen. I'm not writing an article about two good people and destroying their reputations. I told you that before, and you don't seem to be willing to listen. So I quit." I opened the door to leave her office.

"You can't quit because I'm firing you." Gretchen shouted above the noise of the rest of the office.

I turned back to her. "That's fine with me. Either way, I'm not working for you or any editor who wants to print lies in order to sell papers."

"Every paper does it. If you think you're just going to walk away and find someone who's telling the truth, you're a fool."

"Then I'm a fool, too," Mike said, standing from his desk. "I'm not going to hold back, but you better believe I'm not going to lie and open myself up to a lawsuit because you can't figure out how to run a successful paper."

"Oh, please. You don't care about that. The paper will protect you," Gretchen said.

"Maybe they will, and maybe they won't. But I'm not putting my name on something I don't believe in. I quit, too," Mike said. He gathered his things and walked to the door.

"I quit," Stephanie said, following Mike.

"I quit," Jose said.

"What is wrong with all of you?" Gretchen screeched. "Don't you want to sell papers?"

"We do," Jose said, stopping before he left. "But not like this. We love this town. We love the people who live here.

We're not going to be your pawns to ruin lives. Erik did enough of that, and we all agreed we wouldn't let it happen again."

"You can't leave. You're all fired!" Gretchen shouted after them.

None of them stopped, and I felt a swell of pride and joy. I didn't want them all to quit, but knowing they had my back, that they agreed with what I was fighting for, was a great feeling.

"You," Gretchen snarled. "You did this. You put them up to this."

I shook my head. "I did nothing. You did, Gretchen."

She growled, but she didn't argue.

I followed my coworkers out of the office, not wanting to be alone with Gretchen, and found them waiting for me in the parking lot.

"Are you okay?" Mike asked.

I nodded. "Yeah. I'm sorry you all had to quit because of me."

Mike shook his head. "We quit because of her. I filled them in on what was going on, and we all agreed we weren't going to let her do what Erik did. It's not what this town is all about."

Jose cleared his throat. "None of us are okay with what Gretchen did a few weeks ago. That's not how this is supposed to be."

"No, it's not," I agreed.

We all nodded, sharing sad smiles. I never expected Gretchen's arguments to come to this. I thought she'd back off.

I thought I'd get a full-time position working for the paper.

But instead, I was down to two jobs and very little hope I'd be able to pay my bills in the next few months.

I got in my car and lowered my head to the steering wheel. I was supposed to meet my match for lunch, but that wasn't where I wanted to be.

I parked outside Blossom & Grow and drew a breath. Everything was going to change. Everything already had, but it would change again.

Landon was talking to a customer. His smile was genuine. Just like the man himself.

I slid my hands over my belly. Landon was nothing like Kyle, but it wasn't any easier to tell Landon he was going to be a father than it was to tell Kyle.

I knew it as soon as I got sick in the grocery store. The last time I threw up was when I was pregnant with Mikayla. I went back to my cart and added a pregnancy test, then raced through self-checkout so I didn't have to face anyone when I bought it.

It wasn't a surprise when it was positive, but it wasn't entirely a good thing either. Landon wanted kids, and he wanted a wife, but I wasn't sure he wanted any of those things with me. And I refused to marry another man who didn't really want to marry me.

The big change with this pregnancy was I loved the father of my unborn baby. I'd known it for a while, but I'd been fighting my feelings for him. It was time for me to be honest with him and find out if we had a chance at a future.

I opened the door to Blossom & Grow. The chime above the door told him I was there, and he looked up with a smile.

His face froze when he saw me. He wasn't happy to see me.

Shit.

He said something to the customer he was talking to, then approached me. "Hey. I thought you had plans."

I nodded and wrapped my arms around my belly. "I do." I shook my head. "I did. I wanted to see you."

"Are you okay?"

"I quit my job," I blurted.

"You what?" He cupped my elbow and led me through the store. He nodded to a young woman. She smiled at us, then went to help the customer Landon was talking to when I walked in.

He pushed the door to the consultation room closed and pulled me into his arms. "Are you okay? Which job did you quit? Why?"

I shuddered in his arms. "I'll be fine. My editor wasn't happy with the article I wrote. She wanted me to make up drama, and I refused."

"Good for you. That article was amazing."

I smiled. I sent it to him when I sent it to Natalie, Daisy, and Amelia. "Thanks."

"I mean it, Casey. You're a talented writer with a knack for capturing the emotion of a day. You made me feel their love. It was exceptional."

"Thanks."

He tilted my head back. "Were those your lunch plans? You had something with work?"

I shook my head. "I... No. I was supposed to meet the guy I matched with."

"Oh." He drew a breath, and I hurried to continue.

"We set it up a while ago. Weeks ago. I told you he was the one I was thinking about with flirting lessons, but when we started sleeping together... I haven't talked to him in a while. We agreed to meet today, and if either of us didn't show up, it was fine. I doubt he's going to show up because we haven't talked, but I felt like I should go so I could tell him..."

"Tell him what?" Landon whispered.

I looked up at him. "Tell him I met someone else. Someone I... Someone I am not ready to end things with yet."

"He's a lucky guy," Landon said.

I snorted. "When I walked out of the paper, the only person I wanted to see was you, Landon. I know you're working, and I know we agreed to get through the wedding, but I want to keep seeing each other."

"I want that, too."

"Good." I smiled. "Um, there's something else you need to know, though."

"There's something you need to know, too."

"Oh, um, okay. What is it?"

He took my hands, then let go and paced away from me. With his back to me, he said, "I never meant to lie to you."

Sadness washed over me. My entire body flashed hot. I was getting ready to tell him I was in love with him, and he was going to tell me everything between us had been a lie.

"I know I should have said something weeks ago, but I didn't know how to tell you."

I swallowed. "Just say it, Landon. I can take it."

He turned to face me, his gaze sliding past mine before he drew a breath and met my eyes. "I'm DirtyLife."

I tilted my head to the side as I tried to understand what he was telling me. He was… "Wait, you're what?"

He released a shaky breath. "I'm your match, Casey. My screen name is DirtyLife. You're TooBusy, aren't you?"

"Holy shit. Are you serious?"

He nodded. "I should have told you as soon as I figured it out. Andre told me to. I was scared. I thought you'd stop talking to me and that I'd lose you. I wanted to get to know you. I was falling for you. I did fall for you. And I know starting a relationship with a lie between us isn't a good idea, but I thought it would be okay. I was going to meet you for lunch today and tell you, but—"

"You're DirtyLife. You're my match. I asked you for flirting lessons so I could… flirt with you."

He rubbed the back of his neck. "Yeah. I… I didn't know right away."

"When did you figure it out?"

"When you asked me out. The other me."

My eyebrows shot up. "That was weeks ago."

He nodded.

"Did you… All those conversations. I feel like I should have seen it."

"No," he said. "I… When we started talking, I had no idea who you were. We hadn't met, and I didn't know. When you showed up here, that first time, I thought you were beautiful. And then when you asked me to help you learn to flirt, I wanted to spend time with you. I didn't know we were talking until you asked me to meet. I couldn't. I knew if I did, you wouldn't talk to me anymore. On the app, you were different. I wanted to get to know you. And there, you were a different version of you. More relaxed. I didn't want to lose the chance to get to know that woman."

"Were you laughing at me the whole time?"

"Never. Not once. I wanted to get to know you."

"I… Were you going to meet me for lunch today?"

"Yes. I was going to tell you everything. I wanted to get through the wedding. And then we started to get closer, and I didn't want to ruin things. I… I love you, Casey. I know it's fast. I know it seems crazy, but I do. I fell in love with you, and I didn't want to lose you. But I know I will if I don't tell you the truth."

"Is that really the truth?"

"Why… What? Is that I love you the truth?"

"Yes. Or did someone see me yesterday and you know?"

"Know what? What happened yesterday?"

I stared at him. I had to know. Maybe it wasn't fair to him, but I had to know if he was convinced he loved me because I was carrying his baby or if he really meant it.

"What happened? Are you hurt? Is something wrong?"

I shook my head. "I… I'm pregnant."

"You're… Are you kidding?"

I shook my head again, the emotions rising up. I swallowed them back. I had to stay rational and reasonable. I couldn't let my hormones rule me. I had to be smarter than that this time.

His hand covered his mouth, hiding his emotions from me. "Are you okay? I know that's not what you wanted."

I exhaled a laugh. "I don't know how I am yet."

"What…" He exhaled slowly. "What do you want to do, Casey?"

"You're not… You don't have an opinion?"

"I have a lot of them. Five minutes ago, I thought you were going to run out of here angry at me. Ten minutes ago, I was terrified to tell you I love you. Thirty minutes ago, I was looking at engagement rings and wondering if I'd ever be able to convince you to marry me. All of that has changed now. All that matters is what you want."

"You wanted to marry me?"

He nodded. "I did, and I still do. We didn't go into this with that plan, but I want that more than anything else. I want you in my life for good. But only if you want that, too. I don't want you to feel trapped."

My hands shook as I brought them to my face. "Landon."

"Casey."

"Say it again."

"Say what?"

"Say you love me," I whispered.

"I love you, Casey White. More than I've ever loved anyone in my life. And if you'll have me, I want to build a life with you. With Mikayla and our baby."

"A dirty life?" I asked.

A laugh popped out of him. "Very dirty."

"Are you going to stay over there or are you going to kiss me?"

He stalked across the room and wrapped me up in his arms, but he kept his lips off mine. "I love you, Casey. Not because of the baby. Because of you. I will always be here for you, but I never want you to feel like you have to marry me. I know you're not in the same place as me, but I hope you'll give me a chance to show you what it's like to be loved."

I laughed. "You silly man. I am so in love with you."

"You are?" he blurted, truly surprised.

I nodded. "I am. I love you, Landon Boyd."

"Well, damn. I didn't see that coming."

"I never saw you coming, but I'm so happy you're here."

"I love you, Casey."

"I love you."

He kissed me hard, spinning me around and setting me on the edge of the table. He kneeled in front of me and kissed my belly. "Hi, baby."

My emotions swelled and overflowed.

He was going to be the best father ever.

And he was all mine.

LANDON

My baby. She was carrying my baby. And she was happy about it. I'd almost lost hope of ever experiencing that, but there it was. In front of me. Sitting on the table in my shop.

"I need you," I whispered against her ear.

"We're not exactly in private."

I looked around. The door locked, but I wasn't going to risk exposing her or making her uncomfortable. "Upstairs. You can say no."

She shook her head. "I don't want to." She pushed me back with a hand on my chest and slipped off the table. "But there are people here, so we have to be quiet."

"I'll try," I said, opening the door for her to walk out ahead of me.

Gail and Carson were handling customers, not paying us any attention as we snuck to the back stairs and hurried up to my apartment.

"They're going to know what we're doing," Casey said when we made it into the apartment with the door closed and locked.

I pressed her against the door. "You're pregnant with my child. They're all going to know soon anyway."

She chuckled. "True."

"Are you sure you're okay with all of this? A baby and me?" I wasn't sure I'd ever feel like we were secure. Not when I worried she felt stuck with me.

She sighed and cupped my jaw. "When I found out I was pregnant with Mikayla, I was scared. I..." She shook her head. "I guess I loved Kyle, in a way, but we were young. We weren't really ready for the realities of life. Together or with a baby. I was working full time, but we weren't talking about getting married. Then I found out I was pregnant, and we both felt like we had no other choice."

"That sounds a lot like what's happening right now," I admitted. I wasn't looking to push her away, but I didn't want it all to end.

She nodded. "Yeah, but the big difference between you and Kyle is I was already thinking about a future with you."

"What?" I blurted.

She chuckled. "You scared me. A lot."

I took a step back. "Why did I scare you?"

"Because being with you has been so easy from the start. When we met, I knew I needed to stay away from you because of Reegan."

I opened my mouth to interrupt her, but she held up a hand.

"I know. But at the time, I didn't know things were really over. I thought you two were on the way to getting back together, like everyone else in town."

I sighed, knowing she was right.

"When you asked me to be your date for the wedding, a part of me still thought you wanted to use me to make her jealous. And I figured that was fine because I was interested in the online you, and I went into this with my eyes open.

But the more time we spent together, the more I wanted to see you."

"I feel the same."

She grinned. "I couldn't stop myself from loving you, even though I figured it would end up with me on the outside and you and Reegan back together. When I saw her yesterday—"

I sucked in a breath.

Casey smiled. "She said she was happy for us. She's a really good person."

I nodded. "She is. It was part of why I stayed with her so long even though I knew we weren't right for each other."

"I don't want you to do that with me."

I breathed a laugh at the absurdity of that statement. "I want you more than I ever wanted her. Letting you walk away every day was like watching a piece of me leave. With Reegan, she was one of my best friends. I care about her, I loved her, but it never came close to how I feel about you."

"Yeah?"

I nodded. "Yeah."

"I know all of this didn't go the way we expected, but I am happy about it. I always wanted more kids. My dream was to have four or five, but after Mikayla, I couldn't imagine it."

I tucked her hair back and cupped her jaw. "Why not?"

She smiled sadly. "Kyle was never really there for either of us. He worked, came home and did whatever, then went to bed. He wasn't involved when Mikayla was a baby and never got more involved as she grew up. He used to say he didn't know what to do with a baby. As she grew up, he said she liked me more."

"If you're the only parent there for her, of course she does."

She laughed. "That's what I told him. He just wasn't all that interested in being a father. He felt trapped, just like I did. Trapped with me, trapped with a kid, trapped in a life he never wanted."

"I don't feel trapped, Casey. I want this. I want you, this baby, a marriage. I want to be there for everything. I want to go to appointments with you and hold your hand and get you ice chips in the delivery room and do everything I can for you and our kid and Mikayla for the rest of our lives. And if you want more kids after this one, I want that, too."

Tears rolled down her cheeks. "Thank you."

I wiped her tears with my thumbs. "What do you need right now?"

She looked up at me, fire and passion in her gaze. "You."

I didn't need to be told twice. I picked up the woman I loved and carried her to my bed. I laid her down, keeping my weight off her body so I wouldn't hurt her or the baby. I kissed her, my cock hardening as her softness molded to my hardness.

Casey wrapped her arms around my neck and tugged at my shirt, lifting it inch-by-inch until she couldn't pull anymore.

I sat up and yanked my shirt off, tossing it behind me, then helped her up to shed her clothes. Standing in front of me naked, I looked at the swell of her belly and felt a surge of pride and possession I'd never known.

"Mine," I whispered, sliding my hand over her belly. "You're all mine."

"I am," she said. "And you're mine."

"All yours, Casey. Everything I am and everything I have is yours." I reached for a condom, but she stopped me.

"I've only been with you in more than a year. I've been tested, and I'm clean. You can say no, but since I'm already pregnant…"

I sucked in a breath. "I've never… I've always used a condom."

"Okay," she said, removing her hand from my arm and moving toward the bed.

"I… Being inside you without one might have me embarrassing myself."

She chuckled. "I love you. You can't be embarrassed around me."

My dick surged at her words. "Fuck, I love hearing you say that."

"I love you, Landon."

My cock throbbed. "I need you, Casey. No condoms. Just us."

"Just us."

She laid back on the bed, and I pulled her to the edge. I kneeled in front of her and pressed her thighs wide to see her dripping wet and ready for me. "You're soaked."

"The man I love said he feels the same. It's kind of a turn-on."

"Then I guess I'll have to tell you more often."

"I think you should."

"I love you," I whispered against her soaked flesh.

She trembled.

"I love you." I licked through her folds, whispering the words as I loved her body with my mouth. My hands kept her thighs wide, my thumbs teasing her entrance as I took my time enjoying her.

"Landon," she breathed. "I love you, Landon."

Fuck. Her soft declaration was a shot to my dick. It throbbed and jumped, wanting in on the action. I groaned and flicked her clit with the tip of my tongue.

She moaned and pressed her hips to my face.

My balls tightened up, giving me no option but to make her come fast. I sucked her clit into my mouth, flicking the tender nub with my tongue. Three fingers sank into her channel, and Casey fought to let her release out.

"Landon. Oh, fuck. Landon. I love you. Love you so much. Landon. Oh, yes. Love you!"

I didn't let up on her, feeling possessed as she came with my name and her profession of love. My tongue traveled through her folds again, then returned to her clit. I licked over it with the flat of my tongue, making her hips jump.

She whimpered, then moaned.

I added a fourth finger to her core and teased her clit until she stilled, her entire body rigid for a few seconds. Then she released, thrashing and moaning and grabbing my head.

She tugged my hair, pulling me up her body until her lips greedily sucked on mine.

I eased my fingers out of her and lined my bare cock up with her entrance. The feel of her direct heat on me was almost more than I could take.

"Love me, Landon. I want to feel all of you inside me."

"Fuck, Casey. I love you."

She pulled my lips to hers again and rocked her hips to take me inside her.

The feel of her soaked channel beckoning me had me slamming into her. Instantly, my body recognized the difference. My balls pulled up tight, my spine tingling, heat flashing over all of me.

"Fuck," I breathed, tearing my lips from hers. "Fuck."

"Are you okay?" she asked, worry in her voice.

"I'm trying not to come yet."

"What do you mean?"

"You feel so damn good that I almost came just now." I drew a breath and let it out against her throat. "I want to enjoy this a little longer."

"You can enjoy it for as long as you want. And even better, you can enjoy this every day for the rest of our lives. I know I will."

"Fuck, Casey. I can't… I need…"

She tightened her core around my dick, and I lost the fight to hold back.

I pushed back to stand, holding her ankles as I stared at my bare dick disappearing into her plump folds. Her pretty pink flesh was soaked, letting me slide easily into her.

"Landon," she whispered.

I looked up at her and found her watching me with a look I'd never seen in her eyes.

Love.

She was looking at me with love.

With the kind of love I'd always wanted to find.

"I love you, Landon. Let me feel you come inside me."

Her words shot straight to my cock. I pounded into her, losing my mind and needing her. My body took over, slamming so hard the bed shook and her tits bounced wildly.

I looked back at where I entered her, and I lost it. My balls clenched at the same time as her channel, both insisting I stay where I was.

"Casey!" I roared as my orgasm rocketed through me. Every cell flashed hot, then let go, taking all my strength and energy and love and pouring me into her.

She responded with an orgasm, her legs holding me to her and supporting me in a way I didn't know I needed until they were there. Her core vibrated around me, adding to my orgasm and joining us.

"I love you," I whispered.

She smiled up at me, a dazed and sated look that told me she was feeling all the same things I was. "I love you, Landon."

I leaned forward, kissing her gently before slipping out of her. We cleaned up, then got dressed, and I talked her into sitting on the couch with me for a little while.

"I want to buy you a house," I told her.

"No. You don't need to do that."

"My place is too small for four of us, and so is yours. Plus, I don't want you going up and down the stairs all the time. It'll be even worse when we have a newborn."

She drew a breath and let it out slowly.

"Is this moving too fast for you?"

She shrugged. "I don't want you to feel like you have to change everything right now. And I don't want to leave everything to you. I need to contribute."

"I will never tell you what to do. If you want to work, I'm good with that. If you want to stay home, that's okay, too. The only thing I will ask is that we make decisions together."

She snorted. "And you saying you want to buy a house is making a decision together?"

I laughed. "Fine, you're right. But at least I told you and didn't just buy it."

She laughed. "True."

"I do want to buy a house, though. I've been thinking about it for a while, but I…"

"You're comfortable here."

He nodded. "I am. But that doesn't mean I should stay here."

"We have a lot of decisions to make in the next few months. Let's add that to the list."

"Okay," I agreed, only because we had time.

A WEEK after Casey quit the paper, she got a call from one of her former coworkers. Mike told her they'd reported the editor to the owner of the paper. He was going to be the new editor, and he wanted Casey back full time.

"What are you going to do?" I asked her when she told me.

She'd been exhausted and was having trouble being on her feet to clean houses. She assured me it was normal for the first trimester, but I didn't like her working so hard when I could provide for her. She was stressing herself out.

"I love being a journalist. Especially in MacKellar Cove."

"It sounds like a pretty easy answer then. Why are you hesitating?"

"Because of the baby."

"Why?"

She slid her hands over her belly, something she'd been doing frequently. A protective thing, I assumed. "If I don't disclose the pregnancy, it'll feel like I'm hiding something. I'll be taking a few months off when the baby arrives, and bosses don't always take too kindly to learning that information, no matter how early they find out."

"What do you think about this guy? Mike?"

She nodded. "Mike has always been a bit of a shark. He won't let a story go when there's something to share. But he's fair. He was the first one to tell me he'd walk out when Gretchen wanted me to make up things about Omar and Natalie."

"Do you think that means he'll be on your side?"

"I don't know. But I think the sooner I talk to him, the better."

"Call him now. Put your mind at ease."

She hesitated for a second, then returned the man's call.

I listened from the kitchen, watching her on the couch as she spoke to the man who might be her boss.

She told him about the pregnancy, and when she thought she was due. She listened, and by the time she spoke again, she was smiling.

"Thanks, Mike. I really appreciate it. I'll see you next week."

"Well?"

"He wants me no matter how many kids I have. He said my integrity and talent are worthwhile, and people have babies all the time. It shouldn't be a reason not to hire someone."

"Good. I told you it would be okay."

She stepped into my arms and tilted her chin back for a kiss.

I obliged, lingering against her lips.

"Thank you for supporting me."

"I always will."

"I didn't know love could be like this."

"Neither did I, but I guess when it's right, it's different."

"It's definitely right."

"Yes. Yes, it is. I love you, Landon."

"I love you, Casey."

24

I woke to the sound of laughter. It was muffled, followed by a shushing sound. I smiled into my pillow, wondering what my girls were up to.

Casey and I were still searching for a house for our soon-to-be family of four, but until we found one, I was mostly living with her and Mikayla. We took things a little slowly for Mikayla's sake, but she and I bonded quickly. Casey and I attended all the showings of the musical, and we spent Thanksgiving together. I loved the kid like she was my own, while doing everything I could to respect that she had a father.

But damn, I loved her. I didn't know my heart could be so damn full. Every time I looked at the two of them, I felt like the Grinch and my heart grew three sizes. Love was a crazy thing. It was pretty damn awesome.

The laughter got louder, and I knew my girls were plotting something. I pretended to be asleep until I heard them right next to the bed. I cracked one eye open just enough to see what was going on without letting them know I was awake.

Casey held a tray, and Mikayla crept toward me, hands empty.

I surged at Mikayla, grabbing her and tackling her onto the bed.

She squealed with laughter, cackling when I tickled her. "No fair! You were supposed to be asleep."

"I warned you we were going to wake him up," Casey said. She set the tray down, and I seized my chance, grabbing her and pulling her into the fray. "Landon!"

I ignored her protest and tickled her ribs, maybe copping a feel when Mikayla wasn't looking.

Casey's eyes went wide in protest, but the smile tilting her lips said she didn't mind at all.

"We wanted to surprise you with breakfast in bed," Mikayla said when she could breathe again.

"Why do I get all the surprises?" I asked.

"It's Christmas! Mommy wanted to tell you we love you."

I hugged them both to my chest and kissed Mikayla's head, then Casey's. "I love you both. So much."

Casey heard the tightness in my voice and sighed against me.

"I don't need anything special, though. I thought we were going to spend the day together."

"Yeah, but we've been up for a really long time," Mikayla said.

"Someone isn't super patient about waiting to open her gifts," Casey said.

I snickered and winked at Mikayla. "It's your mom, right?"

Mikayla laughed and nodded. "Yep. She's always waking me up early."

I laughed with them, loving what my life had become in the last few months. It was only going to get better.

"How about we carry this breakfast to the other room and let your mom open her presents?"

Mikayla nodded and scrambled off the bed. She raced ahead of us to the living room.

"She's so excited. And you went a little crazy," Casey chastised me.

I scoffed. "Not even close. I love her, and I wanted her to have everything. Trust me, I held back."

Casey laughed. "I love you. But you don't have to do this all the time."

"I won't. Just most of the time."

She snorted and shook her head. She reached for the tray, but I grabbed it. "I can carry that."

"I know. I'm not taking over. But as long as I'm here, I want to do things for you."

"Are you planning on going somewhere?"

"Only if you're with me."

She smiled and led the way to the living room. Mikayla had the presents all split up and in front of a seat for each of us. I sat where I was told and put the tray on the coffee table so we could all enjoy breakfast while we opened gifts.

I picked up my coffee and sat back while my girls got started. Mikayla tore through all her gifts, exclaiming her joy with each thing she opened. I knew it was important to Casey that Mikayla have more than just things, so when I shopped, I was careful. Games, art supplies, and experiences were all in there. Her big gift was tickets to a Broadway play, something Casey argued with me about, but something I was adamant we do together.

Mikayla went crazy when she saw the tickets. "No way. Seriously? How can we do this?" She gawked at her mom.

Casey shook her head and pointed at me. "It was all him. I said it was too much."

Mikayla jumped up and threw her arms around me.

"Thank you, thank you, thank you. I've always wanted to see a play on Broadway."

"I know. After seeing you in the musical, I thought it could be fun. It's over your mid-winter break in February, so we need to find other things we can do when we're in New York City."

"We can do other things?" Mikayla asked.

"Of course. What do you want to do?"

Her eyes widened. "I don't know. But I'll find out."

I laughed, loving her excitement.

"Is it my turn?" Casey asked.

"Yeah, Mom. You need to open your stuff." Mikayla sat on the floor at Casey's feet, staring up at her.

"What is with you?" Casey asked.

Mikayla glanced at me, and I did my best to play it off, but Casey was on to us.

"What did you two do?"

"Nothing," Mikayla said, the word not at all sounding innocent.

Casey shook her head and started in on her collection of gifts. I held back with half the things I wanted to get for her, too, but there was one thing I couldn't pass up.

The last box Casey picked up, the one intentionally at the bottom of her pile was wrapped in paper different from the others. It was silver and sparkly, as requested by Mikayla, with a garnet ribbon. Casey toyed with the ribbon before she slid it off the box.

I held my breath as she tore into the paper. The box didn't give anything away, but it was only a few seconds before she opened it.

I set my coffee down before I spilled it on myself with how badly my hands were shaking. It didn't matter what we'd talked about in the last few weeks, all the plans and ideas and frustrations, it was time to get an answer.

Casey lifted the lid on the box and slid a glance my way. "What is this? A picture frame?"

I didn't say anything. My throat was tight.

She lifted the tissue paper from the front of the frame and looked down at it, her gaze scanning the words in the fancy script.

Her hand flew to her mouth. "What? Landon?"

"Pick it up, Mom," Mikayla said.

"Pick it up. Why?" Casey lifted the frame from the box and unknowingly pulled out the ring tied to the back. It swung and hit her hand, giving me a chance to drop to one knee.

"Casey White. I love you. I love everything about you. I love the way you make me laugh, the smile in your eyes when I say something dumb. I love the way you love Mikayla and our unborn baby. I love that you never give up on things that matter and aren't afraid to quit when you know that's the right answer. I want you to know that you will always matter to me. I will never quit on us. I want to spend the rest of my life with you. If you'll have me."

"You know I love you. You didn't have to get me this ring. It's all too much."

I shook my head. "It'll never be too much, Casey. I love you. I don't care if I have five dollars or five million dollars, it's all yours. And so am I."

"Is this an invitation to our wedding?" She gestured to the frame.

I shrugged.

"You know this is in six days, right?"

"We need twenty-four hours to get a marriage license, and I couldn't get one without you there. I don't want to go through another year, or another day, without you as my wife. Everything is already planned, if you're okay with getting married on New Year's Eve."

She stared at the invitation and the ring, and I started to panic.

"We don't have to do it next week. We can get married next year sometime. Or not at all if you don't want to get married. I wasn't trying to pressure you into it. I just thought if it was all planned and done, then it was easier on you, but I didn't think about you wanting to plan it yourself. I'll call it all off. It's fine." I swallowed against the pain in my chest and pushed to my feet.

"Landon," she whispered.

"It's all good. I promise. I told you we needed to make decisions together, and then I went and forced this on you. I shouldn't have done that. I'll let Melody know we need to cancel it."

"No, you won't. Because I love you. And I don't want you to cancel anything."

"What... Wh... How... I don't understand. You didn't say anything."

She breathed a laugh. "You have a tendency to surprise me. I'm not used to it, and it takes me a few minutes to catch up. That isn't me saying no, it's me saying my heart is full and my head is trying to snap all these pieces into place. There are days I still can't believe you're here."

Mikayla hugged me around the waist. "Me, too."

I hugged Mikayla back and kissed the top of her head. "What are you saying?"

Casey stood and completed our circle, holding both of us. "I'm saying there's nothing I'd like more than to marry you. As soon as possible."

"Are you sure? We can redo everything for the wedding. It doesn't have to be—"

"I know you, Landon. You took care of everything. Every detail. And you probably chose things I didn't even know I wanted. And you made it possible. That's… Thank you for taking care of me. Of us."

"I love you. I will always take care of the two of you. All three of you."

"Even me?" Mikayla asked.

I rubbed her back. "You're mine now, too, kid. You can't get rid of me."

She hugged me tighter.

I kissed Casey. "Thank you."

She chuckled, tears dangling from her lashes. "Thank you for loving us."

"I always will."

She let me slide the ring on her finger, then read the invitation and asked for all the details. We spent the rest of the day talking about the wedding and planning the rest of our lives.

"I, Landon Boyd, take you, Casey White, to be my lawfully wedded wife. For better and worse. For richer and poorer. In sickness and in health. When you're under deadline or in labor. Every moment of every day, no matter how much you want me to leave you alone. I vow to love, cherish, honor, and adore you all the days of my life, till death do us part."

The guests chuckled as Casey's cheeks turned red. She shook her head.

I winked at her.

"Casey? Do you have your vows?" Ramsey asked.

Casey drew a breath and smiled. "I, Casey White, take you, Landon Boyd, to be my lawfully wedded husband. For better or worse, in sickness and health. When you go overboard and do too much. When you drive me crazy with your endless love. When you ask for nothing from me and don't let me know what you need. I vow to love you, cherish you, honor you, and adore you every day, till death do us part."

I grinned at my bride. She was stunning. The smile on her face made my heart full. All over again.

"I think we can all agree these two are a good fit for each other," Ramsey said. "Now, the rings?" He offered the book he held to our attendants.

Andre, my best man, set the ring I bought for Casey on the book. Melody, the matron of honor, put my ring next to Casey's.

"These rings are a symbol of your love and commitment. Whether you have them on or not, these rings are a gift to show your dedication. Just like your love, these rings have no beginning and no end. They continue forever and will never be broken." He held the book closer to me. "Landon."

I picked up Casey's ring and held her hand. "With this ring, I thee wed."

She repeated the process for me, not releasing my hand.

"By the power vested in me by the state of New York, I now pronounce you husband and wife. You may... Well, he took care of that," Ramsey said.

I ignored him and kissed my wife. Chastely. Mostly. A little church tongue. Because I couldn't resist her.

My wife.

I took her hand and led her to the back of the space, giving us a minute alone before the crowd descended. "I love you."

She smiled, her face brightening. She was finally feeling better, the second trimester giving her energy she hadn't had during the first. "I love you. Husband."

"Fuck," I hissed, resting my forehead against hers. "You need to watch that, or I'll skip this reception and take you home."

She chuckled. "I'll make sure to say it often later."

"Please do, wife."

She shivered. "Yeah, I like that."

"God, I love you."

"I love you."

"All right, you two, there are children here," Andre said, grinning and clapping me on the back. "Congratulations." He hugged me tight, then turned to Casey. "And condolences."

My wife giggled.

"Some best man you are." I shook my head at him.

"Just bringing you back down to earth before you run out that door and disappear," Andre said, all too observant.

"Just wait," I told him.

Andre winked. "Trust me, I'm not questioning you. Just making sure you enjoy the rest of the day. I hear it's fun."

"It is fun," Melody said. "And we're all here to celebrate with you." She hugged Casey. "I'm so happy for you."

"Thank you," Casey said.

"And I'm so happy you found each other." Melody hugged me.

Being welcomed into the group of friends so completely was something I never expected. Casey and Melody were close, and Ramsey accepted me without question. With his friendship, the rest of the men who met every week became my friends, too. Ian, Hudson, James, Nico, all of them. And they all showed up for our wedding, to celebrate Casey and me.

"Thank you for being here," I told Melody.

She grinned. "There's nowhere else we'd rather be. I told you that when you asked me if I thought this was a good idea."

"And I appreciate that you said yes," Casey teased. "He seems to know what I want and need without me even knowing, and I thank you for going along with it."

"You two are perfect together," Melody said.

"She's perfect. I just bask in her glow." I hugged my wife to my side and kissed her. "The flowers are pretty good, right?"

"The flowers are amazing. Just like you are."

I smiled at her. Everything worked out the way it was supposed to. It was hard to end things with Reegan. To think I would be alone forever. To wonder if I'd ever find someone who turned me inside out and made me want more.

But then Casey walked into my shop and tripped over my display and stole my heart when I wasn't even looking for her. She gave me a happiness I didn't know was possible.

TRENT AND FINLEY MacKELLAR offered their house for our reception since their group usually spent the evening there for New Year's Eve. It was an easy choice to go with the flow and let our wedding reception be a party that we didn't have to stress out about. Melody assured me Casey would be okay with it, and once Casey found out, she loved the idea of a family event that didn't make her the center of attention.

We ate dinner, and all the kids ran around and enjoyed their night. Trent and Finley invited all the kids to spend the night as one giant sleepover, giving the parents who wanted a night off some time to themselves.

Casey watched Mikayla laugh with Amber and rested a hand on her slowly expanding belly.

I wrapped my arms around her from behind and kissed her neck. "What do you think about our life so far, Mrs. Boyd?"

She chuckled and threaded her fingers through mine. "I think it's pretty spectacular. We're surrounded by family and friends, and we already have something special to look forward to next year."

I rubbed my thumbs over her belly. "We do. I just hope we find a house before this one arrives."

"We will," Casey said. "I have no doubt there will be more houses for sale once spring rolls around. It always happens."

"I hope so. I want you to have everything you've ever dreamed of."

She turned to face me and wrapped her arms around my neck. Her fingers teased the short hairs on the back of my neck. She looked up at me with a smile in her eyes. "I already have more than I ever dreamed of. I have you."

"I love you so much, Casey."

"Enough to sneak me out of here?"

"You're ready to go?"

She nodded. "I am. Let's—"

"Thirty seconds to midnight! Everyone grab their sparklers and we can go outside!" Finley called out.

Finley and Blake walked around handing out sparklers to everyone. A crowd gathered in their backyard, with the kids running through the snow and the adults sticking to the patio.

"Do you want sparklers?" Blake asked us.

Casey looked at me, desire sparkling in her eyes.

"I think we're going to call it a night," I told her, taking my wife's hand.

Blake grinned like a woman who understood very well. "Happy New Year!"

"Happy New Year," we said as we hurried toward the door. I grabbed our jackets as the countdown started.

"Ten!"

I helped Casey into her coat.

"Nine!"

I threw my coat over my shoulder.

"Eight!"

I opened the front door.

"Seven!"

We walked out into the cold.

"Six!"

I grabbed her hand.

"Five!"

We hurried toward the car.

"Four!"

"Three!"

"Two!"

"One!"

I pulled my wife into my arms.

"Happy New Year, my wife," I whispered.

"Happy New Year, my husband."

Fireworks went off over the water, cheers rang out all around town. And I kissed the woman I loved, my wife, my forever.

My happiness.

EPILOGUE

REEGAN

I smiled and waved as the last buses pulled away from the curb. It was finally summer vacation. I exhaled like I hadn't taken a full breath in months. I had the entire summer ahead of me.

My gut clenched at the thought. I couldn't remember the last time I had a summer completely free. Working for Finley and Trent MacKellar for the last few years kept me busy. Before that, I stayed busy with school. Before that…

I couldn't even remember. But a full summer off…

Too much time on my hands was not a good thing. Too much time would remind me of all the things I didn't have.

Happy fucking birthday to me.

I retreated to my classroom and packed up the last of my things. My fellow teachers were hurrying for the door, excited to start their summer. I waved to a few as they walked past me. I was not in a hurry to spend my thirty-sixth birthday all alone.

I stalled as long as I could before heading to my car. The weather was perfect, so I took a minute to lower the top on my convertible. It was an early birthday present to myself.

Cherry red with a black top and shiny new. I'd never bought a new car before, and I loved it.

I also loved cake, and if I was going to spend my birthday alone, I was going to buy one for dinner and not feel guilty about eating the whole thing myself. I pulled out of the school parking lot and turned to cut through the neighborhood to get to the grocery store.

Buses were dropping kids off, and I slow-rolled it through the busy family-friendly neighborhood, smiling at the kids racing off the bus to waiting parents. The bus turned left, and I went right, then immediately stopped behind a moving truck backing into a driveway.

I paused and waited for them, not minding the delay, and looked over at the house.

It was cute. A brick ranch with a picture window out front and huge trees in the backyard. A perfect family house. The kind I never wanted. The life I never wanted. But someone did.

I was staring at the house when the front door opened, and a very pregnant woman walked out. Right behind her was a man who was all too familiar to me.

Landon Boyd.

My ex. The man I thought I'd spend the rest of my life with. The man who wanted that picture-perfect house and family that I bristled against every time he mentioned it.

"Reegan?" Landon said, catching sight of me staring at him and his house. "Um, hi."

The truck was in the driveway, and I hadn't moved. "Hi. Sorry. I didn't realize you guys bought this house."

"Yeah, we're just moving in today. We closed yesterday, but it didn't make sense to move in late in the day. Casey's moving a little slow these days."

"Are you complaining?" Casey asked from right behind

him. She blanched when she saw me in the car. "Reegan. Hi. How… How are you?"

"I'm good. I was just heading to the grocery store when I got stopped by the truck. Congratulations."

Casey rubbed her belly. "Thanks. We've been looking for months, but this place was worth the wait."

Landon smiled at her like she was his entire world.

Casey was a lucky woman.

"I'll get the movers started," Casey said. "Nice to see you, Reegan. Enjoy your summer."

"Thanks. You, too." I smiled as she walked away, dragging my gaze to my ex. "You look really happy."

Landon's gaze was stuck on his wife. At my words, he slid it to me. "I am happy."

"That's good, Landon. I really want that for you two. You're really good together."

He nodded, a sadness in his eyes. "I'm sorry things between us ended the way they did. I know it was the right thing, but I want you to find your happiness, too."

"Thanks. I will. Maybe." I shrugged. "Either way, it's good one of us found our other half."

He drew a breath. "I never knew love could feel like this."

Ouch. I knew it wasn't intended to be an insult to me, but it stung. "I guess when it's right, it's different."

"Yeah." The movers emerged from the truck with a large piece of furniture. "I should go help. It was good to see you."

"You, too."

He started to walk away, then stopped. "Hey, happy birthday."

I exhaled a laugh. "Thanks."

He smiled, nodded, and then ran off to join his family.

I spared them another glance, then continued toward the grocery store.

I parked and was about to get out when my phone rang. I

considered ignoring it, but when I looked, it was my bestie calling.

"Hey, Ash! What's up?"

"It's over, Ree. Rob left." She sniffed.

I sighed. I'd gotten the same call three other times before. Ashlyn and Rob were like kerosene and matches. "He'll come back, Ash. He always does."

She laughed mirthlessly. "Not this time. This time is different."

"What happened?" Her tone was resigned. Not sad. Past sad. She was giving up.

"He said he can't do this anymore. Told me he doesn't want me, doesn't love me, isn't sure he ever did."

"What an asshole."

She coughed on a laugh. "I thought he was the one. I know things haven't always been perfect between us, but I thought we would figure it out eventually."

"Are you okay?"

She whimpered. "No."

Fuck. I stared at the grocery store. My solo birthday cake dinner plans faded before my eyes. "Would you feel better if I came for a visit?"

"What? No. I can't ask you to do that."

"I have the entire summer off. School is over. I'm totally free."

"You don't need to clean up his mess."

"I'm not cleaning up his mess. I'm spending a few weeks or a month with my best friend. We're going to swim in the bay you keep telling me about, kiss hot men, and have the best summer of our lives."

"Yeah?" Ashlyn already sounded better.

"Yeah, Ash. I need to run to my place and pack some stuff, but I'll let you know when I'm leaving. You're only about three hours from me."

"I love you, Ree."

"I love you, Ash. I'm always going to be there for you. We can have a bonfire tonight. Do you have any of Rob's stuff?"

Ash snorted a laugh. "I can find something."

"Good. You deserve better than someone who makes you cry and breaks your heart."

"So do you. Our exes have no idea what they walked away from."

I exhaled a laugh. Mine knew exactly what he walked away from. He walked away from a life that would have made him miserable. A life he didn't want. He found what he was looking for in another woman who made him happier than he ever was with me.

It was a good thing. Even if I was a little jealous and a lot lonely.

But I'd fix the second one. Spending the summer with my bestie? There was nothing better.

"Hey, Reegan?"

"Yeah, Ashlyn?"

"Thanks."

"You're welcome. I'll see you soon. I might be bringing cake."

"Oh, shit! It's your birthday. Oh fuck. I'm the worst friend ever. Don't come here. Enjoy your birthday. What were your plans?"

"I was about to walk into the grocery store and buy a cake and eat the entire thing for dinner and feel sorry for myself."

"What? Why would you do that?"

"Because I have no plans for the summer and nothing to do. I want to come see you, Ashlyn. It'll be fun. And it's the distraction I need after seeing Landon and his pregnant wife move into their new house today."

"But you're over him."

"Yeah, I am. I don't want him or their life, but I don't want to be alone anymore."

"Then I guess it's a good thing you're coming to see me. We can be not alone together."

I snorted. "Sounds perfect."

"I'll bake a cake. Don't buy one. Just get your sexy self here so we can eat cake, kiss hot men, and not be alone."

"Sounds good. I'll see you soon."

"Be safe, Reegan."

"I will. Bye, Ash."

"Bye!"

I hung up and smiled. I guess I had summer plans after all. With the one person who never judged me and never tried to change me.

If only she had a man for me, the summer would be perfect.

THANK **you** for reading Casey and Landon's story! I can't believe this series ends with them. I loved bringing Casey back into the series, and Landon was just right for her. It felt like the right place to say goodbye to Book Boyfriends Wanted, even though I'm going to miss all these characters so much.

Reegan is getting her book, and starting a whole new series! Amethyst Bay, a cute little bay on the New York side of Lake Champlain, is a small community with quirky characters, spectacular summers, and all the feels. When Reegan goes to stay with her bestie, she doesn't expect to find a silver fox next door who makes her heart beat faster. And not just when he yells at her to get off his dock. Preorder *Crazy Love* today!

. . .

WANT MORE from Landon and Casey? They have the rings. They have the house. Now they need the baby! Their bonus epilogue is available to subscribers only. Sign up now!

WANT to see where it all began? Mandy is a curvy girl who doesn't need, or want, a man in her life. Xander is sexy and determined to get to know Mandy, no matter how many times she runs away from him. Read Chubby & Charming for free now!

USA TODAY Bestselling Author Mary E Thompson spent most of her childhood wishing she had a few less curves. She hid in the pages of books because her favorite characters never cared what size her clothes were. Now, neither does Mary, and she writes stories that celebrate women like her. Real women who have curves, chase dreams, and find love, because we should all be happy, no matter our dress size.

Mary spends her non-writing time with her husband and two kids, watching too much TV, cheering for her hometown football team (Go Bills!), and hiding chocolate from her family.

Visit https://MaryEThompson.com/ to sign up for Mary's newsletter, **Romancing the Curves**. Subscribers get free ebooks and other fun stuff, like exclusive, members only content and giveaways, plus are the first to know about new releases and sales!

www.ingramcontent.com/pod-product-compliance
Lightning Source LLC
Chambersburg PA
CBHW060702190726
48289CB00002B/504